For John

Walk in a

Lost

Sheila Barrett

WITHDRAWN

WITHDRAWN

POOLBEG

Published in 1994 by
Poolbeg,
A division of Poolbeg Enterprises Ltd,
Knocksedan House,
123 Baldoyle Industrial Estate,
Dublin 13, Ireland

© Sheila Barrett 1994

The moral right of the author has been asserted.

The financial assistance of the Arts Council is gratefully acknowledged.

A catalogue record for this book is available from the British Library.

ISBN 1 85371 401 1

Cover photograph by Mike O'Toole
Cover design by Poolbeg Group Services Ltd/Bite Design
Set by Poolbeg Group Services Ltd in Garamond 10/13
Printed by The Guernsey Press Company Ltd,
Vale, Guernsey, Channel Islands.

Acknowledgments

I should like to thank my husband, John, for his unfailing encouragement and generosity; our children Niamh, Bronwen, Denis, Tim, Michael and Grace, for their endurance; Renate Ahrens-Kramer, Alison Dye, Cecilia McGovern, Joan O'Neill, and Ann O'Sullivan, for their valuable support over the years; Mary and Dermot Brady, Mary Rose Callaghan, Joseph Kearney and Phil McCarthy, who read the whole manuscript so helpfully; Eamon Colman, who showed me his wonderful paintings of post-nuclear landscapes; and Adi Roche of Irish CND, who responded so graciously to my requests for information;

Jonathan Williams, for his excellent reading, help and advice; and my marvellous editor, Kate Cruise O'Brien, and Philip MacDermott and the fine staff at Poolbeg.

I should also like to thank the Arts Council of Ireland for two travel grants to Arvon Foundation workshop in the U.K. There I met Frances Molloy, whose unstinting kindness and encouragement meant more than I can say.

CHAPTER ONE

I REMEMBER THE LAST WEEK OF THE OLD TIMES VERY CLEARLY. IT
starts with my mother, Conor and myself on Killiney Beach.
I was eleven. Conor was one and a bit, not quite walking.
My mother had him on her back in one of those carriers, I
remember, and she regretted it – he was too big for it, and
a ton weight.

We were collecting driftwood for the sitting-room fire,
going for colour, not warmth; for warmth we'd central
heating and coal, or turf. No, we were out freezing
ourselves for the sake of colour. There was a biting wind
off the Bay, and my mother's nose was bright red. Even
that didn't make her less beautiful: I can see her now,
staggering a little each time she'd lean over to pick up a bit
of wood, Conor laughing and waving his arms, the sea
furling and unfurling like grey silk on the shingle.

"When are we going to Dalkey Island like you
promised?" I shouted.

"How can you even think of it on a day like this?" Her
trousers flapped against her long, slim legs, and her hair
flew back into Conor's face as, delighted, he batted and
pulled at it with his hands. "Look, Maura – here's a whole

pile of them – "

"Don't change the subject, Mum!"

"Ask Dad!"

"When's he getting back?"

"Stop it, Conor! Today … "

"I know, Mum!"

" – at four. Don't interrupt. Get these, Maura, I'm not stooping down again – !" pointing at the small cluster of driftwood that had collected at the tideline.

"Dad's always working."

"Well, you work on him, Maura – oooh!"

I prised Conor's fingers out of her hair while she leaned towards me, our pile of silvery wood at our feet. I blew a goodbye kiss at Dalkey Island, which as always seemed deceptively close to the land. My mother saw me and laughed. "You might as well go to Antarctica!" she said. But Antarctica never had any people in it, and places like that didn't interest me, which I told her.

"Dalkey Island hasn't, either."

"Well it had once."

My mother liked places with no people in them. She was a landscape painter, and I suspect she thought people got in the way.

Home. We opened the door and warmth poured around us, coaxing out all the smells of the house. My mother always slipped in quickly to turn off the alarm while I hovered on the threshold savouring the medley of polish, cooking, wool, the hints of varnish, of turf and genteel age – our house was old, built almost two hundred years ago on the coach route to the South. When my parents moved in and dug the garden, they found a sword under the roots of a tree they cut down. It wasn't the kind people fought with, they said.

This day, my mother set Conor in his playpen for me to

unwrap while she rushed upstairs to wash her hair. My father was coming home. He had been away six days on this business trip, and we'd missed him. My mother worked and did everything too hard when he was gone, and there was always an unspoken apprehension when he was away – my mother was afraid of criminals, and I was afraid for my mother – she was delicate.

Dad was an hour late getting back; we heard the door of the taxi around five. My mother's hair was like a cloud again, soft and dark, her nose no longer red. She was wearing perfume, the kind he always brought her from the Duty Free. She never bothered with it when he was gone, but she kept it in cut-glass atomisers – he brought her those, too – that were always chilly when you touched them, and which clinked when I put them back on her dressing-table, no matter how careful I was. The smell! I don't know why my mouth should water, thinking of it; perfume tasted horrible.

Dad smelled of wine, cigars, aeroplanes, and America. He was no sooner in the hall than the alarm went, so he was turning it off under the stairs when my mother arrived down in her new blue dress.

"Expecting the bogeyman, were you?"

"Um."

They gave each other one of their long looks, and I turned into the sitting-room to bring Conor from the playpen. When I got back with him, Dad's cases were on the floor and he was holding my mother's hands palms up, looking at them and sniffing them. "Working?" Sniff. "Not working." His coppery hair had been rumpled. Then he kissed her hands, dropped them, took Conor up, hugged me. I half-noticed the hug wasn't as squeezing as usual, and that his face was lined and pale; but everything was grand until he picked up his cases to bring them upstairs and said, "The worst of it is, I have to go back again this day week."

My mother said nothing, and he looked around and saw her face.

"Can we keep it until after dinner, Sylvia?"

She shrugged and moved off to the kitchen, tigerish, like a model. Dad, after one harassed look at her back, continued up the stairs.

Conor gave a shout of annoyance.

"Come on," I muttered. I brought him back into the sitting-room and closed the door. The day was destroyed.

The fire was ready to be lit, so I lit it. There was a gasp from the firelighter, and then the flames began to take hold. Conor crawled over to the playpen and pulled himself up, looking at the toys inside. I lifted him into them. The room began to quieten; its thick walls lulled away noise, and the only sounds came from the fire and the grandfather clock.

I didn't mean to gaze into the fire – I wasn't allowed to, indeed, because of all the incidents. That day, though, my guard was down. Dad was home, even if he was going off again in a week, and Conor and I were sleepy, after all the fresh air down at the strand. I still feel guilty about it after all these years; I still half-believe that if I hadn't looked into the fire, nothing would have happened.

The coals had reddened, and the flames were full of wraiths, blue and green from the driftwood. Conor lay on his side in the playpen watching them, heavy-eyed, his finger in his mouth. I remember putting on another stick or two, then curling up near him on the carpet. There was only the sound of his breathing and the little noises he made sucking his finger, the thrum of the clock, and the soft sighs and wordless complaints from the fire.

I was just beginning to see the red cities, half-dreaming them, when something seemed to drop out of the middle of the coals and roll towards me. Before I could move, it shook itself and struggled onto its feet. I saw it was a grey squirrel, scruffy but unscorched. It was an odd shape.

I sat up, speechless. The bulge over its shoulder was a second head, eyeless except for swellings under its fur; the other, proper head, from which its bright eyes looked at me so intently, had no mouth. Now I could hear my father coming back down the stairs, but I couldn't move or interrupt the silence. The squirrel seemed to give me a knowing look, the eyeless mouth to smile.

"Maura?" My father was in the room.

I pointed.

"What is it?"

"The squirrel. Look at his ... "

My father hesitated, then took my pointing hand and shook it a little in his warm one. "Daydreaming are you, love?"

I rubbed my eyes, expecting to see the small shape under a chair or beyond the playpen. I lay down on my side to see if he'd gone underneath the playpen itself. "Where did he go?"

"What, Maura?"

"The squirrel, he – " Even then I didn't realise it was that kind of dream.

"Where'd he come from?" said my father, quietly.

"The ... fire."

"You see? What little squirrel could come out of the fire?"

"He had ... "

"What, Maura? What had he?" His voice was still gentle, but he'd straightened up. I moved away from him.

My mother stood in the door. "Will you ever come when you're called?" She'd put her annoyance with my father to one side and looked almost happy, but even as he smiled and said "We're on our way," her face changed.

"Maura."

"We're coming, Mum." I hung over the playpen to wake Conor, but she was at my side.

"Look at me," she said. She put her hands, still smelling of lotion, on either side of my face. She looked into my eyes.

"Sylvia ... ?"

"Wait, Dan, please. Maura? You were doing it?"

"I wasn't, Mummy. I didn't mean to."

"Maura, don't lie!"

"She'd a nap, Sylvia," my father said in a bored voice. "She dreamed she saw a squirrel in the room, isn't that right, love?"

I nodded, numb.

"A squirrel?" Her shoulders sagged with relief. "Oh, well!" She shook her head. I put my arms around her waist, and she hugged me back. "God, I'm losing it, aren't I?" she mumbled into my hair, but her voice was warm.

At dinner, though, the food tasted like cardboard and my head ached, just like the other times. "Mum, I don't feel very well. Can I go to bed?"

"I'll just tuck her up," she said, smiling at me.

"You can get to bed yourself, can't you, Maura?"

"Of course, Daddy – "

"I won't be a tick," said my mother firmly. "Don't wander off, Dan, Conor can get out of that now." She meant the high chair.

"I'll see you into the bath, then I'll go back down," she said upstairs, helping me lift the jumper off over my head.

"I love this dress," I said, rubbing her sleeve. Everything was perfect, except for my head with its sick throb.

"Tell us about this squirrel." She threw salts into the bath water, and it started to foam.

"Mum, it's – "

"I'd better know, Maura. Because of the headache." She ran her long fingers very gently over my head.

6

"It wasn't a person. Nothing's dead, or ... "

"There's no problem then, is there, love."

I told her about his two heads.

Her eyes widened, and her face became brittle-looking. She said nothing, though, only "I see," very softly.

"Is something wrong, Mum?"

"No. No, pet, not at all." Then, "You won't drop off to sleep in the bath?"

"No."

That was all. I was relieved, thinking I hadn't really upset her, not badly – not like the other two times.

Houses were never really quiet in those days when you think of it, not even when everyone was asleep. There'd be a rush and a click, and the central heating would come on (if you had it), and if you hadn't you'd still hear a car passing or a plane overhead. A radio. Something.

Our house seemed perfectly quiet that cold, still Saturday morning, the next after Dad arrived home. I took the key off the hook by the back door, careful not to make any noise, and went out to my mother's studio in the back garden. My father had it built of concrete blocks, with big windows, a good sink and lots of heating. Then Mum paid him for it with the money she made from her pictures. His feelings were hurt by this, and mine were devastated – she sold my favourite picture to raise the money.

It was semi-abstract, of the sea at evening when the water goes milky and luminous and merges with the sky. In the foreground she'd a ruined jetty, a flurry of wide, dark strokes against the glow of the water. The picture made me cool, thoughtful and a bit sad, but most of all, I felt safe in it. Somehow the brush had made tracks that refracted the light, tracks you didn't so much see as feel in your mind's eye, that led you to where you belonged in that perfect, ruined scene and held you there.

I asked my mother how there was so much light in the picture when the actual colours were so dim, and she said, "Layers. Undercoats."

I cried when she sold it. She was puzzled; makers are entranced by their work while they're in it, but then they move on. I was just a child, and no other picture welcomed me like that one did. She promised that when she painted another I liked as much, she'd give it to me. She thought I was growing, and it would become harder for me to empathise in that total, childish way, but then she always underestimated her work – not its skill, but its power.

The studio that morning had its chilled, inviting smell of paints and oils. I closed the door behind me to keep it in, then turned on the strip lights and paused, astonished. There was the usual orderly clutter of supplies, the canvases leant against the wall, the metal cabinet whose shallow drawers held sketches and water-colours, the refrigerator where my mother kept her working palettes under cling film, the cleaned brushes in their jars – all the same. But the big landscape she'd been working on was off the easel and propped against the wall.

This was the one we called 'the Dutchman's picture' because it had been commissioned by a Dutch industrialist. The man, who was tall, dark and skinny ("Not at all like a 'real' Dutchman," my mother said, giggling), had arrived at the front door with a friend of Mum's he had commandeered. This man stood a little behind him, shrugging apologetically, while the Dutchman explained what he wanted. Dad missed all this, arriving home the next day, so my mother had recounted the scene to him. I could tell she was very pleased, but there was ambivalence in the air.

Dad pursed his lips when she told him the amount, but he still said nothing.

"He's mad! If the paint isn't completely dry by the twenty-eighth of May, he won't pay for it."

"Sure, what odds? Somebody else'll buy it."

"Not for what this boyo is giving me," my mother said. There was a sudden clatter of sleet against the window.

My father rose, looked out, sat down again. "It's sticking," he said.

"What a little capitalist I've become. Well … "

He looked at her, frowning. "You can hardly start now."

"I wasn't thinking of today, Dan. Actually." Another blast hit the window. "There's snow in that. Damn it to hell."

"The long range forecast says we'll be having this for the next fortnight, Sylvia, and there's already ice all over Wicklow – "

"If the worst comes to the worst, I'll resort to John Hinde," said my mother.

"Oh, sure you will."

"I know exactly what I want to do, Dan! I've only to take the odd photo and make a few sketches. I'm just going up to the Featherbed – "

"The Featherbed!"

"I'll do the outdoor bits in one or two visits – "

"Sylvia, will you ever cop yourself on? Two visits, me – " He looked at me and stopped.

"Who's John Hinde?" I said.

"They make postcards, chicken. You'll spend a week just communing with the bloody place," he went on to my mother, "which has to be about the most exposed terrain in Ireland – "

"That's exactly what I like about it," said my mother. Her eyes went the colour of slate.

My father made one of his sudden, brilliant capitulations. "Why not?" he said, shrugging. Then he got up and filled the kettle.

My mother bit her lip and looked anxiously at the window while his back was turned. She hated working under pressure, and she was vulnerable to cold; and she feared arthritis more than death.

"You'll do it, Mum," I said.

She gave me a doubtful smile, and I could already see the picture in her eyes.

Now, three months on, the canvas simmered against the wall. It was of the place in the Wicklow mountains up beside the turf allotments. The view swept across the road to the lonely confluence of slopes and emptiness at the Sally Gap. Save for the rich quiet colours of heather and bog and stone, there was nothing, just nothing but the cold interior of the sky. The picture was hypnotic, like the Featherbed itself, and I knew it was her best ever. For me, it could take the place of the seascape. Knowing its value, I didn't dare ask for it; but what if the Dutchman's deadline passed? We were in mid-May, and I knew my mother didn't consider the picture finished. She was using oils, too, not acrylics.

Something else was on the easel. It was a sketch, a mere jumble of childish shapes. There were a number of cones that looked as if they'd been squeezed above the middle, almost as if they'd high waists. To the right, and a little in the foreground, was a large circle almost nestling among the cones; on the left, a squiggle of convoluted shapes that looked like something I'd seen in *Science 5*, like a digestive system, but which must be pipes of some sort.

A city of queer shapes, like something from another galaxy; I didn't like it. It was different from anything my mother had ever started, and the crude draughtsmanship showed that she didn't like it, either. Whatever was on the easel dominated the studio, and the ugly drawing seemed to spread its pallor over the colours in the room, trapping all the energy in its own coarse lines. I turned to leave.

Only then did I see the two strong cardboard boxes under the table. The flap on one was loosened. Inside were tins of baked beans. She had two whole boxes of baked beans.

I studied her at breakfast. She ate, she took toast and two cups of tea. She wore her red silk dressing-gown, the one I loved. Her face was pale always, but as smooth as a child's; she seemed thinner that day, but she always was when she was working.

There were no real signs of the quiet wasting she'd suffered after Conor was born, that time when people said she was 'tired', 'she needed a rest', and I knew it was something worse. There she had sat, getting thinner and thinner, content to hold Conor all day long as if he were a doll or a pillow, that vacant, clown's smile on her face.

She had been well again for months, and when my father arrived down in his old jumper and denims and put his hand on her shoulder, she put her own hand over it, smiling. I like to remember them like that, my father standing behind her, his face smoothed with sleep, his hair reddish-gold and slightly unruly, my mother leaning her dark head against him, both of them looking at me with calm approval. At that moment there was a commanding squawk from upstairs, Conor waking up, and we all laughed.

Even while I was laughing, I was frightened to death, and as always at such times, I wanted Lizzie.

CHAPTER TWO

LIZZIE WAS MY FATHER'S ONLY SISTER. SHE HAD THE O'KEEFFE determination, the blue eyes and the red-gold hair. She was slight, though, not stockily built like my father. Also, she was a nun.

My father never understood this or accepted it – that is, he never accepted that Lizzie was religious. "Has to run things, couldn't be bothered with a man," he'd say. They were very close growing up, and her vocation was a complete shock to him. My grandmother, a 'relaxed' Catholic who'd been widowed for years, was more bemused than upset by Lizzie's vocation, but she saw Lizzie was happy, so she stopped worrying.

Dad took it hard. He wasn't impressed by Mamo's sheepish suggestion that it might be 'some sort of thingamabob, grace … a sign'. He summoned Lizzie to their sitting-room, and Lizzie perched on the arm of the sofa and heard him out. At this point in the story, Dad would always stop and remark that she'd already developed a professionally kind, patient look, and it was all he could do not to pull her hair.

He tried everything – her age (twenty-two), her temperament, her looks, and all she'd be missing –

children, a man, relative independence – .

"Relative to what?" she had asked, eyes glinting.

"Relative to – to landing yourself in some dump – some bloody backwater – why you, Lizzie?"

"I just want to!" she had said. "And I doubt I'll miss sex as much as you think. And Ps. Dan! I'm not a lesbian." He would end this anecdote with a shout of laughter, but his eyes were still confused.

All that was long before Dad and Mum were married. By the time Conor was born, Lizzie had been happy in her 'backwater' for fifteen years, and Dad had accepted her vocation as he would a slight handicap in somebody he loved. What he still didn't accept was the way she lived it, 'rearing the flintiest scrapings off the streets of Dublin with the help of three madwomen'.

She was always different, fun, but I only grew to depend on her when my mother was ill after Conor. I'll never forget opening the door and finding Lizzie smiling down at me, the little suitcase in her hand.

It would be wrong to say I never trusted my mother after that illness, but I did stop feeling that she could look after us. Dad was away. He hired a nurse, Mrs Quinn, to stay with us and help – Mum was very listless.

La Quinn wasn't in the house three hours before I hated her. She was continuously between me and my mother, but worse, I didn't like the way she held Conor or spoke to him. It wasn't that she hurt him in any way; she just didn't seem to see what a person he was. At the same time, she refused to see that something was wrong with my mother, and it was up to me to niggle and prowl and try to get some response from her.

"Will you leave your mother alone, Maura love, she needs to rest!" Smile.

"She's rested all day."

"She's very tired, pet, she's had a little baba … "

"Mummy."

"Now, Maura – " Taking me by the arm.

"Excuse me, darling," to my mother who, pained and confused, was moving her lips to protest. "Now – !"

But I wrenched away from Mrs Quinn, half tripping over her large foot, and ran up to my room and locked the door.

Later that evening the doorbell rang and there was Lizzie, slightly quizzical, like a subversive Mary Poppins.

The atmosphere of the house rearranged itself around Lizzie, just as the mood of my mother's studio flowed from the picture on the easel. Lizzie's coming didn't alleviate my mother's uncanny despair, but it relieved my own panic and frustration. Afterwards I saw Lizzie as a rock I could cling to when everything else was shifting underfoot.

I couldn't understand why I longed for Lizzie on this ordinary Saturday morning when my father was home again and my mother was healthy, or why the air in the house was cold and crawling. I had never felt frightened like this, not when I looked in the fire and saw Auntie Pat smiling in her chair asleep but not asleep, not even when I saw my mother's dead baby inside her, perfect, never to grow, my sister. Loneliness, loss and disappointment – those pained but felt natural, not like this.

I could make nothing of my 'dream' of the grey squirrel, and neither of my parents had mentioned it again. It hovered, though, chilling my thoughts, like the harsh sketch that had replaced the landscape in my mother's studio. It felt like that day two years ago when I was nine when I'd told my mother about my little sister and had seen the look in her eyes. Lizzie came then, too.

All that week – the last week of the Old Times – seems now to have been a bundle of these old and new hauntings, a last ditch attempt to prepare for the unthinkable. In the meantime, I was starting my mental countdown towards the day of my father's departure.

Monday morning I felt sick, but nothing discernible was wrong with me, and Mum sent me to school. Dad went to his office early and returned late. I waited in my night-clothes for him at the bottom of the stairs.

"What's this? An owl! A nine-o'clock owl."

"Where were you, Dad?"

"Putting food on the table. Where's your Mum?"

I pointed towards the sitting-room.

"Well, now – were you waiting up for your goodnight kiss?"

I nodded.

He put down his briefcase, picked me up and gave me what he called a bear hug, a growelly squeeze redolent of suit, car, and evening air. "Now – bed for you!"

He swung me onto the first step, gave me a launch smack on the bum, and stood watching me.

I climbed slowly, emphasising my failing health. I could hear him in the sitting-room saying, "What's up with Maura?" and my mother's voice answering him. Her low, indifferent tone scuttled my hopes for staying home from school the next day. Later that night their voices woke me.

"Would you even read the papers, Dan? Just read them!"

His voice, tired, sharp – "I'm going to sleep now, Sylvia."

My mother's footsteps on the landing and the creak of the hot press door. In the morning her pillows and blankets were still tumbled on the sofa downstairs and her eyes were as dull as my own.

Tuesday, leaden, drizzling, my father out at the crack of dawn and my mother still in her dressing gown. I walked to school awash with self-pity, scuffing my soles on the rough pavement. There was real rain advancing. The Bay was hardly visible; I might well be soaked before I reached the school. It would serve them right! My mother would have to nurse me through pneumonia instead of finishing her picture for the Dutchman.

The thought of the landscape with its lonely magic stopped me dead in the middle of the footpath. Then (I thought), a sign: a gleaming fan of water leaped from the road, drenching me. The cause of this, the Minister's long black car, continued sedately toward the school. The Minister's daughter, my classmate, stared out the back window at me, pale faced, hand raised in apology.

That afternoon I flung my schoolbag down in the kitchen and ran out to the studio to see how the picture was coming on. The room was cold: the landscape still leaned against the wall. The sketch of shapes, the queer pinched cones and the circle, was gone from the drawing board on the easel. Then I saw that it was crumpled, lying under it on the floor. There was no other sign that my mother had been there at all.

Dad didn't get home that night until after I'd gone to bed. By this time a terror had taken hold of me; I imagined my parents were going to separate. Vague stories about my friends' families came back to me. Nuala Browne lived with her mother; her father lived in England and was married to someone else. Evelyn Higgins's mother was dead – that didn't count. Orla MacPherson had a stepfather. She didn't like him. In fact, she hated him. I got out of bed, put on my dressing-gown and sat on the stairs to listen.

" – fool!" my mother said.

"Do you not think, Sylvia, that a man who has his office six blocks from the White House might be better informed about this than you?" Dad was speaking in the patient tones that always made my mother furious.

"Murray Jarnagan? – a donkey beside the White House would know more! What if there were no crisis, Dan! Isn't it still outrageous for him to insist – sure wouldn't he lift the phone? Use the Fax?"

"He does all those things, and well you know it. Just as you know there's no crisis – "

"No crisis!"

"He puts me up in his own house – "

"The palatial estate in Virginia, magnificently situated in twenty-five acres of woodland – "

"He's naive, yes, Sylvia, a bit crass perhaps, but – "

"'Bit' nothing! And you dance to his tune like an organ grinder's monkey!"

There was a short, dreadful silence.

"Three hundred thou," he said softly, tiredly. "Three hundred thou a year, Sylvia, and that's the bottom line – "

"Before tax – "

"Let me finish, Sylvia!"

"The bottom line is we could probably live on what I make."

"If you want to live on what you make, Sylvia, that's perfectly all right, but my children won't scratch along on subsistence while I'm alive – "

"Ninety thousand pounds is subsistence?"

"You've made that once in your life – "

"Anyway, this isn't it at all! This is totally meaningless – "

"Too bloody right!"

" – because any time now, we'll be paying with beads and beans – "

"Well, Christ knows you're ready with the beans!"

"You've been sniffing around my studio?"

There was an electric pause.

"'Sniffing around your studio'."

"Oh, Dan, I – "

"Aren't you being a bit paranoid about your accumulated wealth? If our future really does depend on beans, love, or your earnings, you'd want to get on with the Dutchman's picture. A mere – what? – ninety-eight tins won't even get us two seats at the theatre – "

"You bastard," she said brokenly. "You stupid man. If you won't read the papers, will you – will you at least pay attention to your own tribal – Jesus, Daniel, your own daughter saw an animal with two heads!"

I threw up on the landing. I couldn't make it to the loo.

They cleaned up, grimly watching one another being kind to me. My mother sat on my bed for a while, loosely holding my hand, her expression remote.

"Mum ... would we be getting a stepfather?"

It was an unhappy laugh, but a laugh. "Not if I can help it," she said.

My father drove me to school the next morning, Wednesday. He drove with special care, as if I were sick or very old. He parked opposite the school and walked me across the road, solid, watching oncoming parents in their cars with calm menace. Only when we stood on the gravel did he look doubtful. "Do you feel all right, Maura?"

"Well ... " I ducked my head and stared at our shoes, his large, polished and my scuffed ones.

"You look all right, so," he said lightly. "Give us a kiss – I'll be off."

"Daddy!" I dropped my school bag, held his arms.

"What, Maura?"

"Why did the squirrel have two heads? – I mean, why was Mum upset about it?"

His face went blank. After a moment he said, "I don't know, Maura. Tell you what. Get Mum to explain it herself."

He leaned towards me, kissed me, tipped me under the chin. "But you know Mum, now don't you?" Then he turned and walked off, his hand up waving goodbye. I'd still like to shake him.

" ... warmer today, we'll have rounders at break ... "

It was Sister Imelda, the Assistant Head, smelling of

paper and casting little kindnesses around me. Her hand on my shoulder. Paper and clean wool, and the starch you sprayed out of a tin. Grey eyes and a young-old face.

That was a kindly day in school, a bruise in my memory. It's the soft, sweet memories that twinge the most. I'd forgotten my lunch or my mother had, and Mrs Mulcahy, my teacher, gave me an apple out of hers. Then my friends started competing over what they'd give me. Jane gave me the end off her Penguin bar. Aoife gave me half her peanut butter sandwich, and Margaret, the Minister's daughter, gave me a little iced cake, a 'petit four' she called it.

Many of the girls were mean to Margaret because she'd lovely things, but no aggression; she was too timid, pale and decent to terrorise us with her father's money and State Mercedes, so she led a dog's life in our class. I liked her.

My mother was in the kitchen when I got home from school. The radio was on. The whole house seemed mildly disarranged and cleaned. There were piles of clean clothes on my bed upstairs and swirls in the rug where the hoover had lifted the pile. She had a hot dinner prepared, too, which was unusual, and Conor, in his high chair, had his fists sunk greasily in the mushed-up version of it.

"Have you finished the picture?" I asked carefully.

"Not yet. Why?"

"I like it."

"Good," she said, smiling at me.

"Why aren't you hurrying?"

"Not in the mood." She always raised her voice a little when she didn't want to talk about something any more.

Shepherd's pie. Milk to drink. Two cod liver oil capsules, and two others.

"Not them again!"

"Oh, yes!" She pulled the stool over to the worktop and

ate her own lunch there, the radio beside her. There was no music, only a steady rumbling of voices. It sounded like the news, so I didn't listen much, but I remember being surprised by her absorption; she almost never listened to the radio. Now she ate her food absently but determinedly, as if it were a duty. Conor was the only person I loved, I thought, who wasn't slightly peculiar.

I did my homework in the sitting-room, my back to the fire. That evening I found another book to read, *Grimm's FairyTales*, from my mother's girlhood collection upstairs. The stories were reassuring – two-headed squirrels were no problem in their world.

Some part of my mind registered the radio in the kitchen, the incessant voices, my mother's light steps here and there. The telephone rang in the hall.

"Ah, Mr Jarnagan," my mother said. Her voice was all edges. In my mind's eye it rattled off some satellite and whizzed like a javelin towards Mr Jarnagan's head.

"He isn't, I'm afraid. He must be on his way. Mr Jarnagan, it's really a very bad weekend for him to – "

There was a longish silence, and then she said, "I'm so surprised you don't keep up with current affairs, em, Murray. I thought one had to, in business."

Another pause.

"Where will you be meeting, then? Under the Pentagon?"

I heard my father's car in the driveway.

"I assure you I'm not joking, Mr Jarnagan. I really thought *you* were, asking – "

"Mum!" I ran into the hall, gestured at the front door.

My mother, who had been glaring into space with the phone clutched to her cheek, jumped as if shot. "You'll have to excuse me – there's a slight emergency here." She plunked down the receiver. "Maura, take the phone off the hook upstairs. We'll at least have our dinner in peace."

I was up like a rabbit.

"Hello?" Dad called in the hall. My mother, breathless, answered him in the kitchen.

I picked up the receiver in their bedroom and held it to my ear. It hummed impersonally. Mr Jarnagan had rung off. I hid the whole telephone under the bed, receiver off and gagged with a cushion.

Mr Jarnagan had come to dinner months ago when he was visiting Ireland. He had a long, tanned face, small brown eyes, very white teeth, and he talked and talked while the other people smiled politely. That was the difference between my father's friends and my mother's – my mother's friends would have told him to shut up. But the people at the party weren't really friends, she told me afterwards, they were 'associates'. The dinner was my mother's best ever, but nobody did it justice; it was as if they had to stay alert at all costs. I laid this at Mr Jarnagan's door. He wasn't nice, he was only enormously rich. I was disappointed, because I liked Americans on the television.

I changed Conor's nappy without being asked. I was half-hiding from Dad; I didn't know how to look at him.

At last dinner was ready, and I brought Conor down. Dad was leaning against the kitchen table with a glass of beer in his hand. He put it down to follow my mother into the dining-room – she brought a casserole, he brought salad. Then he took Conor from me, nuzzled his middle, and put him laughing into his high chair.

My mother was still serving the plates when he asked if 'Murray' had phoned him.

There was a small pause while my mother passed a plate to him. "Will you chop that up for Conor please, darling?"

My father took the plate from her and began mincing the soft casserole with his knife and fork. Then he put it in front of Conor, who pounced on it with both hands. "Well, Sylvia?"

"He rang."

"Does he want me to ring him back?"

She took a small bite of her casserole. It was my favourite. "When didn't he?"

"I take it he does?" My father looked at her. He didn't frown, but somehow his face looked very – distinct – and his eyes too blue.

"I'd to put the phone down," my mother said coolly. She took another bite.

"You had to put the phone down."

"The pasta boiled over." She shrugged.

"I see." Dad looked at his watch. Then he got up and took his plate into the kitchen.

"Are you afraid to even finish your dinner? Are you afraid he'll fire you if you finish a plate of casserole?" my mother shouted after him.

Conor's face crumpled. The Fax machine whined in the hall; my mother dropped her knife, and it bounced off the table and onto the floor. She retrieved it and continued eating. Her hands had the slow, graceless movements of a robot's.

The telephone in the hall made two soft, chiming sounds as my father picked up the receiver and cradled it. He went up the stairs and across the bedroom over our heads. A thump.

"I hid it under the bed, Mum."

"It's my own fault," she said. "Lizzie's able to talk to him. I should have got on to Lizzie."

"Mummy, are you sick? Is he going off while you're sick?"

"I'm not sick." We could hear the rumble of my father's voice above our heads.

"What's Dad doing? What's the matter?"

"Grown-up stuff. Man stuff." At this, Conor, who had been pushing food into his mouth with one hand, watching us anxiously, flung his plate on the floor. My mother, face impassive, scraped food back into it with her knife and brought it into the kitchen. I followed her, and Conor howled. She gave me a wet cloth to clean his face and hands and asked me to put him to bed when I'd done. This was to get me out of the way.

It didn't quite end there. Later Dad talked to Lizzie on the phone in the bedroom.

"Fuck it, Lizzie, how did you get into this?" I could hear him pacing angrily beside the bed while he listened, then an exasperated squeak of the springs when he sat down. "And when is all this supposed to happen?" Another pause. "It's in the grapevine? World War Three is in the sodding grapevine? ... Are there any hints as to why no governments seem to have picked it up?"

There was a long pause here, so long I thought they'd stopped talking. Then Dad gave an outraged snort. "That old woman! For Jesus' sake! ... sorry. Look, Lizzie, your man is off the wall. Is he still in the eighties or what? What? ... Then somebody should let the rest of us poor bastards know about it ... Oh, I do take it seriously!" Now his voice was savage. "My job's on the line, Sylvia is well on her way over the edge, assisted by you! Listen to me! – I've got to go this weekend." It sounded as if he'd kicked the bedside table. "Right. I've listened. Now you listen. Margaret Kilcoyne was at school today. In Maura's class. Right. State car, the lot. And you know and I know, Lizzie, if there was that kind of trouble coming, Kilcoyne'd be in that bunker in Athlone with a pillow over his head and two over his daughter's ... "

"Lizzie, stay out of it. Unless you want to come and hold Sylvia's hand till Tuesday ... What do you mean? Maura's dream? Do you know what she's been reading,

Lizzie? The Brothers Fucking Grimm!"

"I've got to go now, Lizzie … No, Maura's gone to bed. Goodbye, Lizzie, now, goodbye."

He put the phone down with a bang. "Oh, for God's sake!" His voice was faint in the empty room.

CHAPTER THREE

THURSDAY MY FATHER ARRIVED DOWNSTAIRS IN WHAT MUM CALLED his 'power costume' – cleaned suit, white shirt, silk tie. His shoes shone; his hair gleamed like copper. He was all sharp lines and danger. His suitcase and briefcase were in the hall.

My mother hadn't seen him packing. She was in the kitchen, making breakfast, walking around silently between fridge and cooker, cooker and table. She was wearing the red silk dressing-gown. Today it showed how pale she was; there was something agonising about the colours. She was polite, as if Dad were a kind of awkward paying guest. He in turn looked at her as if he were a doctor; he seemed cautiously satisfied.

She wandered out to see if the post had come. I knew she was looking at the suitcase. Dad kept eating his breakfast, but his hands slowed. I couldn't eat.

My mother came back in and said, "I wish you'd bring my car to the airport and leave the Volvo today, Dan. Would you mind?"

"Of course not. Any special reason?"

"I may go to the cottage."

"Good idea." He took the keys out of his pocket and

tossed them across the table. She left them there, but took hers out of her bag and set them down near him.

"Well. Enjoy your trip." She turned to leave the room, then looked back at me. "Keep an eye on Conor, will you Maura, until I get dressed?"

"I'll be late to school," I said sullenly.

"You won't. I won't be long. Bye Dan." She went out.

He said nothing for a moment, only sat at the table, quite still. "Well," he said. He stood up rather heavily, as if he'd dimmed all over. I went to him and hugged him, hugged the bleak going-away smell of his cleaned suit. "Maura, you know I won't be away long?" He squeezed my shoulders. "If you're worried about anything, you'll phone Lizzie?"

"Yes."

"I'll be back Tuesday. You'll help Mum, sure you will?"

"Yes, Dad."

His eyes were sparkling again. He was beginning to look very angry. "If you think Mummy's not well, or if something she says upsets you, call Lizzie right away."

Like now, I thought.

"Kiss Conor goodbye for me – I won't wake him."

Then he went. He backed my mother's small car out of the driveway, going, going, gone.

My mother's door was shut; there was no sound of her walking around dressing. Conor was wide awake after all, cot creaking as he bounced around in it. I'd get detention at school, shuffling in late without a note.

Face-splitting beams and chatting from the cot. "Ma! Ma!" about the best he could do with my name.

I swung him up, recoiling as the whiff of the nappy leaped out to meet me. There was nothing for it but to change him, school or no school. He was like an eel. "Stop it! Haven't I troubles enough, without – "

His eyes widened with reproach.

"There, I didn't mean it, I didn't mean it, Conser." When I'd finished, he held both fists beside his middle, poised, and gave me a commanding look.

"All right. Just one." I put my face against his plump sleep-suited middle and blew hard.

He shouted laughing and went still and expectant again.

"Can't now, Consy-pie. Got to go to school." I picked him up, nearly tottering with the soft, firm weight of him. "Stop it, you!" to his wriggling.

Mum was sprawled over the bed like a crushed poppy, the red silk shimmering with every sob. She was crying out loud like a child, her fists clenched on either side of her head, her black hair spilling over them.

I put Conor down beside her. His face began to crumple; then he sank his fingers into her hair. "Here's your child," I said, and stalked out.

No lunch. Nothing unusual – no need to call Lizzie!

Somewhere between our gate and the turn down towards the sea, I realised the day was mild and lovely, a 'pet' day. Suddenly things were good, things outdoors at least. The pebbledash on the garden wall I was passing sent little currents up my fingers, there were still daffodils in Heffernans' garden, and the sweet, watery smell of spring was everywhere. When I turned down towards the school, Killiney Bay stretched blue and glittering, with that queer clarity the sea has when it shows both its dazzle and its depth. It was a perfect day to mitch.

I'd always wanted to. Killiney Strand was just beyond the school, then White Rock beach and Dalkey Island opposite like a sentinel, stripped of its saints and sailors. The Martello tower, black in the distance, squatted against the sky like a warning. If it were slimmer, high-waisted, it would be like the shapes in my mother's sketch. Even while I thought of Dalkey Hill, with its innumerable hiding

places among the gorse and rocks, its woods and little
paths, I thought of what they'd found there – one of the
Island goats, hacked to pieces. Someone had caught it,
brought it to the mainland, and done that. The girls at
school talked of witches, and the curate at St Stephen's had
spoken against superstition, violence, war, and cruelty to
animals on the Sunday. I turned into the school gate
wishing I hadn't thought of the goat, wishing I hadn't
thought of the lonely bits of mangled flesh on the hill. The
day went strange – everything seemed smaller, even Sister
Imelda hooshing us stragglers at the door. She wasn't
usually so fussy.

Mrs Mulcahy, our teacher, was on high doh. She rushed
through morning prayers and then braked at the end for a
Special Intention for Peace.

"She's like a cat on a hot roof today," my friend Jane
said after Break. Mrs Mulcahy was hunched over her desk,
two fingers pinching the bridge of her nose, listening to
Blanaid reading. "Maybe she's got her period."

"Maybe she's got measles," I snapped. I hated Jane's
smug talk about bodies.

"Then I hope she's not getting a baby."

"Do you mean 'pregnant'?"

Jane looked at me coldly. Josie and Aoife behind us
started to giggle. Margaret, just out of range, stared over at
us, wide-eyed.

Jane shot her a spiteful look and lowered her voice
even more. "Of course I mean – "

Mrs Mulcahy opened her eyes and looked straight at
her. Jane stared meekly at her book. She turned the page.
Mrs Mulcahy then stared at Aoife, who went scarlet and
shook all over. Mrs Mulcahy smiled her wicked little smile,
and Aoife collapsed into silent giggles. We all giggled, half-
horrified at ourselves, because Mrs Mulcahy could go either
way; she could charm us quiet, or she could freeze the

blood in our veins.

Just as she stood up, the door opened and Sister Imelda came in. She took Mrs Mulcahy by the arm and they went out into the hall together. We sobered at once. We looked at each other: someone's parent had been in a crash? Mother Superior had another heart attack?

Mrs Mulcahy came back and Sister Imelda put her head around the door. "Margaret, you're wanted," she said. "Don't worry – no bother. Your parents just want to bring you down the country today."

"I'll miss my maths test," Margaret said plaintively.

Jane put up her eyes.

"It'll be waiting for you when you get back," said Mrs Mulcahy. "I think you'd better bring all your books – ." She stopped suddenly, confused.

Margaret rummaged in her desk in her usual bemused way, awkwardly removing books and dumping them into her school bag. One fell on the floor. "Let Maura there hold the bag while you put them in. Maura … "

I held her bag.

"Lucky!" I whispered. "Where are you going?"

"I don't know! I don't want to go anywhere. I hope it's a mistake."

"Ah, well – see you."

She gave me one of her nice smiles.

Sister Imelda and Mrs Mulcahy were still standing together, almost expressionless. Imelda brought Margaret out, and Mrs Mulcahy paced up and down in front of the room a few times. I remember thinking she seemed a bit like my mother, abstracted in the same distraught way, and I wondered … I didn't know what to wonder.

The next person to put her head around the door of our room was my mother herself.

"Maura, you're next, it seems," said Mrs Mulcahy with a crooked smile. She had gone very pale. Slowly, I gathered my books.

Sister Imelda hurried back into the classroom. "It's all right," she said briskly to Mrs Mulcahy. "Off with you!" Mrs Mulcahy looked at her for a moment. Then she put her arms around her and hugged her. Tears streamed down Mrs Mulcahy's face. "Go on with you, now! We'll all be big fools on Monday," Imelda said.

Mrs Mulcahy looked around the room as if she'd never see us again. Then she left and we could hear her half-running down the corridor. I got my schoolbag on my shoulder and slowly walked out. It didn't occur to me that I should say goodbye.

Dad's big Volvo sat low over its tyres like a cargo ship fully laden. Conor was in his child's seat in the back, surrounded by grocery bags. They loomed all around him – he could hardly move his legs.

Imelda came outside with us, and we stood together on the gravel. It came to me that the boxes of beans must be in the boot.

"I'm probably mad," my mother said, looking sheepish.

"We were going to phone you. We're phoning all the parents now." Imelda was looking past us out to sea as if she expected something to appear on the horizon. She didn't seem particularly afraid or excited; perhaps that's why I kept feeling that my mother was over-reacting to whatever was going on. "You didn't see Brian Kilcoyne?"

My mother's eyes widened. "He was here?"

"Just before you. They took Margaret. They'd the State car with the chauffeur, and the housekeeper was behind them with the family car. It was chock-a-block. Don't go back home and boil a kettle, thinking you're imagining things."

"But there's been nothing," my mother said, "nothing said at all."

"Isn't it terrible?"

They stared at one another.

"Hop into the car, Maura," my mother said.

I opened the door and perched on the passenger's side, the floor of which was layered with soft bags of clothes. I rolled down the window.

"What can we do? We might all be wrong, Mrs O'Keeffe, but better safe than sorry. We've been keeping a bit of an eye on the Kilcoynes, because we heard ... my brother's in the Army, you know, stationed at Athlone ... I don't think Brian Kilcoyne can help it, to be quite honest. I'm telling you Aoife MacBride's sitting in the classroom this very moment and her dad's a tremendous party man. It looks like only the top ones are being warned away. It's that bad."

"I'll be going, then," said my mother.

"You'd best. The media crowd must slip their leads today; I can't think why they're taking so long ... "

"Mind yourself."

"You, too." Imelda leaned towards me. "Mind that fellow, now," she said, nodding at Conor. She held out her hand to me and shook my fingers. "God bless," she said.

Then, to my astonishment, she and my mother hugged each other. It was a day for hugs, apparently. Imelda didn't see me waving at her when we drove out the gate. She was standing where we'd left her, gazing at the sea, her skirt gently ballooning in the breeze.

"Where are we going?"

"To the cottage."

"Why do we have all this food?" I half had it in my mind that Mum was preparing some sort of siege against my father.

"I'm stocking up a bit. Mind your foot, there may be eggs in that, I forget."

"We can't eat all this!"

"We won't have to."

"Where's Poopy?"

"He's in the back seat, Maura, I didn't forget him."

Poopy was my soft dog.

"I don't want to go to the cottage."

"We have to, unfortunately."

"Why?"

"We'll talk about it later."

I craned around to see if I could coax some reaction from Conor, but he was already dozing, his head bobbing with the motion of the car. "Boring, boring, boring," I sang.

"Shush, Maura!" My mother turned up the radio.

"Do we have to listen to that?"

"Yes."

It was her grim voice, so I didn't talk any more. We rolled along, dominated by the sound of the radio. I wished I were in the back seat with Conor.

Outside the car, the air softened and warmed, and I could almost see the buds on the trees stretching and opening over the tired streets; yet something seemed wrong, too, as if a greyness peeked through the sky's blue, or a cruel face waited behind the clouds. That's all hindsight, of course.

I'd have looked harder at everything if I'd known, at every street, no matter how empty, every house, no matter how dilapidated or abandoned, every person on the road. I'd have memorised the faces of the university students pouring out along the Stillorgan Road, the disintegrating knot of them around the boy with the radio, the slowing but still steady traffic along the Canal, and the Canal's greeny-bright water.

Nothing seemed that different – we passed through Lucan, then Leixlip, where the road dipped and crossed the Liffey. My father had always pointed out the pub beside the bridge and said, "The father of a girlfriend of mine owned that pub." The ground sloped gently to the river on the other side, to a quiet green path that we only glimpsed. Today a little brown family of ducks was launching itself into the water.

By the time we reached Maynooth, I was drowsy, floating uneasily between waking and sleeping across the rolling miles of bogland, past windbreaks of pale trees and haggard-looking farmhouses with empty eyes.

I dreamed I saw my father standing beside the road in his fishing gear, but I couldn't make my mother stop for him. Finally I persuaded her to turn around. We retraced our way but he was gone, and we became more and more lost and confused, glimpsing him fields away, but being unable to reach him.

"Surely tractors take diesel," said my mother's voice.

Conor complained gently in the back seat. The car had stopped. We were at a petrol station on a small road I hadn't seen before. Black-and-white cattle grazed in a field opposite.

My mother was standing beside the car, talking to a fair-haired man. She was cross.

"Ah well now," said the man doubtfully. "The boss has gone home for his dinner ... He told me ... "

"Not to sell any petrol?" my mother asked incredulously.

"Well, he said, like ... "

My mother waited, staring at him. She got a reproachful, unbelieving look on her face. The breeze lifted her hair a little.

The man looked at her, blinking when she pushed her hair away from her face. "Ah, sure ... " he muttered. He looked up and down the road, craning his neck. Then quickly and almost furtively, he stuck the nozzle into the Volvo's tank.

"Thank you," my mother said. Her expression did not change.

"It only took eight quids' worth!" The man was chagrined. "Jaysus, you were only topping up!"

"That way the car will take less petrol," my mother said sternly. "And you'd have worried about the amount that was gone, if you'd given me a fill."

"I wouldn't have," the man said. "I wouldn't have given you a fill." He put out his hand. "You can pay me ten," he said.

"You said eight," said my mother. She reached into her pocket and produced a note and some coins. He took them, scowling.

"Thank you," said my mother. She got into the car.

"Don't come back here," said the man. He turned and walked into the small shop beside the petrol pump. Another car drove up and stopped, a green Festina with a young man in it. The pump attendant shut the shop door behind him and turned the sign that said 'Closed'. My mother said something.

"What?"

"Oh, nothing." What she'd actually said was, 'It's starting.'

As we drove away, I could see the sign and the man's shadow behind the glass. The young fellow in the Festina simply leaned on his horn: the noise needled after us when the pump and the shop were out of sight.

"Why did he say not to come back?"

My mother was smiling as she drove, but her knuckles stood out sharp where she held the wheel. "He wasn't very pleased with himself for giving me petrol, and he wasn't pleased with me for getting him to do it," my mother said.

"But you gave him the money."

"I did."

"Then why – "

"It's a strange day, Maura." She turned up the radio. I sulked but couldn't sleep. Conor stirred in the back seat and whinged in a hot, scratchy voice. He's got a cold now, I thought. 'It's a strange day, Maura!' Oh, wow. Jinkers!

There is no news coming out of Damascus at present ...

The interview with Monsieur de Rais has been cancelled ...

"Boring, boring ... "

"Shut up, Maura!"

"I'll bet you didn't bring any of my books."

"Sh-h-h!"

"You're driving too fast!"

She slowed again, driving with taut deliberation. "All right. All right."

She had taken some detour to go to the petrol station, and I wasn't easy until I recognised the roads near the cottage. When she finally drove up the boreen and stopped the car in front of it, my hands were aching. I realised that they were in fists, and that my nails, stubby as they were, had pressed deep grooves in my palms.

CHAPTER FOUR

FOR THE FIRST TIME, THE DAMP-COZY SMELL OF THE COTTAGE seemed wrong to me. It was a holiday smell, an O'Keeffe smell: it wasn't right for now. I paused inside the front door. Everything seemed the same: there was the slow drip from the tap in the sink, and the Sacred Heart picture that had been Auntie Pat's still hung near the door – "too awful to be objectionable," my mother had said. "She loved it; we shouldn't take it away." I remember my father's grateful look.

He had spent many summers with his aunt when he was a boy, and his childhood had always hovered in the cottage like a silent friend. Now something watchful and distant seemed to have taken his place.

I helped my mother put away groceries; every crevice of the car had some sort of foodstuff in it. My mother hated tins, but now she had lashings of them: beans, peas, corn, fruits, meat stews, soups. And she'd four tin openers – four!

"But you've the electric tin opener!"

"In case it breaks."

"Daddy doesn't like things in tins."

"He'll like this." She pushed her hair off her face.

"Conor's crying."

"Will you please bring him in from the car, then!" I heaved a sigh and went to fetch him. Mum had reached her smacking threshold and, besides, I was too uneasy to be cheeky. Conor was howling in the back seat, his face red and angry. I held him tight while he snuffled, outraged.

"She's going bats, but I'll take care of you." I said this loudly so she'd hear me, but she'd turned on the radio again, and I could hear water running.

Conor stuck his small nails into my neck as he clung fast to me. I changed his nappy, shut myself against the radio, grudgingly ate the supper.

Mum listened to those voices. She didn't meet our eyes. She stood up before we were finished, told me to mind Conor, and went outside. I stood up to turn off the radio, then sank down again; I was afraid to turn it off.

London will not be evacuated. In his press conference at Downing Street half an hour ago, the Prime Minister said that any casualties in our cities will be caused by panic. The public are requested to stay at home ...

Was it coming, then, the thing that turned your skin black and made it fall off while you were nearly looking at it, the winds and fires that made matchsticks of houses and skeletons and shadows or dust heaps out of people? We'd heard about all that. I put my head down on my arms.

The door opened and my mother pushed in, dragging a wheelbarrow. I watched her take out the turf, piece by piece, and stack it in the window recess until the glass was covered. She seemed purposeful, almost happy.

She made two more trips. She blocked the windows, the one at the side of the main room facing West; the back window of the bedroom; then that of Conor's and my little room that looked east toward the stream, and finally, the front windows. I sat on the sofa, Conor asleep beside me, and watched her make our cottage into a cave. At last she said gently, "Maura, would you put Conor in his cot now?"

I nodded, dumb.

"I hope none of this is necessary, Maura."

I picked up Conor, warm and sighing, and brought him back to his cot. Our room was smothered in darkness. Even the light, switched on, seemed drained. There was a sensation of dust from the turf in the window, and a faint spill of it on my coverlet. I tucked Conor into his cot but left the light on in my parents' room that led to ours. I opened the two doors wide so we could hear him, though I thought my mother was beyond hearing anything but her horrible radio.

There were no books; she had forgotten them. She'd brought her own things, all right. The easel, folded, leaned in the far corner and beside it stretcher boards and a loose, tall cylinder of canvas.

When I recognised it, I felt a sudden wild burst of delight, followed by fear. Surely she wouldn't bring her paints if we were to stay only a weekend. The picture couldn't dry if she worked on it, not in time to …

"I'm thirsty. Mum … I'm thirsty!"

She held up her hand to quiet me, but rose and filled a glass for me at the sink. Her eyes met mine for a moment, calm, determined, and remote as she listened to the quickening radio voices, but as I reached out to take the glass from her, the voices stopped.

In the blackness, in the silence, the glass shattered, invisible, on the flags at our feet.

"Oh God," she murmured. "Oh, God." Her shoes crunched on the glass. Her cold hands found my shoulders in the dark, the back of my head. She was shaking. We clung together, groping for the door to the bedrooms. Conor whimpered somewhere in front of us. She moved suddenly, and I heard her head hit off the doorframe.

"Don't leave me, Mummy!"

She dragged me forward, stumbling; I stubbed my toe

on their bed, hit my arm on the door beyond, clutching her all the time, and as I felt the shock of her bumping into the cot, something happened under our feet. For two, three, five seconds the floor was gently alive. Then nothing, only Conor's quiet breathing beside us. After a long while, my mother whispered, "Maura … "

I couldn't speak. I held a fold of her dress in my fist, and listened to Conor breathing.

CHAPTER FIVE

I DREAMED THE RIVER WAS MADE OF KNIVES. FROM THE COTTAGE they looked like water in the sunlight, but I drew near and saw steel against steel busily moving and the sound was angry. My father waved, smiling, from the other shore; he was a boy preparing to cross to me. I couldn't make him hear. He smiled with love and jumped into the knives.

My mother stood in the doorway. I could hardly see her; the turf blocked the morning light. Conor heaved up, unsteady, in his cot. The knife-noises were very loud. She picked Conor out of the cot and sat with him on my bed. "Well, it's morning," she said. "But I don't know what kind of a morning it is."

"What's that sound?" I whispered.

"The river. It must be very full."

"Why?"

"Wind … rain … "

I realised I was still in my clothes. "I'll go look!"

Her arm tightened around me. "We can't go outside, Maura."

"Is it raining?"

"No, but I think the air is – " she seemed to be

searching for the word.

"Is it smog?" I asked, not believing it.

"No. Nothing you can see." Her voice was dull. I nudged her arm. "I think it's radiation," she said.

I wouldn't, couldn't ask her more about it. We'd all heard the word and seen the films from that time in Russia.

In our main room, the lights wouldn't come on. "Why do we need that stuff on the window?"

"It keeps out the radiation, Maura."

"Is there any music on the radio?"

"It's – not working. I don't think it's working."

"Why isn't it?" Again, I had to tug at her. "Mum?"

"The radio stations aren't working. I don't think. It's something to do with – but I don't know … quite how it happens." She frowned, as if trying to remember.

"Are you sure?"

"Yes, almost."

My head ached with wondering and trying not to wonder. Now and again she tried the radio, but not even the fuzzy sound came out of it.

"I brought no batteries," she said to herself. "Unbelievable."

"What'll we do?" I said, after our milk and cereal.

She handed me the broom. She wasn't sure whether we should flush the loo or not. Finally she decided we could, unless something strange happened.

"What?"

"I don't know. The water not filling in it, or … perhaps turning a strange colour. I don't know."

Even on that first day, Conor and I slept a lot. There was little else to do, and we knew it. At mid-morning it got very windy, and the noise from the river increased. Conor and I dozed on the sofa. Once I opened my eyes and saw my mother sitting in the fireside chair across from me looking at nothing, her brows slightly lifted, intent. I remembered how the neighbour's cat crouched under our car while the dog from up the road, white-toothed, snarled beside the tyre. Now the river snarled and slithered by our house, and my mother hunched helpless in her chair. There was no other sound.

The night was only the day, darker. Conor fussed until my mother came on bare feet to lift him and bring him to her bed. I lay alone as long as I could and then groped my way to join them. In the morning she lay beside me white-faced, open-mouthed, but sleeping; I held my palm above her mouth to be sure. I don't know what made me do that.

How can I explain how the next days, which were safe, were almost our worst? We were so quiet, so cold: no one came; no car was heard beyond the boreen.

"When is Daddy coming?"

"I don't know, Maura."

"Well, when? He said Tuesday, Mum!"

"Today's Wednesday." I looked at her, then flung into the back bedroom and slammed the door. I cried with my face in the pillow, hoping she would come, but she didn't. Never would I come out of the bedroom and never would I forgive her. Finally she knocked and said she had supper. I decided to come out for Conor's sake.

"I thought we needed a fire," she said quietly. It sparkled in the grate.

"I won't look," I said.

"It doesn't matter, Maura." She put her arm around me and kissed my forehead. I took from this that nothing mattered, and as we ate our supper, two tins of stew and a tin of peaches, we looked different, like a family I didn't know, people pretending to be us.

That night when my mother and Conor were asleep, a helicopter passed over our cottage.

"I would have waked up," she said flatly when I told her in the morning.

"You didn't."

"A helicopter – you were dreaming, Maura! There haven't even been any cars."

"I heard it."

"I'm sorry, Pet – it won't make any difference."

"What do you mean?"

"I mean we still can't go outside." She made me help her tidy and sweep. Our rooms were neat, but the air in them seemed to have died, and I felt irritable and aware of the turf here and there, which made everything slyly gritty. The weather was close and cold, what my father called 'flu weather'.

I slouched on the sofa pretending to be asleep in the afternoon, trying to puzzle things out. As the minutes, the hours of that Thursday crawled along, I began wondering if Mum was crazy. She wouldn't go out after Conor was born; she wouldn't paint. That was part of her illness.

What if, outside, the world went on as usual, what if my father had simply been delayed and couldn't contact us? The whole weight of contrary evidence, conversations overheard, radio, the power failure, the sheer universal skewedness, evaporated for me. Clearly, I'd responsibilities: I must telephone Lizzie. Since we'd no phone in the cottage, I must sneak out and find one.

My mother was dozing in the fireside chair in the main room, Conor asleep on her lap. I slipped back to the bedroom, closing the door gently behind me. There was no sound from the sitting-room. I took the turf away from the window, and the sash moved quite easily; I left it open, because it would be hard to raise it again from the outside.

The afternoon sky was dull and a bit watery. The river, really a stream where it passed us, was still noisier than usual, gleaming beyond the stand of trees where the ground sloped down to it. I went over to look at it.

It had risen above the stony margin where we entered it to swim, and it flowed along its new grass banks with cruel efficiency. It had gone down since my dream and no longer sounded like a thousand knives, but it had a victim; in a place where debris formed a partial dam, the swollen carcass of a sheep, legs upended, bobbed against the waste like some strange table overturned. Caught near it was a black rubber Wellington boot. I couldn't imagine my boy-father ever swimming in that careless desolation. I turned away from it and, staying among the trees for cover, headed towards the road.

I believed in the world's difference by the time I reached the hedge, and that saved me. Partly it was the stream, and the sheep that would have been searched out and removed if times were right; partly it was signs I'd recognise now but could only intuit then, the birdlessness, the stillness below the silence.

I crouched against the hedge when I heard the men. There were two or three of them on the road, walking. Their voices came in snatches on the breeze: they walked soundlessly. Somehow I knew they were too old to be lads walking together, too young, too quiet to be poor bachelors coming from the pub – old men in the country didn't wear soft shoes. And their voices were Dublin voices. They stopped beside our boreen.

"So what's up there?"

" … to find out."

One of them laughed, and at the tone of it I sank lower, shutting my eyes, like a baby hiding.

" … stupid. We could have stayed there."

"With the dogs going mad? … have waked the dead."

"They didn't." Two or three of them, laughing softly together.

" … have a dec" came from a few feet up the boreen. I

thought of the open window and could feel the tears starting.

" … back here!" The voice, deadly, cut through the air. Twigs snapped as the other man returned.

" … broad daylight, you stupid gobshite, and … "

" … starved!"

"All in good time," said the colourless voice of the man who had laughed.

Only a murmured comment from farther down the road told me they were moving away. Still I huddled, shivering. It was a long time before I dared cross the exposed place near the road and then, sweating, run back to the cottage and my open window.

The first thing I saw when I scrambled over the ledge was my mother staring at me, Conor in her arms. She turned, walked into the main room and put him in his high chair. I latched the window.

Then she was back. Without a word she sat down, threw me over her legs and gave me the first spanking on my backside I had ever known. Afterwards she stood me up, seized my shoulders and shook me like a rat. "Don't you ever, ever do that again! Don't you ever!" Then she half-dragged me into the main room, her fingers a circular bruise round my arm. She pushed me onto the sofa, glaring. Then she turned to the sink. Her back was shaking.

"I heard some men."

"Helicopters! Men!" She looked at me, her face white and crumpled-looking. "You could have made yourself very sick – you've probably let bad air – "

"The men weren't sick, Mum. They were just walking on the road."

She took a long breath. "What were they like, then?" she said quietly.

"I didn't see them. I hid."

"I heard nothing, Maura."

"Mum, they were – quiet. And they didn't want you to see them. One wanted to see if we were here, and the other one told him not to come in the daytime. I think they were from Dublin, Mum."

"Why?"

"The way they talked."

"My God. People are out just walking around."

"I heard nothing else, Mum. It's so quiet. And there's a dead sheep in the stream. And a wellie."

She drew her hand across her face, very slowly. I put my arms around her. "Do you think I'm – ? Do you think – nothing's happened, maybe?"

"Something's happened," I whispered.

We sat frozen when the pounding started on the door. My mother recollected herself, rushed from the sofa and tried to quiet Conor, who was in his high chair. She even put her hand over his mouth, at which he screamed with rage.

"Bring me the poker!" she mouthed at me.

"Mrs O'Keeffe! Mrs O'Keeffe, are you in there?"

We stared at one another.

"That's no Dub," said my mother. She moved to the door, hesitated. "Who's there?"

"Mrs O'Keeffe?" bawled the voice.

"Who's that?" she screamed back. A second man's voice was heard. He seemed to be temporising with the first.

"It's Garda Mullen," said the loud voice.

"Please walk to the window," my mother said firmly. I thought of the goat and the seven little kids, but the turf, when she removed some pieces, revealed a man's pale, offended-looking face. Then a hand appeared. It held a Garda identification card. My mother opened the door.

Garda Mullen looked old to me, but he'd have been only in his twenties. He had black hair and a thick stubble of beard. There were great dark rings under his eyes, and his skin was blotchy and pale. Mum gave him a close look, her artist's look, but there was something else, too – pity, fear?

The man with him was older, with sandy colouring and a mild, almost hangdog look. "You're right to be careful," he said softly. "You're right, indeed."

"Mr Coffey," Garda Mullen said, nodding towards him. "Local councillor."

"Haven't we met?" my mother said, staring at him. Then she blushed.

"The Interpretative Centre," he murmured, nodding.

"Ye'll hardly have that to argue about now," said the Guard.

"You'll sit down, won't you … "

They perched uneasily on the sofa, making it look somehow pathetic. They were both wearing strong boots.

"Will you have tea?"

"We'll not take your supplies, so, Mrs O'Keeffe, but thank you very much." Mr Coffey leaned forward, elbows on knees. "It's not often we'd get such an offer. People are very careful now."

Garda Mullen was falling asleep. His eyes glazed, then shut; his head rocked forward.

"Out on his feet," Mr Coffey said, nodding at him. "You'll know how it's been this past while."

"I don't," my mother said. "I don't know anything."

"Ah … " said Mr Coffey. "I see." He moved his big feet.

"I've no batteries for the radio, you see – we've heard nothing since … "

"Thursday night," he said gravely. He peered unseeingly into our cold grate.

"What did happen, Mr Coffey?"

"Your husband's not with you, Mrs O'Keeffe," he said softly, like he was answering a question.

47

My mother looked at me. "He's in Washington."

"I see."

"Mr Coffey … ?"

He cleared his throat, looked at me.

"This is my daughter, Maura, Mr Coffey."

He nodded and gave me a kind look from his tired pale eyes.

"Maura love, take Conor inside to the bedroom, I want to talk privately to Mr Coffey. Please, Maura." She lifted Conor out of his high chair and handed him to me. "Thanks."

Inside the bedroom, I lifted Conor into his cot. Miraculously, he was sleepy and didn't notice I wanted to get away from him. I eased the door open a crack.

" … mainly Westerlies, anyhow. Only time will tell," Mr Coffey was saying. I could see the back of his head. "It's all set up at Athlone, of course. They just can't raise any intelligible signals from anywhere."

"Dublin?" She breathed it, just.

Mr Coffey put his hand to the back of his neck and half-turned his head. My mother looked up and saw me.

"Maura!"

I closed the door. Their voices became muffled again. I curled under the covers on my parents' bed like some hibernating small animal, going drowsy and warm, pretending how by summer the world would be ready for us again.

My mother's words became distinct. "My husband's family was here for generations!"

"Yes, I know – "

"And you're telling me I can't go back to Dublin!"

"I know, Mrs O'Keeffe, but – I'm sorry, but – "

He was standing up. My mother was already on her feet.

"Maura, go back inside!"

Instead, I walked around the sofa and stood beside her. Her hand went on my shoulder, hard and trembling. Garda Mullen's eyes were open now, and he was moving his feet as if to get up.

"There now, lad, take your time," said Mr Coffey. He gripped him gently under the shoulders as if he were a child. Garda Mullen was sweating. He put his hand over his mouth, pressing hard, then lurched towards the door, which Mr Coffey opened for him. We heard him retching outside.

Mum's hand went up to her throat. "He should be home in his bed!"

"He doesn't care," Mr Coffey said, as if apologising for him. "He's lost everything. You know what I was telling you, about, you know … "

My mother nodded.

"The farm next to his. He went back that night, to check on his family." He looked nervously out the door. "The little girl died this morning, and the wife, well, she was in England. His parents are very bad. You're better to be with your own people, Mrs O'Keeffe, while you can still get to them."

He pushed the door open. Garda Mullen stood on the path, unsteady, his face a sick glow in the twilight. The door closed. The room darkened.

I put my arm around my mother's waist. She simply stared at the door, as if waiting for it to open again. Conor woke up with slow, scratchy cries, and neither of us seemed able to move. Finally she stirred, and I let go of her.

CHAPTER SIX

AT FIRST SHE WOULDN'T TELL ME WHAT MR COFFEY HAD SAID. "IT just doesn't concern you, darling. It hardly concerns me, either. In a way." But she put Conor and me into the big bed that night and told me to stay there and keep him there, too. She had to do something in the main room and didn't want to be disturbed, she said.

What she did was cry. While Conor crawled around the bed in the dark, lively as a flea because of his long nap, playing games with my face and hair, she cried. When he finally went to sleep, she was crying. In the morning she still wasn't in the room, and I found her slumped on the sofa, her face white and soft-looking, her lashes gummed shut.

Now our rooms looked twice as forlorn to me. The sofa still sagged a little where Garda Mullen had sat on it, and the fireside chair retained its different angle where my mother had adjusted it, and everything was a thousand times more desolate than before.

I wanted to talk about them. "Mum, what's wrong with Garda Mullen?"

"I'm not sure."

"He'd a weird smell."

"I know. Poor man."

"What was it?"

"How would I know? Something to do with his sickness, maybe, something he wore ... "

"Mr Coffey's nice."

"He's a very clever man," said my mother. Then she rose heavily, took out the broom and started to sweep.

I cuddled Conor on the sofa. He seemed tired these days; he was content to be held for long periods, where before he'd have squirmed away and started exploring or playing. I could see my own bewilderment in his blue eyes. He sat on my lap, his soft hair against my cheek, his heart fluttering bravely against my chest, and I was soothed. We watched our mother moving around the room.

What had Mr Coffey said to her that had her looking like an old woman? My two selves jarred against each other, the one that didn't want to know and the one that had to know or go mad.

That evening there was a sudden loud rapping at the door. Mum, who was standing almost beside it, gave such a start that I laughed. As usual, we'd heard no-one approaching.

"Who's there?" She removed two sods from the windowsill and I could see a shadow across it. She opened the door.

It was Mr Coffey. There were two people behind him, a man and a boy. The boy waited outside the door, gazing back down the boreen as if he didn't care where he was. He was tall, taller than our neighbour Rupert in Killiney, who was seventeen, although he looked the same age. This boy was thin; he'd a beaky nose too big for him and jet black hair. He was like a beautiful starved crow. I wondered why he wouldn't join the others.

" ... John Hughes," Mr Coffey was saying. My mother

nodded at the new man but said nothing, only waited.

"Dominic here needs a place to stay," he went on, tilting his head at the boy behind him. The boy caught my mother's eye and shrugged as if to say, 'You don't have to.' "He's a quiet boy, good with his hands – "

"You sound like you're offering me a serf," my mother said. We all looked at her, astonished, except the boy himself, who seemed to have returned to some bleak daydream of his own.

Mr Coffey's shoulders slumped placatingly, but Mr Hughes's eyes narrowed. He cleared his throat. "If we're to try to support the Dublin refugees, we feel that they should be prepared to help one another, as well," he said.

"What refugees?"

"Well, yourselves! And this young lad."

"I'm no refugee," said my mother, "in my own house, on my own land." She turned to Mr Coffey. "You said you could do nothing for us, and now you arrive up with a poor, starving boy to be looked after – "

The boy began to walk quietly towards the boreen. I pushed out the door after him.

"Wait!" I tugged at his wrist. "Don't go! She wants you, she will."

He stopped and looked down at me. "She doesn't, and she's right, too."

His eyes were hazel. His hair wasn't black now that I was close to him, only very dark brown.

"She's only annoyed at those two. They keep calling us refugees."

"She's right about the food," he said indifferently. "Nobody's handing it out, and it'll be gone – then ... " He shrugged.

"Never mind. What are you doing here? Are you really from Dublin?"

The air fanned past me as he half-fell, half-sat on the

ground. He rested his forehead on his knees. His shoes were trainers, very worn. There was a big split in the right one where the cloth was torn away from the sole. He wasn't wearing any socks. "Are you all right?"

"Yeah. Just tired."

"Why?"

"You don't ask questions, do you?"

"I'm sorry," I said. "You won't go away, sure you won't?"

He looked at me, gave a half-smile, shook his head. "Not yet." His hazel eyes were made up of flecks of green and gold and brown. He'd a nice, thin face.

"You'll stay," I insisted.

Mr Coffey and Mr Hughes came down the path, Mr Hughes puffing slightly, my mother behind them.

"Well, Dominic," she said. Her voice had an edge, but the hand she rested on his shoulder was light. "You'll see how you like refugee hospitality." Then she helped him up.

"Come inside, Maura." She marched off, almost dragging Dominic beside her.

Mr Hughes made an angry noise and stalked down the boreen, but Mr Coffey drifted over to me. "Maura's the name, isn't it?"

I looked at him without answering. Then I turned toward the cottage.

"I'm not asking you to tell me your business or your mam's. Look here to me."

I stopped.

He scratched his head. "T'would be good to persuade your ma to go to your aunt there, the nun. Dominic knows a bit about cars. He'd be a help to you."

"And what if those three men chase us on the road?" I said sullenly.

He went still. "Three men?"

"I have to go in now."

"Wait. What three men, Maura?"

"I don't know."

"Why do you think they might chase you?"

Why hadn't my mother told him about them? I looked towards the cottage, longing for her to come out and give me some notion of what to do.

Mr Hughes was clearing his throat noisily in the boreen, but Mr Coffey's patient, faded eyes did not leave mine.

"I didn't see them. I heard them on the road. They said they'd come to our house at night … maybe. They'd Dublin voices, they … one of them had a horrible laugh." When I mentioned the laugh, Mr Coffey's eyes sharpened in recognition.

"Try to persuade your mam," he said gently, "to go to your aunt. We know that the house and all is your mam's, dear – I knew your Aunt Pat, your great-aunt that is, very well, and your dad, too. It's just – you'll be safer with your aunt the nun there in Wicklow, but your mam shouldn't wait too long to travel."

My face was getting big with tears, but I wouldn't cry.

"Let nobody in, will you?"

I shook my head.

"Good girl." He pushed at the brim of his cap with his index finger and lumbered off after Mr Hughes.

I hurried the few steps to our door, my teeth chattering. My mother was laying a fire. "You'll get some twigs for us, will you, Maura?"

I ran to the back of the cottage to look for them, because nothing on earth would have got me near the boreen. The sky was bright but the land was darkening, and Mr Coffey seemed to have taken our safety away with him.

The gales of the past week had ripped at every tree and shrub, and the area around the cottage was littered with small branches. The cottage seemed deserted from the back, inward-looking and vulnerable, and the Volvo, cluttered with leaves, looked as if it would never move again. I hurried here and there, stooping, panting, until my arms were full.

Our big room was darkening when I stood in the front door clutching my sticks. The only strong light came from the gas ring on the cooker. It softened by the time it reached Dominic on the sofa, blurring the tired lines in his face and the harsh thinness of his body, making him look older and stronger. I got an odd sensation, as if I were about to have a 'dream', but somehow different. It felt physical: something in my chest seemed to move sideways, as if there was now an empty place beside my heart. At the time it felt like a kind of hunger, and I was glad to see the kettle starting to steam on the ring, and the small collection of tins and tired fruits on the worktop. I put down my bits of wood on the hearth, and my mother began to build up the fire.

She gave Dominic a kind look over her shoulder. "How long were you in the podgy clutches of our friend Hughes?"

Dominic stared at her. I squirmed, wishing she wouldn't try to be smart, but he smiled.

"A day. Last night." He shrugged. "They were trying to find me ... some place."

"And would they give you nothing to eat?"

"Ach ... I wasn't really hungry. They weren't bad, you know? They're totally caught out, em, Missus ... "

"I'm Sylvia. This is Maura, and the baby's Conor."

"Hi, Conor."

Conor made a jealous noise. He pulled himself up and held on to the sofa, watchful.

"Anyway ... " said Dominic. He put out his finger and moved it up Conor's chest, as if counting buttons. When he got to the tickly place at the neck, he gave it a gentle wiggle, and Conor offered a half-smile. Usually he didn't like strangers.

"How'd you come to meet them?"

"Mr Hughes? Oh, the Garda brought me to him. The Civil Defence is in the village, see, but there aren't enough of them to ... and they don't want us hanging around. There's been trouble. They're trying to sort out ... You can't blame them, really."

"Do you want Coffeemate in it? We've no fresh milk."

"Sure, I don't mind ... thanks." He took small sips of the tea. His hands began shaking. "It's good. I – "

He put the mug down on the floor and started crying. He looked surprised; then he put one hand over his eyes. He leaned over, resting his elbow on his leg as if he were relaxing, almost, but he was sobbing all the while. My mother sat down beside him on the sofa and put her arm around him.

"It's been pretty bad, has it?"

He nodded, crying.

"Were you by yourself a long time?"

He shook his head. Conor grabbed my mother's skirt, pulled at it. I picked him up, opened his hands, and brought him aside.

"They're all gone, all of them ... "

"Your family?"

"Yes ... !"

"You couldn't get back to them."

"The fuckin' teacher ... the bus driver! ... wouldn't go back. And we tried – three of us walked, we walked from Galway. They stopped us at Athlone and again here. They told us nobody could go near Dublin ... they were all dead!" He rubbed his eyes.

"What happened to the other boys?"

"I left them in Athlone. One bloke's father is a cousin of Fitzpatrick's, you know, some Minister – and the other lad,

Jimmo, got sick. We brought him to a kind of clinic, whatever, they've got going there. Desmond said he'd stay with him. Jimmo wasn't too good ... I went on." He wiped his face on his sleeve.

"What did you hope to do?" my mother said softly.

"Find them." His voice quivered. "Bury them. Just know."

My mother nodded, her eyes shining with tears.

"Everyone in Dublin is dead?" It was my own voice, incredulous and thin.

He nodded, oblivious.

Then there was no airport. Dad could never get back to us, even if he was alive. For some reason I didn't even consider the other airports in the country.

I set Conor down, crept over to the fireplace, and put sticks and sods on the fire until it blazed. I turned the red sods over and over with the poker to coax the heat from them until they were a medley of fallen shapes, blazing, disintegrating.

My mother prised my hand from the poker and led me away. Now my hand and face felt hot.

"Well?" she said.

"I was cold." I curled up on the sofa and went to sleep.

It must have been only moments later when the draught from the door chilled my face and my mother said, "Dominic?" She was turning up the gas under the kettle, not looking. "Did you find the turf all right?" But it wasn't Dominic in the doorway; it was a man. Another came in behind him. They were quiet as two ghosts in their soft trainers.

"Where is the other one?" I whispered.

They looked at one another. "Dominic – " said my mother. She saw them. She'd an apple in one hand and the kitchen knife in the other. She put down the apple very slowly.

"The name's James," said the first man. He looked at her eagerly. His companion giggled.

"And I'm Paddy!" he said.

"Maura ... take Conor and put him in the bedroom." Conor was crawling towards them, beaming. I grabbed him and hurried into the bedroom, half-flinging him into his cot.

I heard the explosion of my mother's breath, her muffled cry, before I even got back into the room. The first man was wrenching her arm, while she flailed at him with her free hand, and the knife, which she clutched like death, flashed in the light from the fire. The other man padded towards them, laughing.

"I'm first," his friend grunted. He was trying to whack my mother's arm against the wall so she'd drop the knife, but she twisted and writhed and kicked at him – she'd only slippers on her feet. Her eyes stared; her lips were drawn back from her teeth.

The other man hovered, his eyes intent. Then he saw me. I stumbled away and huddled near the cooker. The first man hit my mother's arm full against the wall. The knife bounced down beside me.

I put it straight into him. He didn't even know I was there. I was so surprised it would go in that I just stood there with my hands at my sides, looking at it. The hilt stuck out of him like a black joystick. His arms dropped. He looked at my mother, confused. She gave him a violent push on the chest, and he staggered backwards and fell, his back arching a little because of the knife. The other man looked at my mother, then at him. His hand shot out – she crashed against the cooker, the kettle rocking with the force of it. "Maura, watch out!" But I couldn't, because he'd grabbed her by the upper arms and had flung her down. They sprawled together on the floor, my mother trying to break away from him. I remember my arm hurting, but that was the last thing I remember clearly from that night.

My mother told me he slapped her hard with the back of his hand and then reared up as if she had hit him instead. His mouth was opening and shutting and she saw smoke pouring out of his back. Then she felt scalding water on the side of her leg and realised I'd poured the kettle over him. He staggered up and went away; she didn't know where he'd gone. She told me to put the kettle back and turn off the gas, and I did. It was then she heard the third man laughing.

She pulled herself up on the sofa, then rose to shut the door, and he was there. He wandered in as if nothing was wrong; he was so relaxed he seemed normal.

I heard her telling Lizzie this part. She told me what I'd done: she said she had to, in case I remembered one day by myself. But it was the laundered version; she didn't talk about – *him*. He just strolled in.

"Well, well … " He pushed at the man on the floor, the one with the knife in him, with his foot. "Told him women would be his ruin … didn't think they'd be little kids." His laugh was genuine – he thought it was funny. My mother said she found herself smiling and saw me smiling too, and all the time the scalded man was moaning and whimpering outside.

It was only then she remembered Dominic. "What did you do to that boy?"

"Who's he to you?" asked the man in his soft, dead, pleasant voice. Then he had her by the wrist. She didn't know how; he was just holding her by the wrist, quite gently, except she knew that she wouldn't be able to pull away from him. He touched her face with his forefinger, he let it slide right down her face, barely grazing it. The finger then went down her chest, stopping where the swell of her breast began. He raised his eyebrows, smiled at her.

"Let me go – now!" He was still smiling, but he looked

sideways at me, and my mother said to Lizzie, 'I just knew.'

She hurled herself at him with all her strength. He staggered back, but he was up like a cat, laughing outright. He weaved around the table – she'd run around the other side of it – feinting as if to grab her. She said they heard Conor at the same time. He backed across the room, smiling, watching her. "No!" She flung herself after him, but he pushed her; he was into the bedroom and out again, Conor under his arm, before she could reach him. She went mad. She raved, darted, clawed, while he held Conor out to her, teasing.

Conor was screaming. Then my mother saw me coming with the poker out of the fire, and it first landing on the man's neck, then his face when he turned. He dropped Conor and wrenched the poker "and when he hit at her with it – " she said. But he dropped it after, and ran out.

"Oh, Lizzie," she said. "To think she'd do all that!"

"God is good," Lizzie said mildly. My mother made a sound between a laugh and a snort. She hadn't meant that, and I, listening, knew it.

"She was looking into the fire just before, wasn't she? It might have made her particularly strong … it was for the best, Sylvia, that's the point."

I'd become a common sneak by then, listening at doors and behind walls like people used to read the newspaper, my excuse being that only Dominic would ever tell me anything.

After the attack I went back to sleep on the sofa. It remained to my mother to go out in the dark by herself to look for Dominic. They'd kicked him and hit him hard on the head, but he recovered quite soon. Only two people went away scarred; myself and the terrible man. My mother said she saw the mark across his face when he turned to hit me; and I've the tiny mark on my forehead, just below the hairline, where he caught me in return.

CHAPTER SEVEN

I WOKE AT MID-MORNING. MR HUGHES AND MR COFFEY WERE standing near the fireplace, talking to my mother. The turf had been removed from the windows, and yellow light struggled through the small, smudged panes. The room was curiously bare; all our bits and pieces were gone, and the floor had been swept. It was almost as if we had just arrived.

"Are we going?" It was like somebody else's voice, a very small child's.

"We are."

"To Lizzie?"

"Yes." Mum sighed and rubbed at her hair. "Can you get to the loo?"

She had to help me. She moved as if she were a thousand years old; we both did. When I saw us in the bathroom mirror, I cried. My hair was stuck in the angry mark the poker had made, and my face was white and streaked with dirt. My mother had a black eye, and her face on that side looked a slightly different shape. When she washed me – I had wet my pants – I saw that her right arm was a mottle of bruises. She had to leave me there, shivering and crying, while she went to the car to bring back cleaner clothes. We left the smelly ones on the bathroom floor.

I could talk to Dominic about it afterwards. 'Well, what were you going to do?' he'd say mildly. 'Just wait there while they killed you?' But he had not seen me. My mother had. For a while, she was wary of me, I felt, and I was wary of myself. Indeed, I wasn't myself, any more than the world was itself any more.

Mr Hughes and Mr Coffey saw us off. Mr Hughes put a plastic bag full of young cabbages in the boot without saying a word. I sensed they were glad to get rid of us, but me especially, even though Mr Coffey said they owed us for "helping with their problem".

"And, Mrs O'Keeffe – you'll keep the windows up, will you?"

She gave Mr Coffey a frightened look. "What's happened?"

"Garda Mullen. Outside the whole time. Bleeding here." He drew back his lips and pointed, grotesquely, to his gums. "He was almost surely in the wrong place at the wrong time, but better safe than sorry."

My mother helped me into the back seat.

Conor looked at me sadly. He put out his hand, paused, hesitant.

"It's me, Conser," I said. "It's only me."

The morning light dazzled my eyes and made them water, and my last vision of Mr Coffey and Mr Hughes was of two blurred, breaking angels, who waved and turned away from us.

At first, there was little sign of what had happened: even the ruins we passed, the roofless cottages and crumbling outhouses, were old scars left from earlier disasters. The land spread itself beyond the hedges as if it still felt safe; it snuggled green and trusting beneath the shop-soiled sky that waited to smudge it. I thought of Garda Mullen's gums, blackening and bleeding stains onto his perfect teeth.

Our car made the only noise. I thought it must be heard for miles, everything was so quiet, and that the terrible man could track us all the way to Wicklow, but there was nothing until we saw the jogger running towards us on our side of the road, head down, pacing himself. He didn't look up at us, only raised his hand; he was wearing a white singlet, green shorts, white socks and his jogging shoes. His face, glimpsed beside the window, was as tranquil as a saint's.

For some reason, my mother and Dominic almost choked laughing.

"I thought I was seeing things."

"Maybe we were, Dominic."

"I saw him," I said sullenly.

"You miss nothing," he said. He didn't move his head, but it was as if he'd turned and looked at me, or smiled.

Conor sighed. It was a small, patient sound. His eyelids were waxy-looking; he seemed smaller. He'd lost his crisp plumpness of hand and wrist, and his limbs seemed frailer and more supple than before. I watched him until my own eyes grew heavy and I went to sleep, the sickening, closed movement of the car like a spoiled cradle.

Dominic explained the other two incidents to me later, because of the nightmares. First, I woke to hear my mother saying, "Don't get out!" to Dominic, who did anyway.

There was a queer smell in the air of a bonfire and something else. We had stopped opposite a small bungalow whose roof had a great black hole in it and whose black, empty windows had terrible dark swatches flaring around them and up to the eaves. Smoke still drifted idly above the roof. Across the road, cows pressed against the gate and one another, lowing miserably.

The door to the cottage was partly ajar. Dominic gave it

a strong push with his foot, then jumped back.

An orangey-coloured labrador, his coat stained with soot, hurtled out of the opening, followed by two other dogs. He threw himself at Dominic, who, braced against the wall, kicked him solidly in mid-leap. His squeal of pain discouraged the collie, who was scudding here and there, barking furiously; the third, smaller dog, a kind of terrier, slunk back into the cottage and re-emerged half-dragging something in his jaws.

Just as he dropped it, Dominic realised what it was: a blackened human hand. My mother, who was running down the path with a wooden spoon she had found between the seats, saw it, too. They said nothing when they got back into the car, only stopped at a farmhouse a little further on, one that had a yard and cattle grazing opposite. The people wouldn't open the door. My mother shouted to them that their neighbour's house had burned, that his cattle were waiting to be milked, that there were dogs in a pack.

I didn't wake when they stopped in the Wicklow mountains. Dominic described that lonely scene to me only much later, when I was haunted by a vision of a hill, thickly forested, and three birds high to the right rising and falling like kites on a gusty day, three kites on three strings held by the one person. It was Dominic who saw the break in the guard rail beside the road, and the blue Mercedes overturned halfway down the hill; he struggled down far enough to see that the people inside had been dead for some time, and then climbed up again.

Finally they were afraid to stop the car at all; where the road began lowering on its way to the coast, a straggle of men tried to block us, and if Dominic hadn't made my mother drive at them, we'd have walked the rest of the way.

We were in more populous farm country, though the

land was still hilly and clotted with forests. I daydreamed that when we got to Wicklow and met Lizzie, everything would be all right. Even as I wished it, we passed a farm gate, padlocked and chained, then another, and finally a chained gate with a yard but glimpsed, a man sitting on a chair in the middle of it with a shotgun on his knee.

Around the next curve, cars were clustered on a wide verge that had been trampled to mud. "Travellers," my mother said. But they weren't Travellers, or gypsies. Some people sat inside the cars and others squelched around outside; there was nothing family there, no look of order, and one woman, leaning against a dirty BMW, wore a long blue dressing-gown like a coat. Only a little boy paid us any notice; he half-raised his arm as if to point at us, then looked aimlessly around him.

My mother said nothing, but the next time I saw her face in the mirror, there were tears in her eyes.

In Wicklow, the shop streets zigzagged down the hill towards the sea and the old red convent buildings dominated the town, glowering halfway up. But now the streets, that had gleamed dull grey, were brown near the harbour, and farther on was an untidy-looking jumble of mud and sand.

The slate roofs of the houses still shone like pewter in the sun. But I was confused, and decided I was dreaming: down the hill, the red and black prow of a trawler was wedged against the yellow wall of the corner newsagent's, blocking and blotting out the road down to the harbour. My mother and Dominic had been looking the other way. I said nothing.

The road in front of the convent was choked with parked cars. A man got out of one of them and approached us. "They're not taking any more," he said brusquely. "You'll have to go on to Gorey."

"You're not from around here," my mother said coolly.

"I wouldn't say you are, either," said the man. He had wild-looking black hair, the kind that looks dry when it gets dirty, and he was wearing a soiled-looking business suit.

"Excuse me," Mum said, and rolled up her window. She backed down the road very carefully, stopping and parking the car around the corner in a cul-de-sac of ageing semi-detached houses.

The door of the house in front of us opened. A woman came out with a big boy behind her. "You can't stop here!" she said.

"Why not?" said my mother.

"We're keeping the road clear here," said the woman.

"Give it over, Mum," said the boy.

The woman turned and glared at him.

"Come on," said the boy. He put his arm around her shoulders and led her back into the house.

"We should have stayed where we were," my mother said. "We owned something, we'd a roof over our heads."

"Yeah, we could be farmers. No problem," Dominic said.

Conor was whimpering. "His nappy's dirty," I said. "Can I open the window?"

There we sat, yards from where Lizzie was, changing Conor's nappy. "I've only four more," my mother was saying. "I forgot to buy cloth ones. I don't know what I'll do. The last wipe."

"It's in a good cause." Dominic rolled his window down.

"He's got a rash."

I started crying. It was like listening to someone else, someone terribly upset. "I want Daddy, Daddy, Daddy," I howled. "I want Daddy!"

"Maura – " my mother said. Her face was peaked, and

her lips trembled. "I'm going to find Lizzie."

"I'll mind these," Dominic said to her. He licked his lips. He too was pale. My mother left Conor in her seat, and I saw his hand go out and catch Dominic's sleeve, but Dominic looked at me. "Maura," he said, "your mam's doing her best."

"I want Dad," I wept.

He started to speak, then stopped. He shifted as if to turn his back to me, then swivelled around again. "She's all you've got. You'd want to take care of her." He settled back in his seat, taking Conor on his lap.

He seemed so much older than me then; I didn't see him as the half-child that he was. He was steady and resourceful, but he was only seventeen, an orphan who had failed to get himself killed with the rest of his family, a stranger to all and sundry. It explained everything about him, if I'd only known.

My mother returned to the car. A nun had gone to find Lizzie for us. "She's here, anyway; she's alive." Then we sat and said nothing. I began to feel sleepy. I got the sensation of falling you get sometimes when you're tired, startled, and saw Lizzie. She was hurrying towards us, her lips parted, staring incredulously at our car. My mother got out, shaky and awkward, and here was Lizzie half-running, half-falling down the footpath. I laughed, I couldn't help it, and for some reason Dominic laughed too. But when Lizzie stuck her head into the car and looked at me with my father's blue eyes, I stopped laughing and clung to her so hard she gasped.

CHAPTER EIGHT

I HAD NEVER LIKED WICKLOW. WHEN WE VISITED LIZZIE THERE IN
the Old Times, I was always glad to get home to Killiney
again. The town, though pretty, was a sad place; it was
because of its decline that Lizzie, Brigid and Leonie had
been able to buy the old convent and school buildings for
a song, and there they lived noisy, deprived-looking lives
with their orphans.

I disliked the half-empty rooms with their makepiece,
shabby bits of furniture and smells of stark cleanliness and
damp. We never spent much time there; we would take
Lizzie to lunch in Arklow, or in the old hotel outside
Ashford. Then we would bring her back to the convent,
which was almost like a fortress with its red-brick wall and
gate, and we would hear the shrill voices of the children as
they ran to meet her. We never went in with her then; Dad
hated it too much.

The town itself was a bit like the convent, having
shrunk back into older, smaller confines. Now its life
centred in its sleepy harbour and straggle of streets up the
hill. The Depressions, then the Emigrations, had hit it hard,
and everything seemed grey. Dad called it "that dump". I
think it was because he and Lizzie had no money growing

up; it was as if he thought this greyness, if it kept expanding, must swallow them back again. I didn't want to be swallowed by it, either: I wanted to go home, home to the Old Times, really, though we didn't call them that yet. We weren't in the convent a day before I vowed to get back to Killiney by hook or by crook.

I don't remember much about our first week or two. We were gingerly absorbed into the routine of the orphanage, along with some other refugees, and there were gloomy suppers in the fading light of the huge refectory in the basement. We had eaten better in the cottage; our tinned food was exotic compared to the cabbage and carrot we were given now. Lizzie explained that perishable produce had to be eaten, while whatever could be stored had to be set aside for the winter. I saw this as a Wicklow approach to our problem: somewhere else, people must be eating sausages and chips and using salt and pepper. It's strange how you can re-believe things, or how you can ignore what's most obvious.

That first fortnight has a sad, evening quality in my memory. I see the long corridor in the west wing in my mind's eye, and Dominic at the end of it, hunched with grief. The red sunset slants through the windows, and it is still cold. I put my arms around his arm, my head on his shoulder, and he says nothing, the tears sliding slowly down his face.

Another picture is of my mother and Conor near the end of the table in the enormous kitchen. My mother is knitting ugly green socks. The kitchen is the warmest room, and Mum and Conor have been installed there, along with two or three other refugee women with small children. We older children were given chores of tidying, sweeping, and scraping vegetables; for all intents and purposes, we had become orphans.

The days, however, were a blessing compared to the

nights. The nights were not grey. They were spattered with dreams so vivid that they clung about me like bright, bloodstained scarves for half the morning. The third man – the man who had laughed – dominated all of them with his weird assurance and good humour, the wound I'd given him flaring across his face. In one dream he licked his finger and ran it along the scar, smiling at me all the while. Another time he had Conor in his hands, and he was slowly turning him around and over as if he were a thing, not a child at all. I would wake up screaming and crying, with Mum, exhausted, comforting me. After these bouts, I pleaded with her to go home; I knew there was enough petrol left in the car, because she had said it to someone. But it was always, "No, Maura. We can never go home again."

I asked Dominic if he knew how to drive a car.

"The cars we've got now, that sit still, right? You could drive one of those yourself."

"I mean our car. That's got petrol in it."

"Why not? We'll go for a spin."

"I mean it, Dominic!"

"What are you on about?"

"Home."

"Maura, have you not heard people talking? Wouldn't I have gone home if I could? You can't live in a place with that many dead people in it, you'd soon die yourself."

"There are no dead people in our house, we're all gone."

"We wouldn't be let there," he said. "I don't want to talk about that any more, Maura."

"All right then. Don't!"

I tried to remember the roads we used take from Killiney, and cried. And how long had it taken us to drive from there to Wicklow – an hour? How long would it take to walk?

Dominic came to our room on my second day in bed. "How's it going?"

I couldn't answer him.

"Hey!" He jiggled my arm. "Hello!"

His face swam through my tears. I clutched his thin, warm hand and went to sleep.

He came other days. "What is this? An effin' hunger strike? What are you at?"

"Nothing."

I hated getting out of bed, and the food wasn't worth eating. My mother was distraught. She and Lizzie talked about me as if I weren't there. "It isn't radiation," Lizzie told her. "She'd be sick, with stomach cramps and a temperature, like, you know … "

"Yes, but – a milder form – ?"

"Sure, the readings aren't high. Mr Rooney was out with his machine again this morning."

"Are you sure he knows how to work it?"

"It's the shock, Sylvia. That's all it is."

I whined, "I want to go home."

"This is your home now, pet, where your people are," said Lizzie warmly. I turned away. Mum started crying.

That evening Dominic arrived, glaring. "We can't go home," he said through his teeth.

"I won't stay here, I can't!"

"You're a spoilt little bitch!"

This was the final straw. I couldn't even cry.

He muttered something and flung away.

He was back at mid-morning the next day. "Where does your mam keep her keys?"

When he'd found them in her handbag, he dressed me as if I were a hateful doll. Then he carried me downstairs on his back. "Where are you going?" said one of the little children, who was standing by the front door.

"To the circus."

"You can't go outside," said the little boy. "It's raining." As we closed the door behind us, we could hear him calling Lizzie.

The Volvo was parked between the convent and the school. I leaned on it, soaking, while Dominic opened the door. "I'm telling you one thing," he said, pushing me inside, "this fucking car will have a dead battery, right? And we won't be able to go to Dublin. Then will you get it through your head?"

The engine caught immediately. The car leaped forward, then stalled. Dominic started it again, releasing the clutch with great caution, and scraping the passenger side as he shuddered out the gate. A voice called behind us.

"Jesus, how do we get out of here?"

"Go down and to the left. I know that's the way!"

We were off. "Stay on the left. No, that's too close – !"

"Shut up!"

"You are the circus," I said. "You'll have to go faster, Lizzie's running after us."

At this he slewed left into the main street, the hubcap shrieking against the kerb, and somehow we were off.

When he had manhandled the car past the edge of the town, a strange exhilaration took over me. Save that it was Dominic's profile beside me in the front seat and not my father's, it already had the feel of our real, proper life. I would find the key under the graceful tangle of driftwood beside our front door, I would … "Oh, I wish it weren't raining!"

"I wish it wasn't, too," said Dominic dourly, "because then someone would be out to stop us."

I started to tell him about our house, how beautiful it was, but he cut me off. "We are not going to reach your house, Maura. That's what we're going to see, that we'll never reach your house or my house."

"We will."

He didn't respond, only frowned ahead. I wanted to thank him, but I didn't know how. He was too angry at me. "Do you want to hear a tape?"

"We'd better. It'll be our last chance, won't it? Ach, never mind, Maura. I'm just thinking whatever electricity will be going won't be used for tapes and discs any more. Give us something with a big orchestra, right – something we'll never hear again."

There was a selection from famous operas. I won't forget Dominic's pale profile against the rain, and the beauty of the music. We played only the one side. More would have been unbearable, like being shown my mother's painting again, the one of the jetty, just to be told I'd never have it back. In a while, Dominic saw I was shivering, and he found the heater and turned it on.

"The warmest place in the universe is now the last car in the universe," he said.

There wasn't a soul out in Rathnew or Ashford, and Dominic had to stop for a few moments when the rain became so thick he couldn't see. We had started passing the odd abandoned car when, suddenly, the rain stopped. The sky didn't clear, but kept its flinty colour.

The mountains were now on our left and at our backs, and we were on the dual carriageway in the familiar, rolling countryside near Kilmacanogue. We would pass Bray, and then we would cut over towards Killiney and the sea.

"We're almost there!" I cried. At the very moment that Dominic's mouth tightened and he began to press on the brakes, I reached across him and, wild with joy, pressed hard on the hooter. The sky seemed to lighten and fragment, and a second later, we heard the keening of hundreds of gulls.

Dominic slewed to a stop. The road in front of us was

choked with cars, all heading towards us, on both sides of the highway; they were on every verge and shoulder, on every flat surface they could find. Packed solid and dully shining, they were red, orange, blue, magenta, green, black, yellow, every colour you could name, all the way back to the horizon. The great mass had loosened at the front, where the drivers had drifted off at strange angles when they lost control. Those behind were simply crushed together, end to end.

The gulls' cries cut like acid through the silence. They plunged and hopped, hurled themselves against windscreens, or perched and craned on wing mirrors as they tried to get at what was inside. The gulls were like dirty white washing rising and falling over the river of cars, their screams corroding the air.

Dominic opened his door and got sick.

We ran out of petrol just beyond Rathnew. It was a relief to leave the Volvo; as we turned back from the barricade of death, the wind had shifted, and the terrible stench from the cars crashed down on us like a weight, pervading every surface. It coated our lips, our nostrils; it hung in our hair.

We didn't see much of one another for the next while. I found it odd that Lizzie was so much angrier than my mother; after all, it was Mum's car we took. My mother was grateful to Dominic, because that afternoon ended my plan to go home, and with it my illness.

I couldn't forget the look on Dominic's face when he saw the cars.

We were closer than ever after that. Very few people saw what we had seen; it was as if we lived in a slightly different reality from then on. But now Dominic had a new friend – a "worshipper" would describe him better. He was a hulking fourteen-year-old named Mark Meehan, hulking but not awkward, and he attached himself to Dominic like a limpet. I prayed that age would improve me, and I'd get Dominic back again for myself. In the meantime, there was nothing but harder and harder work, the convent library, and bloody Wicklow.

CHAPTER NINE

I WAS IN THE LIBRARY, SO IMMERSED IN A REGENCY ROMANCE THAT Lizzie had to shake my shoulder to get my attention. "Now where did you get that? she said, taking the book gently out of my hand and looking at it. Flora, the heroine, was on the cover in a long, glistening dress; she held up a candelabra, and behind her Lord Ellingham stared angrily.

"She's pretty," said another voice. I looked up into the eyes of Lizzie's companion, a sandy-haired girl, who put out her hand for the book, held it and stared at the picture. Then she gave it back to me. She had kept the place with her finger. "Michelle's got a dress like that." She nodded towards the shopping bag beside her. Four tiny feet stuck out of the top of it.

"This is Sinead Kenny, Maura. Sinead, this is Maura, my niece I was telling you about."

Sinead was only eleven, like I was, and almost as scrawny, but she was the most assured person I'd ever met besides Lizzie. She'd an intense, freckled face and stern blue eyes, and that day she wore her carroty hair in a single plait. Inside her shopping bag she had two Sindy dolls and their sexy, grotty clothes, an old Ladybird Book about dinosaurs, which she calmly assured me were coming back, and two battered-looking jelly sweets. "They're pre-war. You can have one."

I had once turned up my nose at jelly sweets. "Delicious!"

"Have you got any sweets?"

I was embarrassed, but she didn't mind; and to my amazement, she even admired Poopy, my old soft dog, whose muzzle was threadbare. "Oooh, he's lovely," she said, and gave him a kiss. "I've a teddy, Barry. I've had him forever. Will we go out, Maura? This place gives me the creeps."

"Me, too." All the same, I brought her to the kitchen to see Dominic. He was there with Mark Meehan, scraping vegetables. Sinead gave Mark a haughty look in return for his own blank stare, Dominic an interested one. I moved towards him and found a long, dirty stripe of carrot on my sleeve. It puzzled me until I saw Sinead glaring at Mark.

"This is Dominic," I said. "Dominic, this is Sinead."

"Yo, Sinead."

Sinead gave him an inscrutable smile.

"This is Mark."

The boy nodded as if to humour Dominic. I removed the peel of carrot from my sleeve and dropped it on his shoe. He grinned and, although it was the nastiest grin I'd ever seen, it was as if someone had turned on a light.

Dominic was having one of his bad days. He went on peeling vegetables as if he'd forgotten us, his eyes sorrowful and remote. Then Lizzie bustled in and hooshed Sinead and me out of the kitchen.

Sinead was the first person who really tried to explain the war to me. It reminded me of the time Jane told us about how babies got in, then out, in the school yard back in Killiney. There were important bits missing.

"The Russians – or was it the French? Wait," she said. "I've got it. The 'Rackeys and the Surgeons bombed the

Jews. Then the Jews bombed the Surgeons and the – wait now. The English and the Americans bombed – oh, I forget! Then the Irans – the Irans – wait, now. Somebody bombed the English, and our electricity … and somebody else killed Dublin. And maybe Belfast." She shrugged.

"But why?"

"Who knows? Well. Mad Marian says they want us to be their religion, but sure … where are they, then?"

She had heard all this at the shop, the one where the trawler had come to rest. Now that there were no papers to sell, the shopkeeper posted whatever news came to hand on a blackboard outside the door. The latest was STILL NO NEWS FROM THE U.S., in huge, chalked letters. Sinead dived back into her bag and produced a barnacle that she had prised from the trawler's hull. It smelled fishy. "Come on, take it," she said, waving it at me. "It won't hurt you."

"I don't really like them," I said. It looked like a sort of solid bird dropping.

She put it back into her bag with a sigh. Then she looked at the white digital watch she was wearing. "I've got to go soon. Where's your brother?"

Up in our room, she admired Conor even more than Poopy, cooing to him and tickling his warm neck. "My brother's his same age. Morrie. Can Maura come to my house tomorrow, Mrs O'Keeffe? My mum says I'll walk her up and back because she's strange. To the town, I mean. 'Strange!'" she added, nudging me and laughing. I walked with her to the door, and the last thing she said was, "You never told me your mam was so beautiful!"

It was strange to be looking forward to the next day again, maddening when it rained heavily in the night, and nobody was allowed out until Mr Rooney had been found and brought up the main street with his geiger counter. The town was like a pressure cooker, with the children wanting to go out and the parents screaming every time they went near the door.

Mr Rooney had said, "Well, it's no worse," glared and gone off.

Sinead hadn't her shopping bag, only a small black patent purse on a long strap. "I'm sorry!" she said. "They took years finding Mr Rooney."

She brought me through the centre of town where the narrow streets zigged up and down the hill, and we trudged east towards the harbour. She showed me the terrace of houses where she lived. It had been neat; now there was a stink of the sea's underbelly, and the footpath in front of the houses was still rimed with salt and sand and darkened with mud.

"Flooded," she said briefly. "The night of the storms. Wait while I leave this in." She pushed open the hall door, threw her patent bag inside and shut the door hurriedly again, just as someone called her name. "Come on!" she said.

Lizzie had shown me the harbour when we'd visited two or three years before. It was a small but efficient, workaday place with a long concrete jetty. An enormous gray shape in the water between the jetty and the harbour wall showed how the legs of the huge storage tank had buckled, flinging the tank itself, weighing hundreds of tons, onto the slipway. The three men on the jetty didn't seem interested in the damage, but in something out at sea.

"I'll show you the castle," Sinead said.

We negotiated a spongy field above the harbour that led to the rise where the remaining gable of the castle held out against time and the wind. A ragged window in it still watched the sea. I wanted to get close to it, to examine its endurance, its queer, shattered permanence, but I fought back the thought and the dizziness that came with it. It was just as well; down a steep drop on our right was an inlet which I remembered as having a sandy beach. Now its floor was a heaving tangle of kelp and bright blue timber. Some of this debris had lodged in crevices far up the cliff.

Stone steps, down and up, connected the hillock on which we stood and the far edge of the headland where the castle clung. Sinead tried one and slipped down two more, releasing her breath in a puff of pain and surprise.

"Let's not go today," I said. "We'll go when it's dry." I was afraid of skidding sideways down the cliff face into the cove, of being swallowed up in the sucking spidery jumble of weed.

"All right," she said. She used her hands to get back up the steps. We found a dry rock to sit on.

I pointed at the stony wall of the cove. "Did the water go up that high?"

"Higher." She shivered.

"Did you see it?"

"If I'd seen that, I'd be dead," she said. "My two friends are dead. Monique Conlon and Dara Byrne."

"Oh."

"They lived too near the sea ... Loads of people were drowned. Packs of them, when the wave came." She frowned at the horizon. "Is it true that everybody in Dublin's dead, except for the people that escaped?"

Her saying it made me see it, made me see the cars and hear the silence over everything I'd known. I saw the school, empty – then, horribly, not empty: I thought of Nature Studies and decay, and the rooms in my mind's eye filled with heavy air, phosphorescence, soft huddles of clothing, a white hand, clawed, that had once touched me in kindness.

"Are you all right?"

"Yeah."

"I'll tell you what happened to us if you tell what happened to you."

"You'd better start."

"All right." She sighed and let her shoulders slump, as if I'd told her I would carry something for her, settling herself on the rock, and hugging herself with her thin arms.

She told me that her father was a security guard in the chemical factory nearby. He had gone to work that evening in spite of the radio reports, because he couldn't get the manager on the phone, and he reckoned the manager wouldn't forget about him. But the manager was rushing all over town trying to stockpile supplies for his family – "he didn't remember Dad until late that night when his wife said, 'And the factory can take care of itself now.' He lifted the phone and sure enough, there was Dad at the factory, with his sandwiches and all. He apologised, but – oh, my mam was raging when she found out. Dad just locked the doors and started home ... He says it was always creepy there on his own, all the lights on and nothing moving but himself. I mean, it used be ... It looked like a big birthday cake at night," she added, and she made me see it, blazing and festive beside the dark wasteland of the sea.

"He was pedalling his bike for home, and the road doubles round so he could see the factory and then the Wicklow lights on the other side of him, and all of a sudden the factory lights went out. He says there was this grey fog in front of him where the lights were, and he squeezed his eyes and opened them again and sure, the whole factory had disappeared. Then Wicklow disappeared as well.

He kept going on the bike, but he could hardly see the road. There was a bit of a moon, remember? We thought it was the ESB! My gran was at the top of the stairs ... "

"What happened her?"

"Oh, Janey ... !" Sinead leaned her head on her knees. "She fell. It was ... gross. Mam sent me next door." She took a long breath. "The Johnstons couldn't phone – the phone wasn't working – they were all in their sitting-room together in the dark, crying. They said, 'Go home and stay indoors!' They asked was my mam listening to the radio, and I said she wasn't. They shut the door after me so quick they tore my skirt, and I had to go home and tell Mam the Johnstons were saying to hold tight and make Gran as comfortable as she could because 'the balloon was up', and Mam started crying and cursing Dad's manager."

I shifted uncomfortably. There was a cold wind on the headland. Sinead went on as if she had to finish her story no matter what happened. She didn't seem to feel the cold at all, though her clothes were lighter than mine.

"The street was black when I was out there. Just black. The ground shook. Did you feel that?"

I nodded.

"Dad fell off his bike. There were cows beside him in a field and they were all bellowing, but when he got up he thought he'd been knocked out because there was this – brightness – in the east across the sea like the sun was coming up. But there was no grey like at dawn, only blackness on the sea and this queer yellow light over England. Well, Wales."

"Did they all burn up?"

"Not at all! Some came here in a yacht, didn't you know? They stayed in the convent. It was before you got here." She paused a moment and said, "Their baby couldn't see."

I was shocked. I had heard about the people from England, but I hadn't known their baby was blind. We plucked and plucked at the salty grass and made two little piles of pickings. A gust came at that moment and tossed them away.

"Then that night we'd the hurricane, and the sea came up from the harbour and killed Monique and Dara and all the other people. So ... what happened to you?"

I told her about the cottage, driving there, and the long, slow days we'd had, about Garda Mullen and his gums, and how the stream flooded and snared a sheep.

"Is that all?"

"Well ... we got Dominic." I knew this was a feeble account compared to Sinead's, but I had left those times in the cottage behind me, I hoped, forever, and the child I had been on that night. Half-frozen on the headland beside the ruin, with all the wreckage below in the cove, I longed for power; some different kind, that made things good again.

Sinead gave my arm a little shake.

"I just started thinking – you know – about things."

We stared at one another, shivering. Suddenly Sinead's face crumpled. Her eyes blazed with tears. "I miss Dara and Monique! I miss them, I miss them, I miss them!" she screamed. My eyes prickled until I was wailing, too. We faced one another, crying bitterly, until finally we shuddered to a halt, sniffing and staring piteously, understanding one another.

Sinead walked me back to the convent as she'd promised.

"Will you come tomorrow?"

"Yeah." Then her chin went up. "One day," she said, "we'll get back at them!"

I looked after her as she marched down the hill, brittle, holding herself straight, and I wondered if we would ever even know who "they" were.

CHAPTER TEN

JUST AS WE WERE SETTLED INTO THE CONVENT, LIZZIE DECIDED TO move us on. It was useless complaining to Mum; she wanted a place of her "own" again. Dominic was to stay behind with the others; I knew why – Lizzie found him useful. I was devastated. This was tantamount to handing him over to my rival, Mark, with a ribbon round him. Lizzie told me not to talk nonsense. My mother didn't say much; she got our few bits and pieces together and waited until the house was ready.

The house itself was an old brick semi near the convent, musty and smelling of damp. We had it under one of the odd arrangements that sprang up all over the place; it still belonged to the old woman who had lived there and would belong to her family when she died, but her daughter had come to fetch her to her own home in Wexford. "Put someone in the house by all means," she'd told the Council. "It's just that if any child of mine should want it one day, I'd like to have it back."

This was agreed, and the daughter brought her mother and some of her belongings back to Wexford in a horse-drawn vehicle, almost like a high trailer attempting to be a trap. The horse still wasn't used to being in harness and sweated and rolled its eyes. "Poor old thing, she'll be shaken to bits," people said, watching them leave. "What option?" said others, shrugging. All the petrol was gone or guarded and hidden away.

The old woman's valuables were in boxes in the loft. We were left with her furniture, her steel cutlery, her faded delph. It was like scavenging from the field of some dreary battle. I hated the smell of mildew, the dark, worn chairs, the damp beds.

Conor stared around the place big-eyed for a day or two, then settled in. He was off and running now, and talking a fair bit. He seemed to have learned what things were overnight, and would point at the chair, the table, the drooping curtains, if you said the words. This cheered my mother. We spoiled him to bits, and so did Dominic, though he was kept very busy the first weeks after we moved. Lizzie even sent him, and sometimes Mark, out of the village with messages, and this worried my mother. She felt the roads weren't safe any more; there were too many unknowns, natural and human. She wouldn't elaborate on this, which was maddening.

Then we began seeing more of him again. I was a bit deflated when Sinead told me the reason. "Eva Maher has dumped him," she announced.

"The mean old bitch!" I cried, astonished at myself.

"Lovely." Sinead hated strong language.

"What do you mean, she 'dumped' him?"

"She loves Mark Meehan now."

"Mark! He's younger than her!"

"But he's very good-looking," Sinead said, screwing up her eyes as if she were appraising a horse in her mind. "And he's very tall. He looks older than Eva."

"He hates girls."

"He hates everyone. Well, he likes Dominic all right."

Dominic was quieter than usual for the next few days. I

told him Eva Maher was silly to throw him over, but to my amazement, he laughed. "Ah sure, it'll be my turn again one of these days."

"Your turn?"

"I didn't say that. Forget it, Maura – "

"I suppose I'll have to ask Sinead. If I want to know anything about you, I have to ask her."

He burst out laughing. "If you believe what Sinead tells you, you'll believe anything!"

"Well, she always knows more than I do!"

"Come here, little mouse." He dragged me unceremoniously onto his lap. "Am I your friend or not?"

"I don't know," I grumbled. I put my arms around his neck.

"No goosh here," he said, taking them back down again. "Am I or amn't I?"

"All right. You are. I love you, Dominic."

For a moment, he froze. "Sure you do," he said then, "but didn't I tell you no goosh?"

"All right," I said, snuggling.

The easiness had gone out of him, though, and I, hurt, could feel him holding himself away from me.

"Will we stay friends?"

"Just no goosh, right?"

"You gooshed all over Eva Maher."

He whooped laughing, and plunked me back onto my feet. "Eva and I weren't friends," he said, grinning.

"You're teasing me!"

"What are friends for?"

I chased him around the room and out the front door, he lifting his knees and flailing his arms in mock terror, but always ahead of me.

Sinead and I were in our usual rallying-place outside the shop, where an interesting message had been scrawled on the news board. By the time we got there, some member of the Council had managed to scrub it off, but everyone in town already knew what it said: ARMY SPLIT! NEW MILITIA BEING FORMED IN ATHLONE! We hovered, hoping to pick up tit-bits of information, but we had missed the main excitement. Then Mark appeared, carrying a bag of spuds on his shoulder with his usual catlike ease. "Here's who'll know," I said. "Mark!"

"What!" he said shortly.

"What is it about the Army? And a Militia?"

He looked at Sinead, and I saw that she had turned her back on us.

"Ask her," he said, with a bitter twist to his mouth. "Doesn't she know everything?" Then he went inside.

"Come on," Sinead said. She grabbed my arm and half-tugged me down the street.

"What is he talking about? Sinead!"

"Jesus, excuse me, trust you not to know!"

"Know what?"

"About Mark! How can you talk to him!" She shuddered.

"Why? What's he done?"

"Done? He is."

"Is what?" I was starting to feel uncertain and very angry.

"Queer! Gay! Homo-sex-u-al!"

"I'm going home." Rage was the wind, I was the sail.

I don't remember a thing until our front door, pushing it open and finding Dominic and my mother in the sitting-room. They turned serious faces to me.

"Sinead is after telling me that Mark is – 'queer', or 'homo, homosexual' – "

"Oh, the little bitch," Dominic groaned.

"She wouldn't talk to him, and he – "

"What did she say to him?"

"Nothing, that's just it! What is it, Dominic?" He didn't

answer me, only looked at my mother. She gave him an encouraging look, nodded, and he was gone.

I ran to the window, and he was already at the end of the road and turning down towards the town.

"Mum!"

Then she explained to me that Mark would always love men instead of women, that this was the way he was made.

"And Dominic?" I whispered.

"No, Dominic likes girls. You know that. Remember he went with Eva."

This didn't give me much comfort. "Will he and Mark stay friends?" I asked her, thinking of the look in Mark's eyes when Sinead turned her back.

"Yes, I think so. Would you like that?"

I nodded, but I went to bed that night very confused. Mark had never liked me much, or so I thought; and yet I'd wanted to defend him from Sinead. Sinead was my best friend, and yet I felt somehow more akin to Mark.

I didn't let myself think too much about what it would be like for men to love men; wouldn't it bring thoughts of what it was like for a girl to love a boy? I reckoned I knew a little about that already, and I cried myself to sleep.

After a while I was resigned to living in our sombre, solid house, and there was no doubt that it was good for Mum. She had maintained a fragile optimism until shortly after we arrived in Wicklow; then she realised she had left "the Dutchman's picture" behind in the cottage. It was rolled up in the broom cupboard, and Mr Hughes and Mr Coffey had overlooked it when we were leaving. She didn't get ill like after Conor's birth, but she did seem aimless, diminished, and much older. I, too, felt the loss. I didn't understand why it was so bitter to me until I saw the picture again years later.

Then Mum discovered a large quantity of white latex paint. I found her coating the walls of her bedroom with it. There was a box of tiny sample tins beside the door. "This is my current canvas," she told me. She was animated and relaxed, her grey eyes shining, her dark hair tied back. The room whitened hourly in the north light from her window, the bed a dark sag in the middle, the dressing-table a bulbous lump, a shadow beside every imperfection in the wall. I didn't think I could bear it.

Sinead came to see. She was ecstatic. "Do you mean you'll do pictures on it?" she asked my mother, incredulous. "What'll you do?"

"Whatever comes to mind," said my mother, flushing.

"Can I see?"

"Oh – sure you can, Sinead. You'll be very disappointed, I expect – " glancing at me.

"Oh, no!"

"Are we going or not?" I said.

"Yeah … " Sinead almost walked backward out of the room, dragging her feet. I wouldn't mind, it was only four white walls, but my mother looked so pleased that I was ashamed of myself.

"You're so lucky," Sinead told me later. We had made up our coolness over Mark without talking about anything much. We were sitting on the low wall across from the shop. The trawler had almost stopped smelling. "Imagine your mum able to paint pictures on the walls! Your aunt told me she's fantastic. What does she paint?"

"Landscapes. Scenery."

"Oh. Well … maybe she'll paint some people, do you think she will?"

"I don't know. Maybe."

Sinead jumped up and glared at me. "You make me sick! The only nice thing happening, and 'I don't know. Maybe!'" and she made an ugly, gloomy face.

"You don't know anything!" Then I grabbed her arm. There was water-light playing over the bow of the trawler opposite, rippling and gleaming, light but no water at all, light that blinded me until it was a relief to be back in the dark interior of the cottage, even though I was alone and for a moment, afraid.

I didn't want to open my eyes, the headache was so bad, but Sinead was giving long, frightened wails. A soft hand patted my face. "There now, Sinead, she's only fainted, see? Shush, Sinead." The light was dazzling, their two faces a welcome shield between me and the sky. Sinead stood wide-eyed, her mouth still squared with panic, and Eva Maher's blonde hair almost tipped my shoulder. "Well now," she said, with her slow, benign smile. "You'd want to eat more, I think."

"No, it's ... I feel sick!" I sat up. Sinead moved away. Eva, though, helped me back on the wall and made me lean my head down.

"You mightn't get sick. Is that better? Sinead, Dominic's just gone up – ah, sure, never mind. I'll bring her home when she's able." She fluffed my hair with her fingers and put her warm, soft arm around me. "Are they working you too hard or what? There now, how are you getting on?"

"Headache," I whispered. She was so beautiful, how could Dominic not be upset by being dumped by her? Mark was always slighting her – "She's like an ivory sculpture, yeah, pure bone from ear to ear." But –

"Eva?"

"Yes, pet."

"Are you going to marry Dominic?"

"Not at all."

"Why?"

"He's too young for me; he's only a year older than me, see, eighteen. But he's very nice. No, I'd want to marry an older boy, Maura."

Sinead, seeing I wasn't going to be sick over her shoes, drew near again. "You'd want to ask him to wait for you, Maura."

"Shut up!"

"Stranger things have happened," Eva said, helping me up. She gave me her slow, sweet smile. "Are you coming, Sinead?"

Sinead started talking to her about my mother's painting, while I remembered my "dream" between throbs. Our cottage, damp and musty, a smell of animals in it, leaves blown in and banked in the big room, blown in through the sagging front door. Kicked it down, but gone. The closet door is shut, but I am going to get the picture; I'm going to look at it again and take it away with me forever. I open the door. The closet is dark, but I'm not afraid. I put out my hands. I touch the four walls, the floor. Nothing.

When I told my mother that night that I had "dreamed" about the picture, that it was stolen, she put her arms around me and said nothing for a moment. "I'm sorry. You wanted it, didn't you?"

I nodded.

"I'm sorry. But ... Perhaps someone will see it now ... hang it up. We might never get back there." She stroked my hair, frowning. "You say the door was kicked in?"

"Yes." I thought of the quiet, and the strange desolate beauty of the place. "But he was gone."

Chapter Eleven

We still don't know who started the War. Sometimes I wonder if there's something strange about our lack of interest in it. Perhaps it's because it's irrelevant – nobody ever arrived to collect the spoils, so our curiosity starved and died after a while, along with so much else.

We're irrelevant too, in ways, those of us who remember the Old Times. Our experience is so alien to that of the younger children, like Conor, that they can't entertain our past at all. It's as if they'll never quite understand us, or we them. They envy us that world of cars and aeroplanes and fast food, that world that seems like a dream. They make us tell them about it endlessly, and it's like talking to people from another country. Our own little brothers and sisters.

The realisation that the change was permanent dawned on us very slowly. Well, if Dublin was gone, or Belfast, there was always Cork. Cork, Waterford and Wexford were mutilated, but not toxic. And Athlone hadn't been hit at all, for some reason; neither had Galway.

"Ach, we Irish are always last in the queue. They were scraping the bottom of the barrel," was the prevailing theory. "Experimenting" was another. "Shifting stuff they didn't want blown up on their own doorstep." "The Iranians." "The Americans." "The Japanese." "The Iraqis." "The British." "The Georgians." "The Chinese." "The Libyans." "The British." "The Syrians." "The French!"

It made no difference: the greater world seemed to have forgotten us.

In the meantime, our own government became more and more remote. This didn't happen right away; for the first year or two, advisors came on bicycles, on foot, and even on horseback, to tell us how to store food, keep warm without electricity, plan co-operatives for farming and food-sharing. For a while two or three would come; then, when hunger and cold weather began taking their toll, a representative might come alone. Finally, they had to come in threes or fours so they could ward off attack; and at this point, they came only once or twice a year.

We worked almost too hard to notice. Men left the harbour in yachts and dinghies to set pots and to fish, tossed like flecks of spume on the waves. Everyone else who was able-bodied weeded, hoed, did whatever the farmers needed and could teach. We were hungry all the time, and cold most of it.

With all that, some of us managed to thrive. Sinead and I didn't soften, like some girls did in their early teens. We were hardy and light. Sinead grew quite tall, but I stopped at 5' 2". Conor had all the colds God sent, but nothing like Morrie, and he escaped the really devastating illnesses that scoured us. We nearly lost Lizzie in The Big Flu, and Mum got an insidious version of it; she was in bed only for a few days, but the thing hung on to her for months. Her skin looked different afterwards, thinner and somehow shinier, and though there were still no lines in her face, she'd a grey look, and there were little threads of white hair at her temples.

Morrie's life seemed more fragile than ever, but to

everyone's astonishment, he continued to live. When he was well at all, he was the maddest child in the town, his red hair glinting wherever the action was, his face alight with schemes. On days when he was breathless but not ill, Mark or Dominic might carry him up to the shop, trips that became less frequent as more and more work was found for them outside the town.

Conor loved Morrie. They were always together. They were hardly out and about before people were calling them "Mind and Body"; Morrie thought of their scrapes, and Conor executed them.

How can I explain that we felt safe? Mr Rooney's geiger counter had stopped working, and the fishermen searched their catch for mutations; harvests were meagre, the sheep often diseased, never mind ourselves, but we felt safe, safe for a while within ourselves as a community.

There were always rumours from the countryside, but that outer world hardly impinged on us any more. I let the rest of Ireland become blurred and distant in my mind, and with it, the violence I had known in the cottage. At seventeen, I wanted only one thing: Dominic. And Dominic was achingly elusive.

That was the only thing that didn't change after we went to the Red House, the name we gave to one of the semi-submerged houses near the sea. Conor had been teasing Dominic for months to bring him there. It was known to be dangerous, strictly off limits, but the wilder lads had enlarged the doorway so that they could enter the house in their dinghies. It was Conor's eighth birthday, and Dominic was about to leave us again, so he was very open to Conor's blackmail.

The Red House was said to be haunted; the family that lived there had never been found after the first storms. I stayed away from it. Sinead went, and said "never again". She said it was the worst place she'd ever been, and it didn't help that Jamie Fallon, who had brought her in his dinghy, tried to paw her up and down. She reminded him of her mother's temper and "Jamie's hands flew back onto the oars, but Mother of God, I couldn't get out of it fast enough, Maura, there's something wrong in there."

This was enough for me; I was still careful about such things. I hadn't had a "dream" for three years now, and Lizzie said she thought passing through puberty might have rid me of them. "Will you miss them?"

"No."

She looked relieved, and I felt a rush of love for her, for her easy insistence over the years that there was nothing wrong with me in the face of Mum's worrying and probing.

I avoided places like the Red House like I'd avoid hot spots or the legendary "hungry grass" of the West, in case the "dreams" were only dormant, so when Dominic said he'd bring Conor, I felt a goose on my grave. "I have to leave tonight," he was saying. "I'll be down the country a long time."

I tried to remember what he'd looked like before he had a beard. The dark beard, cut close, made him look old for twenty-three, and somehow less accessible. It was like going to work on a cross between an apostle and a pirate.

"Maura ... !"

"You weren't to go until tomorrow night."

"Nothing I can do," he said, and the way he said it reminded me of my father.

"Oh, well, then!"

"Listen to me, Maura. If Conor doesn't go with me, he'll go with someone else."

"Oh, right," I said.

"Listen, girl, I met Ciaran McEvoy down the town today, and he told me he'd promised Conor and Morrie he'd bring them to the Red House."

"Wait til Sinead hears that!" Ciaran McEvoy was a

danger to all life, including his own. Sinead thought he was wonderful, but there were limits.

"You see, Maura … If I bring Conor today, I can get him to promise he won't go again."

"All right."

"What's upset you?"

I shrugged.

"You've not been listening to Sinead's old rubbish?"

"Sinead's been there."

"So have I. The creature with the fourteen black tentacles is vegetarian."

"It was your one with the two white tentacles you went with, I'll bet," I said.

"That would be telling."

"Well, she showed her heels to the lot of you." I peered at him, cautious, to see his reaction. He merely looked thoughtful.

"She did that all right," he said.

Eva Maher, having run out of men to love in the town, had finally left us six days ago. Apart from the fact that she'd always had a special fondness for Dominic, I'd nothing against her. It was impossible to be angry with her; she was simply herself, trusting and kind. Some lads took it hard when Eva left them for the next, but not for long. She was a sort of communal blessing, like a good crop or a treasure trove. At twenty-two, she still had the soft, rounded features and white-blonde hair of a much younger girl, and her beauty was so well known that people from miles away asked after her and wanted to see her.

When we realised she was gone, a gentle gloom suffused the town. "She was too beautiful for us alone," said one of the old men. That was the general feeling. "They'll have heard of her in Athlone," someone said. A light coldness entered the atmosphere. Many troubling rumours had come from there in recent times.

"Who do you think she went off with, then?" I asked Dominic.

"God knows. We'll hear one of these days, I'm sure. Anyway, I want you to come with us – "

"My skin's crawling, Dominic."

"Maura … " He waited until I had to look at him. "Don't you believe I'll take care of you?" He said it with mock impatience, but there was real hurt in his eyes.

That was that.

Lizzie gave Dominic his supper at the convent that evening – since he was going away on her business, it was up to her to feed him for the road, she said. Later, missing him so keenly, I resented every moment of that meal.

He came for Conor and me afterwards. Mark was with him. Mark gave me one of his brilliant, sardonic smiles, but I felt too oppressed to counter it, so he relaxed into his usual austere watchfulness. I found myself wishing he were going with us to the Red House.

"See you after, Dom," he said. "'Bye, Con. Happy birthday." He took a twist of paper out of his pocket and gave it to Conor, who ripped it open at once. It was a small, sticky honey cake.

"Oh-h-h … !"

I looked at Dominic. The honey cake would have cost Mark dearly.

"You're the lucky fellow," I said to Conor.

"Yeah … ! Thanks, Mark!" and he gave him a hug.

Mark had to bend almost double to receive it. He twinkled his eyes at me over Conor's shoulder, but I wouldn't rise. "Well, 'bye, Maura dear, for ever so long." He waved casually then, and moved off.

"I hate him and all," I told Dominic when he was out of earshot, "but he's generous." Conor offered us bites of the honey cake like a good child, but we insisted he eat it himself. All the way down to the place where Dominic had his dinghy, he talked, excited, full of questions. How many times had Dominic been to the Red House? Was there really a ghost? Was it true it might fall down?

Down by the river there was the usual stink of mud and salt, sweetened by the summer scents of trees and grass. When Dominic pushed off and we began floating across the quiet water, there was an instant in which the three of us seemed as settled as smiling figures in a frieze. Then we slipped past the roof tree of a cottage that had crumbled beneath the water, and I began to feel caught, reeled in towards the Red House.

We could see it now. It stood on a slight rise, now invisible beneath the water, and it gave the impression of a haggard face with its broken doorway and downstairs windows, which opened like small dark caverns above the water. Part of the roof had caved in, and I could see light coming through the other side of the house upstairs. The façade had weathered and peeled to a scrofulous pinkish-grey, and even Conor drew in his breath a little when he saw it.

Dominic lined up the dinghy in front of the doorway. "You'll have to duck," he said. He gave a few strong, sharp pulls, then drew in the oars. The dinghy shot towards the opening, and I leaned over tight and shut my eyes, pulling Conor down as well. In a moment I felt the dead chill of the house around me. "Oh, yes!" Conor said.

We were in an enclosed square of light and shadow that had once been a sitting-room. There was a hole in a corner of the ceiling through which the evening light stole softly. At first I thought the walls were moving, but I saw then that, miraculously, a little of the wallpaper remained like dark wet skin that undulated where it was loose. There was an almost unbearable stench of mould, stale river and sea-water. Dominic was moving the oars. "Duck again," he said. "We're going to the dining-room."

I heard Conor's happy intake of breath. We moved again, and I felt the lintel of the door touch my hair. I sensed light and opened my eyes. Conor gave a little shout of delight. The floor, then the roof, had given way completely above us, and the light streamed into the space, augmented by the two half-windows in front of us. Everywhere the water's refracted light moved and shimmered on the walls. "No," I whispered.

My dream-eyes saw the twilight forming on the other side of the room, two figures in a boat. I saw the gleam of a bare arm, the sway of a breast, Eva Maher straddling a lover, a man who steadied her, his hands on her upper arms while their boat swayed gently under them. His back was to me, I could only see the crown of his dark head where he half-sat, half-lay against the thwarts. Eva was laughing as she rose and sank, rose and sank; there was something happy and childlike about her even then. I couldn't hear her laughing, though. I could only see her and I couldn't make her hear me either, though my lips kept forming the words. At the last moment she flung up her head and looked at me, her lips parted, and I screamed her name – she heard me, I'm sure of it, but his hands were already on her throat.

Conor was being sick, and my head ached so much that I couldn't open my eyes.

Dominic said, "Don't look again, Conor. Poor Eva. Get your head down again, we'll get out of here. Hold Maura, Con, in case she tries to sit up."

I felt his cold, small hand on my shoulder. I saw the man's big hands on Eva Maher's white neck.

"It's all right, nearly out," said Dominic's voice. "Stay down, Con."

There was good light about us, and the clean smell of

the outdoors. Conor leaned against me. He was shivering. I put my arms around him, wondering if he could possibly have seen what I saw.

We drew away from the Red House, Dominic rowing hard to get us back to his mooring upstream. His face was white, his eyes so intense they looked black. When he saw me staring at him, he shook his head. "I'm sorry," he said. His eyes were full of tears.

Chapter Twelve

THE MAN WHO MURDERED EVA WAS AN OUTSIDER. I HAD SEEN ONLY the back of his head in my "dream," his tanned forearms and white shoulders, but I knew he was not one of us. I told Lizzie, who immediately put about the rumour that Eva had been seen with a stranger with curling dark hair on the day she disappeared. There was no use telling people about my "dream"; nobody would have believed it, and suspicions might have found scapegoats in the town.

Some invisible barrier had been broken, leaving us exposed. We hadn't much crime, only the bit of thieving, and Eva's murder shattered us. Her death forced us to look outward again and to consider the rumours that had collected like a siege force on the edges of the town, rumours about the dissolution of our government, the final disbanding of our Army in the Midlands and its replacement by the Militia, and the rise to power in Athlone of a man named Jack Rourke.

I was too sick to go to Eva's funeral, but my mother told me that the church was packed. The curate was ill and delegated Lizzie to say the Mass, and even the old ones were too distressed about Eva to complain about it.

"Lucky the Bishop came when he did," my mother said.

"It would be awful if the funeral were postponed; there'd be uproar." Bishop McGlinchy, seeing how Father Peter was failing, had ridden into town on his huge, black hunter, ordained Lizzie, and trotted straight out again. It was the only good thing that happened during that dreadful week.

I lay curled tight in my bed for three days. It was a kind of mourning, more for myself than for Eva. I'd been rid of the "dreams", I'd thought, forever, and with them the taint of the awful episode in the cottage. Now the scenes in the cottage haunted me again, and with them, the scarred, smiling face of the terrible man. I would wake to the sound of my mother's gentle movements and the ribboned scrape of her brush as she painted Eva on the other side of the bedroom wall, and then I'd fall into another troubled sleep in which the man smiled and smiled at me, as if he were waiting.

The Council organised a meeting for the girls and young women – they thought Eva's murderer was a sex criminal – and Lizzie was among the speakers. She told us that what had happened to Eva could happen to any one of us who didn't value herself or have some sense about where she went or with whom. She was frightening us into being good, a waste of time where I was concerned; I'd nothing to say when Sinead and the others started in about their boyfriends.

"Well, I think I can keep seeing Ciaran," Sinead said afterwards. "He can't even kill a chicken!"

"You'd want to be careful what he does to you."

She laughed.

"Well, think of Jackie!"

"Will you stop!" Sinead said, shuddering.

Jackie's screams, long and grating like an animal's during her labour, had come flying at us through the bricks and mortar of her house. We were waiting outside for loyalty.

"She's screaming the whole time now, Sinead, it should be over soon."

It was, and all for a dead baby, a pretty little boy with a tiny head. Jackie, who was already a bit simple, and who was very small for her fifteen years, was now almost like a baby herself. Loss and pain had bewildered her.

"All that and nothing to show for it," Sinead said. She drooped against the wall.

"It'll make nuns of us yet, Sinead. Lizzie's counting on it."

She gave a little snort. "No fear of me, anyway," and we parted.

My mother was waiting at the window, her face a light smudge against the darkening room. "Jane Martin passed here ten minutes ago," she said.

"I was talking to Sinead," I muttered.

"We'll have to move Conor again."

"Oh, Mum! – Why don't we just change rooms? It's no problem if you paint all day in yours, I won't mind sleeping there at night."

"I need to stay in that room, Maura. Anyway, Conor'll feel able to go back to his own room soon. He's fewer nightmares now."

I knew this would be her answer.

She sank down carefully on one of the chairs. "What did they tell you?"

"The usual. Avoid men and lonely spots."

She hardly seemed to hear me, only stroked the knuckles of her right hand, flexed her fingers.

"What did you paint today?"

"I worked a little more on Eva," she said dreamily. "Come see? No, don't. It's too dark now. Pop your head in tomorrow morning when the sun's on it."

"I'll be out early again."

"Ach ... ! Let me look at your hands." She could hardly

see them in the room's twilight, but she rubbed her own palms, still sensitive, over mine.

"With respect, Mum ... painting Eva just now isn't ... I mean, I can see why Conor doesn't want to go to sleep in there." The room was overwhelming enough without the addition of Eva. Two sides of it were populated by life-sized figures, full-length and closely grouped. Everyone Sylvia loved or feared was there: Conor as a baby, myself, Dad in his best suit, Dominic, Lizzie. There were Mr Coffey and Garda Mullen, who looked like a medieval martyr, and Morrie, Conor's best friend. She had executed them in shades of umber and charcoal, with materials she had mixed herself, and, despite these limitations and the bizarre confinement of the room, they were compelling. Disturbing, too, because in a corner, slightly crouched, was a handsome man whose face seemed a reflection in a cracked mirror because of the scar that ranged from his right forehead across the bridge of his nose and down his left cheek. I flinched.

"Maura, you've a cut here! We must see to it."

"It's only a graze."

"I'm painting her as she was, love, not the way poor Conor saw her. Now, come here."

She bathed my hand in a sup of water she had boiled and left to cool, and that satisfied her. "I hate you doing field work, darling. Hate it."

"It's all right, Mum. At least it's all of us. It's fair."

"You're too good for it."

"Who isn't? Sure we'll just have to keep remembering Mr BogeyBomb in our prayers. You haven't painted him," I said, teasing.

"I think he's a composite of all his own faces and the faces of all the millions he's murdered and starved and caused to die – he's a composite, of microdot faces. But I don't know what that looks like. Huge, of course. Maybe he's just a few dull little dots among all the brighter ones. Pimples. Maybe all the dots together form the face of God. They never said just the good ones were formed in his image, did they? That's my thought for the day."

"Stop thinking. Stick with painting, Mum," I told her, and she laughed.

We climbed the stairs, both suddenly tired to the point of staggering. I lugged Conor from my bed to hers. He wanted to stay with her at night after the shock of seeing Eva's body in the water at the Red House. Dominic had only recognised her from her hair; she was like some soft sea fiend, swollen, gazing at them from just under the surface, her hair fanning and crawling with the water's movement.

It wasn't long after falling into bed, grateful for Conor's leftover warmth, that I was wide awake again and at the mercy of my thoughts.

It seemed so unlucky to have had the "dream" when I was with Dominic – lovemaking that ended in death. That was the equation that had the women whispering the moment they heard of a pregnancy, and that had them weeping uncontrollably when a child was born. They cried if the mother was living or dead, the child healthy, dead or deformed. All these results were unbearably moving for them.

I'd hoped to be sterile like Eva, but reality was lurking inside me all along, like a stone under the soil that breaks the plough. When my period finally came, with cramps and torpor and – for the first day or two – a feeling of being injected with lead, I hated it. There was a mess, and smell, and the boiling of rags. How did anyone put up with it?

"Don't you want to be a woman?" Sinead asked me, looking at her nails, smiling a secretive little smile.

"No!"

I longed for love, but the rest was mad. After all the

pain, to have a baby that might die, like Jackie's, or perhaps live a while all wretched and higgledy, with people coming to whisper and stare? It didn't matter that I seemed prettier, or that the boys liked me more; I only wanted Dominic, and he didn't come.

Curled tighter and tighter in my bed, I watched the shadows intensify, wondering where he was, and whether somewhere in the darkening land he'd a bed to lie in.

We didn't see him for three years.

CHAPTER THIRTEEN

ON A FINE DAY IN OCTOBER, THREE YEARS AFTER EVA'S DEATH, Conor and Morrie were working on the wall. It was one of Morrie's good days – it had rained but it was warm, and Morrie wasn't wheezing. He was mostly chatting while Conor worked, but nobody minded, least of all Conor.

They were bringing bricks from one of the demolished houses in a wheelbarrow. Their faces were lean and looked older than those of eleven-year-olds, but after that, they were very different. Morrie, despite all his sickness, was taller than Conor, who could still make two of him. Conor's hair was now more brown than copper, but Morrie's was flaming red. It glinted when he turned to call to me, "Tell Sinead that Ciaran's just fallen off the top of the wall!"

"I take it he's all right, as usual," I said.

The wall was nearly finished. It enclosed the central part of the town, where most of us now lived, incorporating house walls and gables, and every kind of building material imaginable. In some places only high, pointed palings, the stripped trunks of pines, were between us and outsiders. The plan was to encircle the town as soon as possible, then go back and shore up the weaker spots.

The wall made us feel more secure, but it made life very intense, too. When the heavy gate swung open in the mornings, letting us out to work in the fields, we smiled encouragingly at one another, whether to ward off fear or to celebrate our freedom, I never quite knew. The wall cut across streets and threw long shadows down new cul-de-sacs, but bit by bit, it began to feel natural. And weren't we lucky, we told ourselves, that our town was in a cluster, so that we could have a decent wall around it?

The farmers, and all those who lived out on the land, had their own problems. Some whose holdings were very remote sent their young children to be cared for in the safe confines of the town. "You'd be mugged for a parsnip out there," people said. "Or half a spud."

I turned towards Sinead's house; she and I were to go blackberry-picking in the hedges just west of the town. I preferred not to meet Ciaran, who had little time for me; he thought I was behind Sinead's having cooled towards him for a while. In fact, she'd spent months slagging him, telling all and sundry he bored her rigid. Then, lo and behold, he started hanging around with the unfortunate Kate Begley, who was flattered to the skies. It took Sinead almost ten minutes to reclaim her property.

It was just as well I'd kept my unkindest thoughts about Ciaran to myself. And what was I anyway, only an almost twenty-year-old virgin, short-circuited by unrequited passion and feeling as autumnal as the October day. I still missed Dominic bitterly. For all I knew, he might have married down in Tipperary or wherever he was, though Lizzie maintained he hadn't. She knew about his movements, but she'd say little to me except that he was well. He and Mark were now willing minions in a sort of semi-clerical spy-ring whose members tramped all around the country liaising, gathering news, and doing some

community work for "cover". One of their jobs was to
advise people about rat control, which Sinead found very
funny. I knew nothing else to hope for, so I kept hoping
for him to come. But three years! He must feel nothing for
me.

The wall was a distraction, odd bockety thing that it
was. We all worked on it when we were able, even in
winter on dry days that weren't freezing. There was
urgency in the air, but we didn't know quite where it came
from.

Ciaran wasn't with Sinead, to my relief. We chatted
easily as we trudged across the graveyard and the field
beyond, making for the hedges and woodlands where the
blackberries grew. Soon we heard singing and the sound of
an axe. It was James McEvoy, Ciaran's older brother,
chopping up branches from a fallen tree beside the ruined
cottage there, singing like a blacksmith. His back was to us
and he'd his jumper off. Sinead started to hail him, but I
stopped her.

"Listen!"

She threw up her eyes, but stayed quiet.

Farewell you lasses who loved young soldiers,
Farewell young soldiers who loved your land,
Farewell poor Ireland, farewell our hopes,
Farewell our freedom under Rourke's cruel hand.

"It's old rubbish!"

"Shh!" I said, but he'd heard us.

"Are you coming to help or to admire?" he called to us.

"What's the song?" I said.

He scratched his head. "What song?"

"So it is about something! Let's hear the rest."

"What'll you give me?"

He was only joking, but the look he gave made me

prickle uncomfortably.

"We'll help you tidy the logs."

"Speak for yourself," said Sinead.

"Don't mind Sinead, she's apolitical. Come on, James, give."

Sinead made as if to go, and I grabbed her. "Don't you leave me here," I whispered.

"You're aunt'll give me a hiding," he said, grinning.

"You're a pal. Come here, Sinead, sit down."

James sat down on a stump with the air of a concert pianist.

The soldiers lined along the roadside
With their cruel orders they'd not agree
T'was on the Curragh in the blackest morning
That lonely Ireland did ever see.

In iron Athlone inside their bunker
Our "heroes" Martin and Kilcoyne
Did tell our Generals Blake and Cleary
To stop our people stumbling on.

Will we forget the dead of Dublin?
Forget the dead of sweet Belfast?
Te dum te dum te dum te dum te ...

He frowned. "I forget that bit."

"Thanks be to God," said Sinead.

"Go on," I said.

"Umm ... "

Why were our brave lads sent to Sinai
To Syria, to cold Russia's steppes,
To stop the killing outside Paris,
Now Ireland chokes in Rourke's mad grip.

Farewell you girls who loved young soldiers,
Farewell young soldiers who loved your land,
Farewell poor Ireland, farewell our hopes,
Farewell our freedom under Rourke's cruel hand.

"Explain."

"For heaven's sake, it's that stupid old business on the Curragh," Sinead said. "You two can chew over it, I'm going home." She had gone very pale. She almost ran away from us down the hillside, her feet crashing through the leaves.

"Has Sinead said anything to you?" James said after a moment.

"About the Curragh? No, she never talks about things like that."

He seemed to find that very funny. James was very good-looking, tall, though not so tall as Dominic. He was nice. He had twice as much sense as Ciaran, too, though not the same flamboyant good looks.

"Sinead should have fallen for you," I said.

"Ach, she's not my type. I like dark-haired women, myself." He pulled on his jumper, which made me feel relieved somehow. "It's enough for one day," he nodded at the logs. He motioned to the fallen tree where Sinead and I had been sitting. He sat on a stump opposite. "Sinead's not looking too well."

"She's tired."

"Mrs Kenny still acting up?"

"Oh, not too bad. She hasn't quarrelled with anybody for a good while. Sure you'd know it if she had. You'd know before I would."

"Morrie's been good?"

"He has."

"Ach ... I'm asking all the questions," he said. He

smiled, but I could see he was disturbed about something
and I realised I liked him. "The song's about the Army," he
said abruptly. "It's about what happened just after the War
when the people poured out of Dublin and onto the
Curragh, heading west. Sure, you knew all about that."

"I know they weren't stopped at the Curragh."

He nodded. "There was uproar in Athlone. The
Ministers hadn't even the cup of tea in their hands when
they heard half Dublin were on the roads out of town and
moving fast in their direction, and they ordered the Army
to keep the people in the Curragh. They panicked ...
You'll have heard all this."

"I'd forgotten some of the names."

"Cleary was on the spot, and he told them he'd keep his
own men there to assist the people onwards, but there was
no question of keeping refugees that close to Dublin – if
there was going to be a nuclear attack, what was the point?
Blake was in Athlone looking at what he reckoned was the
bigger picture, in which a nuclear attack didn't figure at all,
and he and Cleary fell out. The men in the Curragh
supported Cleary, and the guys in Athlone weren't happy
but they stuck with Blake – the officers down in Limerick
did too, but afterwards they split away."

"Well, then, who were the men in Army uniforms who
came last week to investigate the English?" Two families
had arrived from England in a yacht, dehydrated and
hysterical, and a number of soldiers had come to question
them about the conditions they had come from.

"Similar uniforms, right, but they're all Militia. What
we've got these last few years isn't the Army at all. Not the
old Army. Sure, there were hardly any soldiers left here
when the War started, too many out firefighting for the UN
and the EC. We've a rabble now."

"A rabble."

He stood up suddenly, as if he'd heard something.

"James – you go down the country – do you ever hear anything of Dominic?" I said, catching him by the sleeve.

He motioned me up, looked over his shoulder, took my arm, listened. Then he started running, half-dragging me with him down the hillside.

We pounded over the rough hillocks, the slate roofs of the town crouching invitingly in front of us. I could see movement beside the ragged end of the wall. James glanced over his shoulder and stopped so suddenly that I tumbled over onto my hands and knees.

"Sorry," he said, still looking back.

A ragged figure struggled after us. It lifted its scarecrow arm as if to hail us, then clutched its chest and fell.

"Wait here," James said.

I followed him to where the figure lay sprawled on the ground. We could hear his breathing yards away, long, sobbing groans.

"Is he dying?"

James knelt and touched the rough hair. "I'm James McEvoy, Michael. Be easy – I see nobody coming after you."

I recognised Michael Sheedy now. His hair was whiter and longer since his last visit, but his clothes were as rotten as ever. He still lay panting, his face hidden by his straggling hair.

"Where's Charlie?" I whispered to James. "The cart?"

Michael pushed himself up on his knees. His face was bruised and filthy, his beard full of spittle. His eyes were the worst, swollen with crying. He stood up, wavering. "They took Charlie. They took the cart."

"You'd better come to the convent, Mr Sheedy," I said.

James nodded at me to go ahead. He supported Michael Sheedy on his arm. When I was a little way down the hill, he called to me. "Maura! Get Pat Jamieson, will you?"

I nodded, and kept running.

Chapter Fourteen

Pat Jamieson, the Chairman of the Council, cast quelling looks around the convent kitchen, lingering longest on me – I had taken charge of the soup – but nobody offered to leave.

"These proceedings are confidential," he said drily.

Michael Sheedy told his story with halts and stops and many tears. He and Charlie, a young orphan he'd befriended some years ago, were on their way from Rathdrum when men moved out from behind a hedge, blocking the road. "A terrible-looking lot. I've seen poor, sure we're all of us poor, but I never seen the like of those up close. I thought they only wanted the cart. 'Yous can have it,' I said. They were all carrying these long sticks. 'See what's in it,' the ferrety one says, and they tore into the cart and threw the things around."

"What did he look like?" said Pat Jamieson.

There was a brown smell from the range. Mesmerised, I was forgetting to stir the soup.

"Fair dirty hair and one of them frizzy beards like a bird's nest. Red face, light eyes. Tall ... not as tall as you, Mr Jamieson. He'd a lump in his nose here," touching the bridge of his own.

Brigid, very quiet, was writing it all down.

"And the others?"

"Shorter fellow, younger ... cropped browny hair and a wispy little goat's beard. He'd a scar. Over his left eye. Oh, Jesus! Didn't he squeeze along Charlie's arms – the lad couldn't move with the fright. The other one lifted him up to see had he weight on him. You'd think they wanted to eat him, the way they went on."

"The other?"

"The third ... he got behind me right away, but ... He'd brown hair going grey, but he didn't look old. Long. Beard." He shook his head. "I only glimpsed him. He hung back in the bushes."

I burned my hand, jerked it away from the side of the pot, sucked it where it stung.

"They just said, em, 'Right.' They turned the donkey around and tied Charlie's wrists behind his back, and poor Charlie, he always has to be fidgeting with his hands. They said it would be the worse for him if I interfered. They said they'd be watching me all the way here ... !"

"Yes."

"They wanted the cart and donkey, and they're slow. Charlie'd be no use to them by himself."

Lizzie and Mr Jamieson exchanged a look that Michael Sheedy didn't see.

Mr Jamieson conferred quietly with someone outside the kitchen door. It was getting dark in the room. Brigid and Leonie led Michael Sheedy away; they'd prepared a bed for him.

"Lizzie, what will they do?"

"I don't know, Maura."

"Well, won't some of the men go after them? They're bound to catch up with the cart, I mean everyone knows it ... "

"That's true. Pat Jamieson's very cautious, though."

"But, Charlie!"

"I know. It's just possible. There's such upset in the country now, though, Maura, and you'd be afraid … "

"Afraid of what?"

"Well, reprisals, really. The wall's going so slowly, we're so vulnerable at the moment."

"Reprisals from who?"

"Those men … ach, they're part of something bigger, Maura. Surely. I can't explain now, I've to run upstairs, pet, they're meeting. Oh, not a word to Sylvia, do you think? Wouldn't it upset her?"

"She'll hear anyway."

"If she hears it tomorrow, it'll be different from you rushing in tonight telling her."

"Do you know, Lizzie, you treat me like I'm backward."

"I'm tired. I'm sorry. Really, love." She was gone, surefooted in the familiar dark.

I finished washing up, emptied the basin in the yard, left the soup tightly covered on the range. Already, hopeful mice were scuttering near the wainscotting. I hovered in the dark passageway, dreading to go home. Conor would be in my bed, grinding his teeth and having breathless conversations in his sleep. My mother would be waiting stoically in the cold sitting-room.

I saw a feeble glimmer under the door of the refectory. The room was silent. I pushed the door open. There were embers in the fireplace, a dull glow of turf and wood. I heard a rustle and sigh that could only be human.

Someone was in the armchair. Sleeping. For a moment, I was afraid. Then I heard the mutter of conversation in the room above. If I shouted, they would hear me. I drew nearer. It was a man, tall, slumped to one side in the chair. He was wearing a rough cloth coat, and his long legs, shabby and booted, stretched towards the fire. Long, dark hair caught at the nape of his neck with a bit of string. I sniffed the air. He was clean. Not a tramp, then, not one of the clever ones who managed to get in, like the one who had once attacked Leonie. I edged closer, trying to see his face, and he grabbed me. He'd my arm behind my back and his hand over my mouth before I could move, and just as suddenly he released me.

"Who are you?" he said thickly.

"Who are *you*, more like!"

But I knew. I put my hand up in the darkness and touched his face, felt the little scar along his cheekbone and the cropped beard that was still like raw silk.

He didn't resist when I pulled his head down and kissed him, or when I moved close and pressed against him. He was so warm, and he was trembling just like I was. He muttered my name like a question, as if he were still dreaming, and as I held him with all my strength, something seemed to break for him, some resistance, and then he kissed me so hard our teeth scraped. We never heard the door open.

"Maura!" It was Lizzie. She sounded almost frightened. Dominic and I rose shakily from our knees, helping each other.

"You've found Dominic," she stammered.

"I've found him," I said.

"I'm afraid – Dominic, I'm very sorry – something's come up. Pat Jamieson wants to talk to you now."

"He mustn't go away," I cried. "You can't go. Lizzie, he's too tired, surely Pat Jamieson can wait – "

With that Dominic put his finger on my lips, said, "I'll come later," then kissed me and went before Lizzie out of the room.

She turned back. "Go straight home, Maura."

"I'll wait for him. Lizzie, you didn't tell me he was here!"

"Maura, I'm sorry – I can't explain now, there's no time,

and Sylvia – "

"You weren't going to tell me? Has he been here before? Many times?" I was shouting at her.

"I can't talk now, love. Go home, Maura, I mean it. This could take hours." Above us, the scrape of chairs, an increase in the volume of the voices. Jamieson. Michael Sheedy. The men of the Council. Dominic, Dominic.

Fool that I was, I went. I went home, resenting every breath of air that dispersed the feel of him, his smell, the smallest gust that could dislodge one fibre of his clothes from mine.

My mother was waiting, like I knew she'd be, and I scowled on the front step, trying to control my anger against her for being ill and breaking our hearts.

"Maura! What's wrong?"

Useless to hide anything from her when she was attending.

"What's happened?"

"Dominic's here," I said slowly.

"Where?" She was surprised.

"At the convent."

"And is he well?"

"He's all right. He's tired."

"We'll make a bed for him."

"Yes. But Lizzie got him, Mum. And Mr Jamieson."

"I see. Something's wrong."

"Well, yes and no."

"You sound like Dan when he knew something he thought I wouldn't want to hear." I could hear the sad smile in her voice. "You're very like him in ways, do you know that? You look like me, but you're very determined, like … It's a good thing. I've something I want to say to you, Maura."

"Mum, it's late, won't you be tired out?"

But she brought me with her into the sitting-room and

drew me down beside her on the sofa. "I wish you hadn't left the convent," she said abruptly. She felt me start, and she went on, "It's time you settled something with Dominic."

"I'm not sure he … even though … "

She stroked my arm in a dreaming sort of way. "I've watched you both a long time, Maura."

"What did you see, Mum?" I whispered.

"I saw … It's going to be all right. It's just – I think Dominic can't make the decision. You'll probably have to do it for him." Her voice was now calm, almost brisk.

"I don't understand."

"Whatever decision you want to make. Live with him … Marry him … Just don't wait. He and Mark are up to their necks in whatever's going on."

"And how do you know that?"

She laughed. "I've my own sources I cultivate."

I told her about Michael Sheedy and Charlie then, watching her pale face in the firelight.

She looked very sad, but "A matter of time" was all she said about it. "Just remember what I've told you, love. Conor and I will always be looked after here, you know that. So if you have to follow Dominic … He'll always go where he feels most responsible. Wouldn't it be better all round if he felt responsible for you instead of Lizzie and Pat Jamieson?"

"I thought you and Lizzie wanted to keep me away from him," I whispered.

She put her arms around me. They felt so light and brittle; shrug and they'd break. "Lizzie's afraid. It's children, Maura. Pregnancy. I was, too, but … you're old enough to decide what risks you want to take. And you're wretched without him."

I stayed awake for hours, listening for Dominic's step in the hall, reassuring myself that the meeting was to last for hours. I woke to my mother's grave face, and Lizzie at the front door. It was morning. Lizzie handed me a note and stood shaking while I screamed and wept, and Conor hovered wide-eyed, gazing at us from the kitchen.

CHAPTER FIFTEEN

SINEAD TOLD ME SHE WAS PREGNANT WHEN SHE WAS SURE, CRYING, her hair loose and falling over her face. She dreamt of Jackie's baby day and night. "What if they all have microcephaly, from now?" she wept.

"They didn't after Hiroshima," I said. "Only some of them."

"How do you know that?"

"There's a book about it. In the Geography section."

"Jasus, that's Brigid, books about babies in the Geography section."

"It's about Japan, you eejit."

"Why isn't it in History, if it's about the World War II?"

"Ask her!"

"I don't need to. It's part of the Plot, isn't it – the re-populate the world plot. Relocate all those little reminders about the effects of radiation. Keep them bonking."

"Well, Sinead – I'm surprised. I never thought you'd say that word."

"Shut up, you."

"You can bonk all you want now anyway, you've nothing to lose."

She was cheered by this, typical Sinead.

Then something else came along to upset her. It was a few days before her wedding, which was "scheduled" for whenever Bishop McGlinchy came back to town. (Mrs Kenny didn't want Lizzie to do it.)

Some men out fishing were blown off course and saw a black slab like a standing stone looming out of the water. The currents thrust them so close to it that they could hear the hollow thrum of the water against its sides, the only sound in the silence that seemed to encircle it. Well before that, they had recognised it as the sail structure of a nuclear submarine, and they returned home very shaken. The locals near Arklow, accepting that they were stuck with it, decided to believe that the sub had broken up and the reactor was somewhere else.

On the way home, our men noted every small anomaly in the marine life they saw. As luck would have it, they netted some mackerel, and one of the mackerel had a multiple tail. James McEvoy had a look at it when they returned. If you forgave its wrongness, it was lovely, he said, fanning out like a class of explosion, a blossom of fin – a – a dress like a dancer's, he said, that spreads out at the bottom. I went to see it myself on its slab in the back room at the butcher's. It was not lovely, and it already stank. James was trying to make light of it for Sinead's sake. Every night half the street could hear her wails – she'd one nightmare after another about her baby.

My mother heard the talk and was hungry for a description of the fish. She didn't feel up to walking down the town to look at it herself, so I had to describe it to her, scale by mucky scale. The fish found its way to her bedroom wall in due course, and it goggled at me each night when I kissed her and settled her bedclothes round her. She was like a child during these scares – a child who is determined to see the dream to its end.

On that cruel day when I saw Bishop McGlinchy on his

black hunter, I thought many ordeals were about to end. For one thing, Sinead and Ciaran would be married. That, however, wasn't what dried my mouth and started my heart thundering with hope. Mark stood beside him holding the rein, his fair hair gleaming in the sunlight. I watched them, lightheaded, knowing that Dominic must be nearby. Mark looked up and beckoned to me, with a glance that was almost friendly. I approached carefully because of the horse, who, sensing my nervousness, shook his mane and snorted.

Mark looked wild, but well. His hair and his beard were a bit matted, but he managed to look clean – a lot cleaner than Bishop McGlinchy, in fact, who always looked as if he'd been dragged backwards through briars without upsetting himself very much.

"Dominic says hello," Mark said.

"He's not here?"

"Don't get sick over it. He'd be here if he could."

"Is he well?"

"Sure, same as ever."

"'Sure, same as ever,'" I said bitterly. "Gone!"

"There now," said a mild voice from on top of the horse.

I glared up at Bishop McGlinchy. "Hello, your Lordship!" The horse threw up its head.

"Mind now, Maura, mind the horse," he said equably.

"I'm leaving the horse," I said rudely, and walked away.

"See you at the wedding," Mark yelled after me, a grin in his voice. I didn't turn around so he wouldn't see me crying.

Dominic might have come for Mum's sake, or Conor's, if he wouldn't come for me. He had to know the way she was. Even Lizzie admitted she was dying now.

Conor was waiting just inside the front door at home. His eyes were baffled and rebellious – even his coppery hair was contrary. I smoothed it with my hands while he ducked furiously, and stopped him from slipping past me. "Hang on. Tell me about Mum."

"She's been messing all morning with a bunch of flowers," he muttered.

"Painting them?"

"No, for the wedding."

"She knows?"

"Leonie came when you left. Then Sinead. They brought the flowers."

My heart twisted with envy. "My God, you'd think they'd hold off, the state of her. Is she all right?"

"Grand. She's laughing and smiling and all." He made to pass me again. Then he stopped. "Leonie says Mark's here with McGlinchy – "

"Bishop McGlinchy."

" – but not Dominic. Is that true?"

"Yes."

"Well, Jesus, you'd think he'd come." We heard Leonie's voice upstairs, calling. Conor escaped.

Leonie had changed the sheets on my mother's bed. My mother was sitting up in it, looked pretty again; her wasted face had colour in it, and her eyes sparkled.

"It's well for some," I said.

"Listen to her, Leonie. I'm only in bed for a bit, you tyrant. Maura, Leonie likes my fish."

"I wish you'd put your hand to the church," said Leonie.

"Then I couldn't indulge myself. I couldn't have Jack Rourke in the church," she added, nodding at the crouched figure in the corner.

"Is that him?" Leonie said, incredulous. She got up to look closer.

"Is Ireland full of men with scars like that?"

Leonie stared at it, fascinated.

"Mum, what do you mean, that's Jack Rourke?"

She shook her head at me, then lifted the posy she'd made. "Mind you catch this, Daughter – I've fixed it. I've already had a word with the bride."

"You might have had a word with me. Oh, all right," I said when she looked hurt.

"When's Dominic getting here?"

Leonie was gesturing to me behind her back.

"Soon," I said. Then my mother gave me the posy to take to Sinead. It was beautiful, with large, starry clusters of anemones and tendrils of ivy. "Who was up in the hills?" I asked her, because those mutations were found only on the high ground.

"Mark brought them. Enjoy yourself now, Maura. It could be your turn next."

Leonie beamed and hurried down the stairs on my heels. She dragged me into our kitchen, wide-eyed, forefinger of her free hand pressed to her lips.

"I'm staying with her," she whispered. "She'll be all right for the afternoon. Get on now, you don't want to upset her. Bring Conor back with you after," she added.

"You told her Dominic was coming?"

"I did of course. Mark says he is; just not for a day or so. Twisted his ankle or something. No point upsetting her."

I hugged her, holding the posy out of harm's way.

On my way to Sinead's I met Morrie and pounced on him. "Are you meeting Conor, Morrie?"

Morrie put his finger to his lips, nodded, gave a shifty look towards his house and sidled around the corner. I followed him. "Sorry," he said, "Mustn't stay in sight. Mum's – whew!"

"Sure, she is. But it's nothing to when you'll get married, Morrie. We'll all have to leave town."

He laughed. "It's the dress that has her going. Sinead looks like a big, fat Easter candle in it."

"Will you go out of that, Morrie! She'll be gorgeous. Look, just make sure Conor comes home after the wedding. Mum's not good, okay?" Later I remembered Morrie seemed a bit short of breath, but we'd got so used to that, I didn't notice it at the time.

Sinead looked beautiful. She was wearing her mother's wedding dress, which Mrs Kenny had managed to preserve through "hell and high water", as she put it. The dress fell in gentle folds of ivory satin. It had been so many years since we had seen anything like it that I felt a moment of terror looking at her, as if she were opening a door to all the beautiful things of the past, things it would be unbearable to remember. "You look gorgeous," I said. "You look happy."

"I am happy," she said. "I'm not even worried about the baby today. I know everything will be all right. God, aren't the flowers lovely? I can't thank your mam enough."

The little group of neighbours outside was in great form, teasing Mrs Kenny, who really looked very well, and being complimentary to me. When Sinead came out with her dad, they cheered, and we all walked together up to the church.

The rest of the town seemed to be already there. Bishop McGlinchy had recruited Mark as server, and someone had unearthed a vestment I had never seen before, one that hung gracefully from the Bishop's craggy shoulders almost to his heels. I wished my mother could see it. It was the finest bainin, and a crimson cross ran the width of the shoulders and the length of the back. As he moved here and there, it gleamed, and I could see there was embroidery and fine work the entire length and breadth of the cross. In fact, in my sudden happiness, everything seemed to twinkle and shine: the beeswax candles on the altar, the light through the windows, which was alternately cool where they'd been broken, jewelled where they remained, the glints off the odd gold chain or bit of jewellery the women had brought out to wear.

There weren't so many of us after all these years, making those who were there infinitely precious, the more so because we were all there, not just the Catholics. My eyes filled with tears; Sinead gave me a brisk shove in the back. "Walk down now and hold him in case he changes his mind!"

There was little chance of that. Ciaran and James, his best man, were now standing beside Bishop McGlinchy. Ciaran's eyes shone; I knew he would never forget the way Sinead looked today.

Conor and Morrie were perched at the far end of the front pew, as far from Mrs Kenny as Morrie could get. They would melt away until the wedding party went back to the house; neighbours and friends had contributed what food they could, and the result was going to be a feast. Something in the way Conor was sitting made me uneasy. His face was averted. Was he crying? Morrie's thin hand was on his shoulder.

Then my eyes were drawn irresistibly to Sinead and Ciaran, and I became lost in the ritual, the words with their austere and gentle insistence, the choreography of meaning as Bishop McGlinchy and Mark moved around the altar.

Watching Sinead's transfigured face, I began to feel frightened; it was like being stripped of layers of angry strength and left too open to hope and the overbalancing darkness on the other side of it, and I felt disorientated and weak. 'Not now,' I prayed, going cold, 'don't give me a dream now,' though it felt different. There was no dream, but something was wrong.

There was happy confusion on the church steps afterwards, with people coming to offer their congratulations and admire Sinead in her dress. "Maura!" she yelled. "Go down there to the bottom of the steps; I'm throwing the posy."

Bishop McGlinchy took up the cry. "All the eligible women! Bottom of the steps!" I pushed back to the far edge of the crowd, glimpsing Mrs Kenny on the steps, fussily looking this way and that.

Then Sinead caught my eye. She hurled the posy at me with breathtaking accuracy. I had to catch it.

"You're next then, Maura!" the little girls screamed. They looked blank at the same time, because there was no obvious bridegroom in sight. I would cherish the posy because my mother had made it.

"Maura!" Mrs Kenny was at my elbow, red-faced and puffing. "I can't find Morrie and Conor."

"I saw them just after we came out. They were ducking behind people, hiding. Are you sure they haven't gone on to the house?"

"I am. I sent the children to look."

"I have to get back to Mum, Mrs Kenny, I – "

"How is she, dear?" She was still scanning the little groups of people.

"So-so. If they're at our house, I'll send them on to you."

She didn't reply, only nodded and began trotting towards her own house. I climbed up the hill, swinging the posy and fuming. Those two to be causing trouble, today of all days, with a wedding and an illness. I could hear the happy voices down the town. They were moving off towards Kenny's, where there was to be music and dancing. The first notes of the fiddles made filigree on the air.

Our front door was open. Brigid – when had she got there? – was hurrying out. When she saw me, she stood and waited. My legs went stupid. When I passed through the garden gate, she moved towards me and put her arm around my shoulders. I could only look at her.

"Lovey, it was so quick. She was chatting away to Lizzie, and then – "

"I see." That was all I could think of to say.

"Lizzie's with her."

I trudged up the stairs to her room. Lizzie was on her knees beside the bed, head down, praying. My mother lay casually on the pillows as I had last seen her, but her lips were slightly parted now and her eyes were closed. Her beautiful white face looked somehow smaller, and she had the intractable stillness of the dead. She and Lizzie, in their immobility, were almost subsumed among the portraits on the walls. The painted faces drew near the bed as if welcoming her. A trick of the light seemed to point up the scar-faced man in the corner whose ruined smile mocked us, mocked –

"Maura!" Lizzie got up and walked around the bed to me. I breathed out, slowly. "My poor pet."

"When did she die?"

"About a minute after you left. She said, 'Maura's got very pretty, hasn't she?' and she just – " Lizzie opened her hand as if releasing a bird.

"I've got to find Conor."

"We'll find him, Maura. You stay here and have a bit of quiet. I'll go tell Brigid to look for him; I'll stay with you."

I knelt beside the bed and took my mother's hand. It felt odd with the life out of it. It was still just warm, but even while I held it, it got cooler and heavier to my touch, more and more strange-familiar. I felt my breath shudder up and down in my chest as it had when I was a baby and cried, 'Mummy, Mummy,' thinking she was gone when she wasn't. I cried for her, for her loneliness and fear, her lost picture, her life and art shrivelled by our great ignorant catastrophe. I cried for Dominic, cold and hungry somewhere and yet to know, and for Conor, now an orphan. I understood at last the weight of responsibility she felt for him, because now it was mine and it was crushing.

Someone was coming up the stairs. It was our neighbours, Mrs Harding and Mr Comerford. They brought in the small table from the hall and put it at the foot of the bed. Lizzie followed them with two small beeswax candles. She struck at the flint. The little sparks were very bright in the room, and I realised it was almost night. Where had she been?

She helped me up and drew me out on the landing. "Come down to the kitchen," she said quietly.

I stumbled after her, putting myself in her charge as I had when I was a child. The stairs were steeped in shadow. I clutched at her arm. "Where's Conor?"

"That's what we have to talk about," she said.

Chapter Sixteen

THE KITCHEN SEEMED FULL OF PEOPLE, BUT I REALISED AFTER A moment there were just four besides Lizzie and myself. Mrs Kenny sat at one end of the table, distraught, with Brigid beside her, comforting; Pat Jamieson from the Council sat opposite her with our three remaining rush-lights in front of him, managing to look both sympathetic and angry. Behind him, leaning against the wall, was Mark.

"You tell her!" Mrs Kenny said, crying outright. "Let's see you tell her what you told me!" Pat Jamieson made a repressive gesture. "Oh, I'm being very troublesome, amn't I!"

"Mrs Kenny," he began.

"What's the matter?" I said.

"Sit down, Maura."

"Lizzie, what's the matter? Mrs Kenny, where are the boys?"

"They're gone! Stolen out from under our noses, from inside our famous wall and our famous security! They'll tell you now, Maura, they've no-one to spare to go after them." She said "no-one to spare" in a quavering, mincing voice.

"Do you think we wouldn't send someone if we could?" Lizzie's face was haggard. "Maura, I'm sorry, I didn't want you to hear like this, Mrs Kenny said she'd – "

"I understand." I meant I understood Mrs Kenny and why she was raging, even in our house of death. "You're telling me they're gone, and you're doing nothing, just like when Charlie was taken."

"Exactly!" cried Mrs Kenny.

"Mark?"

Mark shifted against the wall. He gave Lizzie a long, brooding look like a question. She looked away.

"Lizzie?" I said. Unbelievably, the refusal seemed to be coming from her as well as from Pat Jamieson. "Sure, you've nearly your own private police force, Mark and Dominic and Pete Mulcahy – ?"

She gave me a wounded look. I stared back at her, incredulous. "I'm sorry, Maura," she said. "They can't be spared."

"They can't? What are they, the honour guard for the Second Coming?"

Mr Jamieson shifted disapprovingly.

"Morrie has athsma, you know! You're just throwing him out on the roads with a gang of thugs – "

"We are not – we did not!" Mr Jamieson said. "Those two brought it on themselves, they slipped out the gate – "

"Are you telling me they got out the gate?"

"How do you know they let themselves out of the gate?" demanded Mrs Kenny.

"How else would they get out?"

"The way every other person under thirty gets out – that bloody tree of O'Bannons' that the Council refused to cut down because of the apples!"

"It'll be cut down tonight, Maura," Mr Jamieson said heavily. "I'm sorry. It makes no odds. There's no-one to be spared."

Mrs Kenny had been glaring at him and shaking her head, and this last was too much. She flew at him, hands clawed, crashing her chair behind her. Lizzie looked at Mark, but Mark did nothing, only settled himself more comfortably in the shadows. Brigid tried to restrain her and got an elbow in the breast. Mr Jamieson, his hair tousled, eyes blinking furiously, managed to grab Mrs Kenny by the wrists. She kicked at his ankles. "That will just do, Mrs Kenny," Lizzie said in her Council voice.

"It was 'Imelda' before you left my son to die," Mrs Kenny screamed. "My son and your own nephew – are you going to call her 'Miss O'Keeffe' from now on?" nodding at me.

"Get her out!" Lizzie said, her lips trembling.

"This is my house," I said. "I hope you'll say a prayer beside my mother, Mrs Kenny."

But she stumbled around the table to me and touched my shoulder. "I'm so sorry, so sorry. I can't, you understand, but I'm sorry for our trouble, sorry to bring mine to yours. Sinead's going over to McEvoys' tonight. I don't want her to know yet. She'll go mad. Oh, what will happen, Maura, I could lose them both!"

I put my arms around her. "You mustn't go home by yourself," I said. "I'll walk with you."

"I'll go, too," Mark said briefly. Lizzie started to speak, but thought better of it. Mark hadn't looked at her, but he was "putting out knives," as Dominic and I used call it. He could subtly alter his stance so you knew you shouldn't approach him, though his expression remained as bland as ever.

It was moonlight outside. Mrs Kenny walked between Mark and me on the cracked footpath. Mark poked my arm. I looked at him and he nodded, as if to say "well done".

By the time Mrs Kenny got to her own door, she was moving like an old woman. She stumbled on her front step. "They've been gone hours," she said, her voice dragging. She put up her hand to feel the light mist that was beginning to fall. "It'll soon be over ... Oh, Morrie, Morrie ... ! Who can I tell? Martin's not fit to go after him. If only he'd be found before I have to tell Sinead."

We could hear voices in the house, and bursts of laughter. The door opened and Mr Kenny came out. "For God's sake, Imelda, where have you been?"

With a haunted look back at us, she let herself be drawn inside.

Mark steered me into an alternate route back to my house. "Sorry about your mother. She was all right."

"She painted you, you know. On her wall. After she sketched you."

"Did she, now," he said politely. He didn't care at all how other people saw him.

We stopped in the black shadow under a gable. "Mark, what in the name of God is going on?"

"Civil War, maybe."

"With what? Sticks and rocks?"

"Probably." The smile.

"Is this why they won't send someone after the boys? Mark, I still can't believe it!"

He gave me a painful, admonitory flick on the top of my head. "Sure, as you said yourself, it's happened before, and keep your voice down."

"So it's the slavers? Oh, Jesus, of course it is. Mark, they'll kill Morrie. What can we do?"

"Morrie will slow them down, of course. They may just let him go."

There was a bleak little silence. "He was breathless this afternoon," I said.

Mark moved restlessly.

"Where do they take them?"

"Sure, to Athlone. To be sold or whatever."

"'Whatever?'"

"Some they keep for hostages. To extort things out of their communities. We could always suggest that Conor and Morrie are more valuable as hostages than slaves, but that could go wrong; if they didn't get their money or goods – " he stopped himself and put his finger on my lips. We heard rapid footsteps, and then we saw Lizzie, hardly more than an anxious shadow, hurrying past the end of the street towards Kennys'.

"What's Lizzie doing?" I whispered.

"Looking for you. Look, this is what you'll do."

"About what?"

"About Conor and Morrie, you daw. Do you want them or not?"

"Of course!"

He motioned towards the wall that loomed black at the end of the street. "Would you be willing to leave the charmed circle to go after them yourself?"

"Yes!" I said, terrified.

"Right. We get Lizzie – "

"She'll never let me out of here. If I'm going, shouldn't I just go?""

He grabbed me by the arm and started propelling me towards the convent.

"You wouldn't last a day without Lizzie's help. She owns all the good shoes."

"But how'll I persuade her to – "

"Two words," he said grimly. "'Margaret Kilcoyne.'"

We waited in silence in the shadows across from the convent. Margaret. Of course. Still alive in Athlone, and her father with all that power. I turned up my roughened palms, looked at them, let my hands drop down to my sides. I thought of my mother back in the house, slowly stiffening in her bed. I had seen her, spoken to her for the last time. Maybe Conor, too. I got an odd sensation around the knees, and found myself on the ground, sitting. "Put your head down," said Mark's voice, testily. "Get it together now, she's coming."

The rest of that night, like the day that led into it, seemed unreal. Someone else stepped into my skin. I was glad of this person; she was me-not-me. She had no loves, ties, or fears. She protected me from Lizzie, whom I would have pitied and finally obeyed. Lizzie had no such helper, and in the end I-not-I extracted from her everything I needed. Mark, seeing that this other me was in control, stretched out on Lizzie's floor like a cat and slept instantly.

"He can do that anywhere it's safe," Lizzie said, looking down at him. "You'll have to learn that when you're outside, learn what it took him and Dominic years to ... You mustn't go, Maura. I'll never see you again."

"Show me the map, please," I said.

She unfolded it very carefully and spread it on the table. It was a map of Ireland. I let out my breath in a long, silent sigh. "Far enough to walk when you're on Shanks Mare," she said, noticing.

"Even farther then for Conor. And Morrie."

She shook her head when I mentioned Morrie. "They're taking them all to Athlone now." She moved the rush-light onto the northern corner of the map. The light flickered over the worn surface with its thousands of veins and capillaries, its frail names of roads, towns, hills and rivers. Ireland. It was enormous. Then the shocked, cool person who had taken charge pushed the anxious self aside again. For hours I listened to Lizzie while she traced the lines on the map with a roughened finger. Laragh, Ballymore Eustace, the Curragh ... Rathangan, Daingean, Tyrrellspass, and finally, Moate. "You must be very careful here," she said. "Be sure you approach Athlone from the south, not the north. If you go astray, you'll wind up at An Fásach, and you don't want that."

"What's there?"

"Has Dominic never told you? It's a hot spot, the worst in Ireland."

"Dominic doesn't say much."

"No, he wouldn't."

"You could have told me things. You could have told Conor, even. You treated us like fools, Lizzie."

Her face reddened, and she looked ashamed. "Ach, it was after the panic that time the rumours got round about the landings." This was the third winter after the War, when people got to hear that bands of Arabs – or Russians – or Chinese – were making their way up the East Coast, killing and ransacking. A number of people fled to the mountains, and a whole family died from exposure before they could be found and told the truth.

"Well. Mark said you'd give me shoes."

She sat silently for a moment, then said, "Come downstairs with me." She picked up the rush-light. When we stood up, Mark opened his eyes, recollected the situation, and went back to sleep.

She led me down the stairs and through the dark house, through the kitchen which hardly smelt of food, being too clean and too impoverished, to a small storeroom. "We've very little now, but with a bit of luck ... Oh, Maura," she said, her voice breaking. But I said nothing, and she held the light up to the shelves, then set it down on a small table and took down three bulky plastic bags, which she placed beside it. "There was one lady's pair, I'm sure," she said.

I was looking at the bag. It was a bright, shiny green. It said "St. Bernard's" on it in black script, and in much larger block letters underneath, "DUNNES STORES", glimmering seductively, a holograph. Conor in a baby chair in a strong wire trolley that my young mother pushed. Aisles upon aisles of shelves of food, soaps, drinks, tins, brightly lit.

And just beyond this, a dazzle of clothes, clothes on racks, on shelves, on tables, and on the far side, other shops. My mother saying we didn't need crisps, crisps in their colourful shiny wrappings. My mouth watered. The salt, crunching melt of them, I'd nearly forgotten it. I could almost taste the crisps, salt and vinegar was the flavour. It was silly because that time I remembered, we hadn't bought them.

Lizzie was waiting. She had said something to me. It was the boots, I was to try them on. They were heavy in my hands, brown leather with thick soles. They had creases; they leaned over at the ankles, still obliging someone who was probably dead, and they'd thick red laces that looked almost new. "Pray you fit into these. They're hiking boots, hardly worn."

I put my feet into them, laced them clumsily in the feeble light, and stood. The firm uppers and uncompromising soles seemed to hold me up and the floor down. "They're a bit loose," I said.

"What socks have you? Show me." She stooped to look, then pinched my sock with her hand. "Paper'd be thicker! Where'd you get these at all?"

"They're old. I threw them on."

"A proper pair of socks and these boots should fit. Hold the light." She rummaged delicately and drew out a shoe-box. This too went on the table. She took off the pasteboard lid and revealed several pairs of hand-knit socks. I had seen Leonie and my mother knitting such socks from wool they had picked from old, frayed jumpers. Lizzie put two pairs into my hands. They'd the humble softness of all such things, things which had been used and then coaxed into yet another shape.

"These look like Mum's," I said.

Lizzie peered at them closely. Her eyes filled with tears. "They are. They won't wear out on you soon, either." She brought me into the kitchen and sat me down at the table, then thought of something else she wanted in the stores and left me in the dark while she went back.

I sat quietly, absorbing the familiarity of that room where we'd worked and taken many meals. It wouldn't do for Lizzie to find out how frightened I was, how reluctant to leave her and the place she'd made safe for us.

When Lizzie returned with the light, she was holding her great treasure, a light waterproof jacket that could be rolled into a tiny ball and crushed into the pocket of something else. It even had a hood. Last, she'd a small backpack, the sort that teenagers used have for their schoolbooks before the War. Into this she put three apples, a large chunk of brown bread and a soft, smelly round of cheese that she wrapped in clean rags. "We'll wake Mark," she said abruptly. "It'll be light soon." She paused beside me. "Sylvia used say you must be let go to find your destiny, she always said that about you and Conor. I don't know if this is what she meant, Maura!"

"It is, Lizzie," said my other self.

In the end, she couldn't say goodbye to me; at least she wouldn't watch me out the gate. "Keep the jacket and the socks in your pockets," she said. "You can't afford to lose those. Try to keep out of the rain." Then, "I'll pray for you," she whispered.

"We'll be all right," I said. Mark opened the front door. I slipped out after him and together, keeping to the shadows and gliding along almost silently, we approached the town gate.

Chapter Seventeen

Mark sent me out on the easier road, taking a more difficult route to Laragh for himself. We were to meet at the outskirts of the town. "Not a place to go on your own," he said carelessly. He would move quickly to see if he could catch up with the boys or find Dominic.

"And what if you do catch up with them?"

"I'll still be back for you. Wait for me."

He left me alone on the road I hadn't seen since Dominic's and my attempt to go home ten years ago. Walking was difficult, and when the sky began to lighten, I could see why. The surface was strewn with twigs and leaves and odd debris, and the bits of asphalt that still showed were rucked and wrinkled like the skin of an old elephant. The leaves and dirt on the road muffled my footsteps, and only the soft snapping of twigs under my boots reassured me that I wasn't in one of my "dreams". It was a relief to hear a little stream beyond the hedge.

A breeze sprang up, then intensified, and somewhere high overhead there was a long powerful moan, a terrible thrumming. Higher voices, screams and whistles cut through it, ebbed, rose. The hedge moved. I backed across the road, the hairs rising on the nape of my neck.

When I looked up, it was rearing right over me, a black tangle of bones against the sallow sky. There was another behind it, and another, in an obscene and jolting march across the meadows. I had fallen to my knees: now I got up, shaking, and flung down my pack and kicked it. My banshees were the huge electricity pylons that the War had turned into useless mysteries on the land.

I felt very alone, but that wasn't all of it. Already I sensed that more had changed than we could discern on our short trips to the woods and fields around the town. There was a different atmosphere; the tangled hedges were oppressive and sad, and so was Rathnew with its rust-bleared petrol station, deadpan shops, and houses that sagged inward on their ghosts.

It was fully light now, though the sky was grey, with a high overcast. At least it wasn't raining on Conor and Morrie; at least my mother wouldn't be lowered into a hole full of muddy water. In an hour or two, the men would start uncovering a place for her in the long trench that served for our many graves. They would gather stones and leave them in a pile beside the displaced earth.

I imagined the little cavalcade on its way through the West Gate, and up past the old housing estate and into the field behind it with its long, straggling hillocks. They'd wrap her in one of her own blankets, and another blanket, folded over, would serve as a stretcher. Lizzie would follow them, leading the prayers, and Sinead and Mrs Harding – would Sinead know yet about Morrie? – and Leonie and Brigid and Mr Comerford, our neighbour, and those who could be spared.

"Let the dead bury their dead." It should have been a comfort, but I could only cry, especially by the side of the road in Ashford. The tea room at the entrance to the

famous gardens was roofless now; so was the little book-
shop, where my parents had bought me an old copy of a
book called *Candy on the DART*, about a little girl who
rode the trains that used run in Dublin before they got the
VoloRail. I always thought the DART sounded nicer than the
VoloRail. They changed it just before I was born.

A gust of wind threaded through the acres of foliage
behind the wall, and with it the fragrance of many flowers,
accompanied by a rank, marshy tang. My mother had
plucked a purple blossom from one of the shrubs and set it
behind her ear and another one behind mine.

Up the rise, in the main street of the town, there was
life, I could feel it. A slow spiral of smoke rose from a
house among trees up the hillside. The buildings facing the
road were shuttered like those in Rathnew, but these had
been cared for, and there was an alertness behind the
blankness.

Just past the shell of a gutted supermarket, a road
intersected the main highway from the left. This was surely
the road to Annamoe and Laragh; I started along it,
suddenly feeling exposed. It began to rise almost
immediately. There were houses on either side, solid
cottages and bungalows, and what would once have been
good estates branching out to the left. It was hard to know
which of the houses were inhabited; their small front
gardens were wild, but almost all the windows were
glassed or fastened shut, and no door hung loose. The
road here, though as littered as the highway, seemed more
trodden. There seemed to be a kind of normalcy, but the
true position was soon made clear.

There was a crash of branches, and a child appeared
around the side of the house I was passing. It was a little
girl, frail but spirited-looking in bundly knitted clothes. She
must have been about five. She froze when she saw me.

"Hello."

Her mouth and eyes widened. "Mam!" she managed at last, a thin squeal.

"It's all right," I began.

"Mam!"

There was another crashing of leaves, and the top of a lilac waved wildly. A woman pushed out behind the little girl. She had a shotgun. She raised it and levelled it at me. It's true what they say about the interior of a gun barrel looking very black. I put my hands in the air, like people did in films long ago. My voice wouldn't work to say anything.

"Go out of here now," said the woman. "We know what to do with your kind. Go back!" she said to the child. "Go get your Dad."

I knew that if a man had been on the premises, he'd have been out with the shotgun himself. "I meant nothing," I said. "I'm only passing. I wouldn't harm anyone." It sounded like a lie.

"Go along now, and don't come back this way," said the woman. Her face was both angry and frightened. She reminded me of my mother. The little girl had already melted into the bushes at the side of the cottage.

I shrugged and started on my way, half-expecting to feel shotgun shells rushing past me or, worse, slapping into my back and bursting out the other side. I blamed Mark for the tone of this encounter. 'You'll be safer if you look like some manky little boy, not a twenty-year-old virgin with all her teeth, worth two pigs and an uncontaminated cow,' and just outside the gates, he had cut my hair to near-stubble with his knife. I must have looked manky all right to that woman with her shotgun; I must have depreciated by at least a pig.

Pure adrenalin pushed me past hedges and fields, some

roughly tilled, as the road rose past cottages and ruins of cottages, places that would have looked sad and friendly if there were only more signs of life. Something pale caught my eye in the garden of one of them: it was the hull of a yacht on some rusted support that was almost hidden by the long grass. There was something unbearable about it, stranded forever miles from its element.

This world had turned itself inside out. All stone things, like the old estate wall on my right and the little bridge where the road dropped and crossed the stream, looked far newer and fresher now than the more recent desolation around them. Everything was the same, and different.

On the other side of the bridge, a low stone wall exposed rolling meadows and a field with a desultory huddle of sheep at one end. On the far side, there was a different sort of activity. Birds rose and fell, landing on something in the grass that I couldn't see. My skin began to crawl. I thought of Conor or Morrie trying to run from the men and escape, I thought –

A man approached the sheep through a gap in the hedge. I let out my breath. The way he moved in that field showed he owned it. He waved his stick, scattering the birds. Then he leaned down and grasped something, the thin, stiff legs of a half-grown lamb. I went on my way.

The tunnel-world of the hedges was becoming more and more oppressive; the sky was defeated by the wild growth that arched over the road. The drifts of forestry that stretched up on my right, the stands of conifers both darkened and lightened by hollies, sycamores and beeches, seemed to be marching down on me. A cypress had fallen but was supported on the other side of the road by the trees opposite, forming an unpleasantly intimate bridge whose dead fingers trailed softly through my hair and over my shoulders when I hurried under it, glad to glimpse the clean, blueish-looking mountains on the left and the soft brown of turf or heather up ahead. I longed for space; leaves, shadows, and patterns of leaves marbled my sight, drifting around me like fragments in a kaleidoscope. I rubbed my eyes and was relieved to find myself in the open, on a bare mountain strewn with stones. The sky was still grey, but it had lightened; it was so bright and cold that it dazzled me.

I crouched on the road as shadows swung overhead. Birds. Black, threatening, they drifted to a place on the hillside and dropped beyond one of the great boulders that jutted out of the harsh grass and heather. I picked myself up and shuffled along the road. I must see what lay on the other side of the rock.

Something hurt my side. I put my hand to it and felt a stick, as if my rib were protruding, twisted to look at it and realised I was sprawled on the road in the green twilight between the hedges, not on a hillside at all. My head throbbed.

"Look, Alan," a voice said. "I believe he's waking up." It was a gentle voice, but it carried a warning.

I saw their feet first, a large pair and a small, both in dull, patched Wellingtons. The man had one of those faces that weather to a pale, uniform brown. It was delicately lined. He was looking at me through light blue eyes, very peaceful; there was something monkish about him, though he was dressed in the worn clothes of a farmer. The child, warmly wrapped in scarves and a woman's aran cardigan, stood at his side. He looked at me quietly, with the dignified, rather doubtful regard that Down's Syndrome children often have.

"Are you ill?" The man had a cultivated voice.

"No, I ... I'll be all right in a moment." I put my head

down on my knees. The pain began to subside.

"What do you suppose is wrong with you?" said the gentle voice.

"Nothing, really. I'm all right." I struggled to my feet.

"Would you mind if I took your pulse?"

I looked at him, then at the child, who smiled beatifically and pulled at his cuff, as if to show me what to do.

"You're a doctor!"

"I was."

"Was?"

"When I lost my medicines, I lost most of my skills," he said. He took an old steel watch out of his pocket, supported my wrist with one hand, peered at the watch in the other. "All right," he said, his eyebrows going up. "Who would have thought?"

The little boy swayed gently from side to side.

"Now then, Alan – this – girl's – very well." Seeing my expression, he went on, "I did think you were a boy at first. I thought … "

"What?"

He looked at me with his quiet, shrewd eyes. Now they seemed bleak. "I wondered if you were one of a party that passed here during the night."

"You saw them?"

"Heard them, more – it's very dark here." He stopped.

"What did you hear?"

"Do you know them?"

The child, Alan, began to whimper.

"I know their hostages," I said. "One of them is my brother."

"I see." He was a doctor, all right. He looked like he was deciding whether he'd tell me I was dying.

"My brother's friend, Morrie Kenny, was taken with him," I said. "Morrie has a bad chest."

He nodded. "Have you anyone to help you?"

"I'm expecting someone … "

"A man? Wait for him. Don't think of approaching that lot yourself; they'd eat you alive."

For a moment, I wondered if he meant it literally.

"They're bad ones. I'm very sorry. I can do nothing. I'm on my own here with Alan. There were three of them; and the two boys."

"Could you hear … ?"

"Only one boy talking to the other, to the boy who was coughing."

"Is it far to Laragh?"

"About four miles. Will you be stopping there?"

I shook my head.

"You wouldn't want to pass Glendalough in daylight, and even Laragh's a bit tricky."

"So I'm told."

"Won't you rest a while with us?"

My legs were aching; there were already raw spots on my feet, and I knew I would get to Laragh long before Mark. However, "I'll push on," I said. "Thank you."

"Stop in if you need to on your way back," he said.

As I moved away, Alan's face crumpled. "Mam," he wailed. "Mam." His father picked him up and carried him up the hillside towards a gate with stone pillars. The wailing stopped. The two small hands met and clasped behind the father's neck.

Just outside Laragh, I picked my way into the forest, out of sight of the road, but where I'd be able to hear anyone who passed. The afternoon was chill, but mercifully, still dry. An enormous chestnut with a thick canopy of leaves provided a good resting place, and I sank down, rested my back against it and nibbled the hard barley cake that Lizzie had given me, making it last as long as I could.

Despite the sneaping breeze and leafy noises, I was

confident I'd hear Mark on the road. Louder in my mind were Conor's footsteps and Morrie's laboured breath, the harsh throbs of their increasing misery and despair. I clenched my hands tight and tried to pray, but all that came was anger and fear. Where was Mark?

I drowsed, feeling mist steal down, then slept as the whole world slid away.

CHAPTER EIGHTEEN

THE TREE'S ROOTS FELT ROUGH AND SLIMY IN THE DARKNESS. MY legs were stiff, clothes heavy with mist. I had slept into the night. Mark would have searched for me in vain. Conor and Morrie would be miles farther on, a step farther for every second I had slept.

I struggled to my feet and felt my socks pulling away from raw spots that had dried. Dominic's voice, long ago: "The first thing you care for is your feet." Cursing myself, I removed the boots, then the socks, keeping them near so as not to have to hunt for them in the dark. Lizzie had given me unguent in a twist of paper. Some of it had melted into my pocket, then almost congealed again. I picked it out and applied it to all the sore spots, then put on the socks my mother had made, and the boots.

Fog crept along the road, reflecting off the weak moonlight that filtered through the trees. The sleep had refreshed me, though it was like a loan I couldn't repay. At least I needn't wait any longer for Mark, but could pass through Laragh in the dark now, and keep going. He could meet me when he wanted. We'd all heard about Laragh. It was where a number of hill roads met, and sometimes the people demanded "tax" from travellers. Dominic said it depended on the size of the traveller as often as not, and he and Mark had never been approached; but smaller people had bits and pieces taken from them or were even made to do "Community Work". I prayed that nobody would delay me while Conor and Morrie melted further into the web of roads and byways.

The trees that met overhead blocked the moonlight, but the footing was not too bad, and the watery murmur on either side of the road showed where the drains were. It was the suddenness of the tree's embrace that stunned me; I couldn't stop myself crying out. When it was clear that no warm-blooded thing was encircling me, but merely another fallen tree, I left what seemed like half the skin of my hand, assorted threads of coat and jeans and every curse I knew on it. Afterwards, hurrying on, I kept one arm cocked in front to protect my eyes. Finally the trees thinned and the mist dissipated, though the sky remained dark, the moon defeated by clouds. There were other sounds now, the swish of an animal's footsteps in the field on the left and, then, the sudden, deafening yammering of a dog. A scraping rattle told me he was chained, and I pushed on, trying to keep myself from making any noise.

I was in Laragh. There was what seemed to be a low grassy knoll in front of me with a long building on the right, "an old shop", Lizzie had said, a slightly lighter place in the darkness. My road was to bear off to the left, past a long row of houses and hedges and cottage gates. I could see nothing. I was waiting for a voice to call, a hand to shoot out and hold me, and I imagined again and again that something – a footfall? a soft rustle? – was sliding just beyond the intelligence of my hearing.

This road passed Glendalough. "Don't go there under any circumstances. Only the dregs of the country go there. It's changed a lot since St. Kevin," Lizzie had added, even managing a smile. "It's a den of thieves, and you don't go there unless you're a thief yourself."

"Isn't that just where the slavers would go with Morrie and Conor?"

"And have them taken off them? They'll run them past there." We both knew there wouldn't be a hope of running Morrie past a post or a stone, not the way he'd been that day.

Surely he couldn't have got so far? What if he was lying beside the road and I had already passed him in the dark? This thought upset me so much that I took a wrong turn. The road, which had been rising, now dropped. This wasn't right, according to Lizzie's instructions. Retracing my steps for a few paces, I found I'd taken the left of two forks. From somewhere behind and below, there was a blood-curdling growl, followed by hisses and snorts. I regained the upper road and ran as quietly as the boots would allow. The terrible snores continued below on my left, the clouds swung away from the moon for a moment, and its tentative gleam picked out a corbelled roof through a gap in the gorse. That was Glendalough, and I was lucky the watchman had been sleeping.

As the light strengthened, it revealed less and less; it was as if all the houses and landmarks had stolen away under cover of darkness, leaving only a few stragglers behind. In the glen below I could hear water; on my right gorse and conifers climbed the horizon. Little precipitous roads bumped down towards old farms on the left; I wondered how cars and animals had ever managed to get up those again.

The land itself slowly brightened, radiating light from thousands and thousands of pale stones and boulders. The mountain ahead was weeping; complex veins that gleamed like pewter ran down its stony face, soft gleams that would harshen to silver as the sun got higher. My mother would have loved this place, I said to comfort myself. I tried to see it as she would, even as I listened for any human sound and strained at the horizon to see if there were figures there. Once she told me stones were very difficult for her. "I'm inclined to make them come forward. They get too light or something, they take over. They have light, that's the problem. When you're looking at them, though, you're always aware of their mass and their texture. That's what I find hard, to do justice to the light, the mass and the texture at the same time."

She'd her head on one side when she said this, and a faraway look in her eye. Her fingers curved longingly when she spoke about the texture of the stones. I examined the tumbled hillside ahead of me and the white, hard bed of the river below, as if to organise them in my head for a picture. I wasn't my mother. There was something missing. Then I saw there wasn't, after all; far ahead on the hillside, there was movement: three birds, black against the sky, rising and falling.

I ran. They mustn't drop behind that rock, that boulder that looks like the head of some monster; they mustn't drop. When I got nearer I shouted at them, waving my arms. Two of them hovered higher; the third stood on the rock, defiant, wings half-cocked. I picked up a stone in mid-stride and fired it off. "Oh please God, not his eyes, not his eyes." Opposite the rock, I clapped at them and shouted. They flew away.

The first I saw was his feet. The men had taken his shoes; they had plundered the rags from his body. His feet were swollen and blistered. They had left his trousers – they were too worn and small – but they'd taken his best denim shirt away. It had two neat patches. Mrs Kenny had used the pocket to make them, so there had been a darker square on the breast.

His eyes, glazed now, weren't quite shut. I could see the clouds moving in them. He was very cold. I tried to shut his eyes, but couldn't; he had begun to stiffen. I said an Act of Contrition, not that he'd anything to be contrite about. "It's to please your mother, Morrie. God, punish them as only you know how."

I pulled him a little away from the boulder so as to make room for a cairn, and then stopped. It would take hours to cover him. A shadow glided over us then, and another, and there was a soft rush of air and scrape of claw at the boulder beside me. I began to assemble the stones.

It was hardest to cover his face and his brave red hair. All the time I talked to him and to Sinead as if they could hear me. "She'll want to come here someday, maybe even move you back home … Sinead, he'll be undisturbed, I promise. Nothing will touch him." In the end, it was hard to leave him. Then I saw Conor in my mind's eye, stripped of his friend and stumbling farther and farther away from me, so I hugged my aching arms to my chest, and started to follow him once more. I looked back once at Morrie's tumbled cairn. It huddled by the big boulder as if sheltering there.

I don't know when the landscape started to soften, but between one moment and the next I heard a gentle music all around me. The whole hill was spouting rivulets of water. They tumbled through the heather, gorse and stones, ending in tiny waterfalls where they dropped the last few feet into the drain, with many tinklings and happy whispers; I set my foot on a stone to balance myself and held my hands under a small cascade whose racy chill numbed them and started my heart beating faster.

I was about to stick my head under, turn my face up, swallow, when I heard a shout. A lean figure was approaching, a tall man with a stick. He was gesticulating wildly. I stepped back into the road and waited, thirst forgotten, until his limping gait resolved itself into something more familiar, and the sun glinted off Dominic's dark hair.

CHAPTER NINETEEN

I DON'T KNOW HOW LONG WE CLUNG TO EACH OTHER. THEN, "DID you drink any of it? Did you?"

"What?"

"The water. Did you drink it?"

"No, I – "

"Thank God," he said, gripping me again. "We must get to the spring, though, and wash it off your hands. That's really all?"

I nodded.

"Hurry now, he said, starting back up the road. "When we get to the spring, we'll talk."

By the time we reached the part of the forest where the spring was, Dominic was calm, even a bit remote. He limped ahead of me between the trees and over the tangled bracken as if he were a guide, turning often to check on me, helping when I needed it. The spring gushed out of a tumble of rocks in a small clearing, cascading a few feet into a little pool before joining a trickle that wandered away to the Glendasan. "It was tested long ago and it was all right," he said. "Did you wet your sleeves?"

I hadn't, and he pushed them far up my arms, then

made me soak my hands in the moving water. They were chilled, then numbed, then white. He rubbed them hard where I'd abrasions from the stones. Finally he was satisfied. Then he made me remove my jacket; he hung it on a branch and beat it with his stick. "The great thing is you didn't drink it," he said.

He gave me a troubled look. "You were a long time coming," he said. "What happened? Wait, now – I'm sorry, Maura, before we talk, I want you to wash. It's best."

"In that? I'll never be warm again!"

"To be safe. You're dusty. I see dust in your hair."

He was so serious that I leant over the stream.

"Wait – "

"Good God, let me get it over with!"

Without ado, he tugged my jumper and shirt off over my head.

"Go on now," he said softly to my back, "if you get that wet you'll freeze all right." I heard him behind me giving the jumper the same treatment he'd given the coat.

I plunged my head into the stream, gasping, my skull flooding with dull pain. In a moment there were cascades of icy water over my back and shoulders as well. I heard Dominic behind me, laughing.

I shook my hair like a dog, the better to splash him back, and turned on him. He stopped and looked stricken in the same moment I realised and clapped my arms over my breasts. He turned blindly to take my jumper from the branch where it was hanging, and threw it to me. I pulled it on.

"What happened your hair?"

"You didn't see Mark?"

"He didn't mention it."

"Mark happened to it. With his horrible knife."

His smile wavered and then was extinguished. "I'm sorry about Sylvia." His face twisted, and I ran to him and held him. "I wanted to see her again," he said, his voice breaking.

I held him while he cried, and told him of her easy death and how she was happy knowing he was coming soon.

The tears streamed down his face.

"I've needed you with me so much, I can't tell you – none of it's been real until now!"

He drew back and looked into my eyes, and then we held each other for a while. Now, I thought foolishly, everything will be all right.

Mark, plunging ahead with his great strength and energy, had located Conor, but alone he could do nothing. He and Dominic thought that, even two against three, they might be able to get the better of the slavers, but it would be a close contest. Mark had hoped to buy help in Laragh and overtake the little group on the road, but he found that these particular men were known and feared more than others. "Mark said they were moving very quickly. Conor looked tired, but all right, Maura. He was more upset than anything. Morrie was already dead when Mark caught up with them."

"Then how did Morrie get – ?"

"Mark said Conor carried him a while on his back."

It was my turn to cry, and I told him about making Morrie's cairn that morning. Already I was worried that there weren't enough stones.

"Everyone who passes will throw on another one." Dominic stirred and got up, protecting his sore ankle. "We've real walking to do now, girl. How are your feet?"

"Not bad. But I'm hungry."

He gave me a barley cake to nibble when we were on our way. If we'd only had Conor and Morrie, and my mother to go home to, I would have been perfectly happy.

My mother used to tell me about a nightmare she had, that she went shopping with Conor and then realised he was no longer beside her, and that closing time had come and gone and he'd been missing for hours. She rushed from room to room in the shop searching for him in the wilderness of plenty; then she looked out and it was night. Midnight. She would wake herself sobbing, knowing she'd lost him forever.

I thought of the slavers hurrying on their way, widening the gap between Conor and us with every stride, disappearing into the byways that were like a tangle of filaments on my map. Conor was somewhere, I told myself. The reality of the road he was on registered itself in his feet, in his legs, he smelled the air where he was, he was thinking something at this very moment, he was utterly, utterly real.

I saw his dirty, tear-stained face; his blue eyes had an arrested look. "We're coming for you!"

"What?" said Dominic.

"I saw him! Conor!"

"Where?"

"Oh, you know – "

"Like in one of your dreams?"

"Nearly. I only saw his face. A good dream, for once. Dominic, it's happening so much now. I saw where Morrie was." When Dominic put his arm around my shoulder, I realised I was shaking.

"I used to worry about Conor, how he'd get on without Morrie," he said quietly. "'Mind and body!' Morrie was always on borrowed time, Maura. Poor Mrs Kenny ... terrible woman! Still, she did everything she could for him, bar push the earth off its course to get us a better climate ... Remember how he'd make me carry him places on my back? No way was he missing out on anything."

Little by little we started the lifelong process of

remembering, grafting Morrie into our souls word by word. I wondered if we would be doing the same for Conor, or for one of ourselves, before this was over.

We hurried for a while in silence. I couldn't stop looking at Dominic. It was as if I'd been born looking at him; then, that I was seeing him for the first time. Thoughts shimmered confusedly in my mind.

"What will Mrs Kenny do, Dominic? Morrie was her life."

"Somebody else will come, or need her, and if they don't – she'll die."

His face was as quiet as an icon's when he said this, and I thought of him that time he arrived at the cottage after the War, when he said my mother would be a fool to feed him. I think he knew when she went out to him on the path that he was taking us on rather than the other way round; it was up to him to decide whether to live or not. My heart clattered with anxious love.

After a while, my tumble of thoughts and feelings subsided; only motion mattered. Dominic's sore leg seemed to be improving, and I had to strain to keep up with him.

Lizzie had once said even *I* would seem tall to the next generation; people would start being smaller again through hardship. They'll look at our clothes and shoes and wonder, she said, just as we wondered about the tiny suits of armour fighting men wore in the Middle Ages, men we thought of as enormous in their size as in their exploits. "It's the opposite with us. For all our size and strength and health in the West, we've tiny brains, and we'll go the way of the dinosaurs."

"But Lizzie, they say the attacks came from the Middle East, not the West."

"Oh, they probably started there. But we meddled and sold. Meddling and selling, that was us. We should have left them in their ignorance and kept our own to ourselves." She never gave quarter to the "troglodytes", as she called them, who had spoiled our lives and spilled us out into the countryside at dawn to hunt for nettles and mushrooms and wild garlic that weren't there because everything had already been scoured.

My parents had protected me from news reports I'd heard as a child. 'Don't worry, it's very far away,' and the car bombs, the hackings, the tortures, the strafings, the starvation, all receded to a darkness on the far horizon. Then the War came and set it all at the end of our road, even in my own face in the mirror.

When survival was the issue, or we really wanted something, we showed what we were made of. I looked at Dominic beside me and loved him for his gentleness.

We walked until it was dark and my feet were so sore I could scarcely touch the road with them, and Dominic's limp was noticeable again. We picked our way through a village as the night settled around us and, as we passed the shuttered houses, every bone in my body yearned for home. For the first time, I realised that "home" had stopped being Killiney years ago; "home" was Wicklow, and as we drew farther and farther away from it, I longed for Sinead and Lizzie, for our ziggedy streets and our empty, bewildered house. I reached for Dominic's hand and clung to it.

"Not much longer now," he said. At the far end of the village, he knocked on the door of a house – I could hardly see it in the dark. There was a scrape and a rustle inside and then a voice whispered, "Who's there?"

He told him, and bolts were drawn back. The door swung open with a squawk. "All for the want of a bit of oil," the voice grumbled, "the whole village will know I've visitors."

We stepped inside into pitch dark. A muttered conversation took place, while I strained to see something, anything. There was a creak and a vibration in the floor, and the door shrieked again behind us. A dirty hand pawed at my face. I pushed at what seemed to be a warm, firm collection of greasy rags. "What are yeh coming to? That's no lad, or he hasn't got a beard."

"There now, Pakky, don't be frightening him."

"This way," said the voice.

I held on to the back of Dominic's jacket and was aware of going in to another room. Behind us, a door shut and a key turned.

"Dominic!"

"It's all right. This is his routine. It's necessary for him. He's been good to us over the years." He passed his hand over my hair. "How are you?"

I laughed.

"We can't stay long. Only a couple of hours. I'm sorry. We need to cross the Curragh in the dark; it's very exposed. We've not made bad time today; don't worry."

I wanted to ask him something, but I was asleep before I lay down on the floor. I was trying to find him and Conor: I knew they were ahead of me on the road, but whenever I drew near to one, the other disappeared around a bend or even a mountain. A different kind of dream woke me, the other kind; it had nestled beside me like a panther while I was sleeping.

In this new place, the light was strong and yet not the usual colour of the sky. There was a fraying, languorous movement all around me, a hypnotic rising and falling, queer swirls and whirlwinds of pale brown dust almost as light as the air itself. They seemed almost intelligent, leaning towards me, forming and reforming as if curious, even affectionate. Then I found myself far enough away to see that it was an area I was looking at, a queer desert covering many acres but bounded all around by a greenish margin and finally by ordinary fields. The desert, however, provided the only movement in that landscape; no animals grazed in the untilled fields nearby.

While I was watching, the wind quickened and the dust began lifting more convulsively, gathering itself into graceful showers and torn, gentle fingers that splayed and stretched longingly towards the green margins. In the midst of it, a mere shape in the dust, was a human being. I tried to draw nearer, sweating with effort and fear, but I couldn't see. It stood, passive, while the dust eddied and stroked.

Someone was hurting me in the dark. I pushed at him.

"Maura!"

"Oh, stop, my head!"

"You'd a nightmare," said Dominic's voice beside me.

I could only groan and cry.

"What was it?"

When I told him, he held me close and I felt the first real stab of urgent desire. I held him tighter and he held me too, for a moment, but then he gently pushed me away and found the door handle. He rattled it, and Pakky came.

I never did see Pakky's face. When we left his house, the village was as black and inscrutable as ever, and the road as notional. Dominic was quiet and I was, too, my mouth too dry with terror for talking.

When later he explained to me what I had seen in the "dream", I told him to leave me and catch up with Mark; I would follow. We kissed, and I didn't cling to him or make him wrench himself away, but when I heard his quick footsteps moving farther and farther up the road, I wanted to run after him, howling like a child. One thing I decided, stumbling alone in the dark: the next time we met, we would be woman and man, even wife and husband if the chance came.

CHAPTER TWENTY

THE CURRAGH WAS A MILLION SIGHS AS THE WIND, UNHINDERED, threaded its way through the miles of grass. Here there were no hedges, no trees, no mountains, nothing but the subtlest undulations in the land to check the winds that blew across Ireland. Its emptiness was as compelling as the emptiness in my mother's pictures – it bulged with absence. The men were gone, and the horses, yet every blade of grass remembered them.

During the first years after the War, the Army controlled the plain from its great camp there; there was safe travel wherever they were. Then even this faithful band of men dispersed. Their superiors couldn't agree; they were decimated by flu and then, it was said, by tuberculosis. They'd been below strength at the outset – most had been away when the War happened, deployed like the monks of long ago to advance the "peace". Their fate was never known. We'd dribs and drabs of news over the years, but the meaning of it all had never come home to me until now, on this vacant, windswept plain.

Lizzie hadn't liked us to talk about such things. She thought they spread uneasiness. I suppose it was harder for her; she felt responsible in some way. We didn't. I wondered how she was coping with my mother's death, and her fears for Conor, Dominic, Mark and me.

I sensed her in her room in the convent, standing at the window looking out. There was something prickly on her wrist beneath the sleeve. A circlet of rough twine, of hemp? A medieval forget-me-not! What next?

She'd have a nice infection for herself if she wasn't careful – and yet I could feel her love, it was like a hand at my back or a car with plump black wheels under its strong, shining body and its interior like a huddle of sofas. And its radio – I'd throw away the whole ludicrous thing and keep the radio. And all I'd hear on it would be what I was hearing now; wind-music, wind-language, absence. Steady now. I must keep my mind on Conor, on Dominic somewhere ahead of me in the darkness, on the road under my aching feet.

It was said that when the wind blew from the east, there was still a stench of death from Dublin; one of the worst tales was of a pony found wandering, his legs in tatters – he'd been attacked by the great rats that swarmed out of the city, and I listened below the wind for the sound of stealthy claws. I'd been so intent on trying to listen that I'd paid no attention to my other senses, and tripped in a rough pothole, not even daring to whimper in case I'd miss something. Lizzie had told me to cross only if Mark was with me, and had fretted about reports of wild dogs, even a wild bull. I hoped the dogs and the bull would meet one another before they met me. The wind was so pervasive that I would hear nothing coming, but that was no preparation for the long, trembling yowl that rose from the darkness beside me. There was a sudden crashing in the grass, and the yowl was repeated, rising into a shriek. I backed away, terrified, as a black shape staggered onto the road and another cry tore the air. This, however, was punctuated by a caught breath like a hiccup, and memory asserted itself.

"What are you doing to that baby?" I yelled.

The figure, that had flapped a few yards up the road ahead of me, stopped. A girl's voice said defiantly, "Who wants to know?"

"Are you pinching it or what?"

"Fuck off!" I could see the girl faintly outlined ahead of me, walking quickly. The baby's howls had lessened, and now stuffy-sounding sobs and growls ensued.

"Did you steal it?" I said, hurrying after her. It started crying again in short, sharp bursts, well on the way to a rigid colicky stomach and sheer hysteria, all signs I remembered well from Mrs Harding's baby back in Wicklow.

The girl gave a harsh laugh. "Like hell – and you'd better not try!"

"What would I want with a screeching baby?"

She stopped. I had an odd feeling drawing near to her, or rather to the baby. There weren't so many healthy ones born; I wished I could see it.

"What they all want – a child with nothing wrong with it. Don't come closer! What are you, anyway? A girl or a boy?"

"A boy."

"I don't believe you. Stay back!"

"Who are you?"

"None of your business," she said.

We seemed to have reached an impasse. At this there was a smacking noise, and she half-cried, half-cursed. "Oh, Jesus, he'll tear the tits off me!"

"Sometimes they do that if they've wind," I offered. "They think they're hungry because of the pain. Or if he's dirty and sore … "

"You know a lot," she said grumpily. "You're a girl, aren't you?"

"I'm travelling as a boy."

"So would I, except for my little problem," she said. She sounded more confident now.

"My name's Maura."

"Hm. Well."

"Don't tell me your name if you don't want. I only trust you because you've the baby."

"Fair enough." She half-turned, as if to start away, then stopped. The baby still whimpered piteously. "How do you know about babies, anyway?" There were tears in her voice.

"I helped mind the two in our town. We were taught."

"See if you know what's wrong with him, then." Now that she was beside me, I could see that she wasn't very big, though she seemed quite fat. She thrust the small bundle at me – I scarcely had my hands up in time to hold it. I caught the baby under his arms, and when I did his entire torso seemed to rid itself of a belch.

I sniffed at him. "He's probably wet, they always are, but I don't think he's dirty. If you can wrap him up, he might sleep, now he's that out of him."

She took him back from me. "Thanks." Then, almost shyly, "Would you be able to tie the cloth around me while I hold him?"

"No problem." It was awkward, though; she'd a length of cloth that felt like old sheeting that we were eventually able to tie over her shoulder and around her middle.

"He'll probably do it again before we're finished," she grumbled. At that we were done, however. "Well. Are you coming?"

That was just what I was asking myself. "I may have to hurry faster than you can walk," I said apologetically.

"We'll see, so. You're going to meet somebody, eh?"

"Well ... "

"Look, Maura, is it?"

"That's right."

"I'm Jennifer. The baby's Fergus. I'm going to have to trust you more than you need to trust me, because look, I've proved I can have a healthy baby and you haven't. And you won't rat on me to any slavers or whatever because my boyfriend Isaac will kill you if you do because nobody – nobody – messes with Isaac."

"*You* did," I said. There was a moment's silence. Then she giggled, a snorting giggle that made me laugh, too.

Soon we were speeding one another along, whispering and listening at intervals, reminding ourselves to be careful because sound would travel miles if the wind dropped. It wasn't long before I knew her story.

Isaac was the son of Dublin refugees who came to help on her father's farm. Isaac's mother was frail and didn't live very long. His father set off for the smith's in the next townland with an old plough that needed to be mended. "It was a ton weight, and he was to balance it all the way on a wheelbarrow." Jennifer's older brother was to go with him but got a dose of food poisoning the night before and was too weak the next day. Isaac was still too young. "So Barry – Mr Marks – set out on his own. He was never seen again alive. When Dad and Jamie got worried the next day, they set out to look for him. They found the wheelbarrow – the wheel was broken – but the plough was gone, and they found Barry's body behind the hedge. Dad nearly sent Isaac away, too, only Jamie and I begged him not to." She walked a while in silence.

"And what age was Isaac then?"

"Oh, it was nine years ago. He was seven; we both were."

"So you're both sixteen?"

"That's right. Sure, you're all right, I like younger people," she said kindly.

"Oh, good!" I said, wondering if I should tell her I was twenty.

"You must mind yourself, Maura. They're always looking for young girls."

"Why did Isaac leave?"

"Why do you think? Dad caught us. Isaac said he wanted to marry me, but Dad was too angry. I think Dad was against the Jews all along. That's what he said to Isaac, did he really think he'd let me marry a Jew. Can you imagine? Jamie could hardly hold him long enough for Isaac to leave. Jesus, it was the worst ... I knew I was pregnant, too, I thought I'd lose the baby for sure, but ... " she lowered her face to nuzzle the baby's head.

"What did he do when he found out?"

"He didn't. He'd a stroke. Now poor Jamie's on his own. I promised Isaac I'd come to him when the baby was born, so I'm off to find him and see will he come back and stay so we'll help Jamie. He and Jamie get on great. We might get married, too, when the bishop's around, or the rabbi. Have you ever seen the rabbi? There's supposed to be one who goes here and there. Isaac's not too pushed, either way. I'd like the rabbi, ach, to make up for Dad, but McGlinchy may have to do." She shifted the sleeping baby, sighing. "Now, you can tell me why you're out here in the middle of the night."

I told her about Conor and Morrie, keeping vague about Dominic and Mark and their part in the search. Jennifer had sharp ears, however, and she said she wanted to see "the boyfriend", as she immediately called Dominic.

Finally we walked in silence, too tired to talk. I couldn't imagine Conor on this featureless expanse – it was as if we were all being erased as thoroughly as life had been erased from the "hot spot" of my dream. An Fásach was all too real; it was the place Lizzie had mentioned and Dominic had described to me before he left me to go faster, to try to intercept Conor at all costs, in case Conor was meant to be the solitary figure in the dust.

"You never want to be downwind from it. It's more toxic than anything you could imagine," Dominic had told me.

"Is it spreading?"

"Just a little, but it's steady. It's a bit less poisonous at the edges, though you wouldn't want to get excited about that. It's on the surface, apparently; it hasn't reached the water table yet. All the same, you don't want any of that to blow onto you. Most things near it have mutated. There's a lot of sickness around there, too."

"Have you seen it?"

"No, and I won't! Mark went up to have a look, and didn't the wind change while he was beside it. He said it was like claws reached out of the dust and groped towards him. He legged it through some trees, and then he noticed that the branches slapping at him had double twigs, double needles – they were like fists. He travelled solid until he got to O'hAnnluain's – it's a place you can wash and get your clothes laundered – and he soaked in the stream there until he was shrivelled."

"Dominic … What would Conor be doing there?"

"I don't know. But you're sure it was him you saw?"

"No."

He said, "Do they always happen? Your dreams?"

"I don't know. The one about Morrie did, and yet … I never had ones about the future. Maybe the person I saw … maybe it's over."

It didn't feel over, though, and Dominic heard that in my voice. It was then he had left me, so he would be quicker.

Chapter Twenty-One

Jennifer sank down on the road, groaning. She looked like a small shrub in the dark.

"What's the matter?"

"I'm so sore … !" She busied herself awkwardly with the cloths around her waist, then pulled up her skirts and rummaged, squatting. "Oh, yuk! If there was only a bit of water … " The baby began to whimper. "Not now, not now," she breathed. "Come on, Fergus, be good."

"Will I hold him?"

"No, I've got … it's all right. You wouldn't have a drop of water, would you?"

Dominic had given me his plastic bottle.

"Just a bit … to wash my hands. Have to be careful. What is this at all? Our Lady! That's not holy water, sure it's not, it would kill us?"

"Spring water."

"Thanks very much. Oh, if we could find a good place, there's nothing here … All right. Thanks for waiting. I'm grand now." But she still sat on the road.

"Jennifer?"

She got up rather drunkenly. "Okay," she said breathlessly, "Okay."

170

"You're sure?"

"I'm fine."

"How old is that baby?"

"He's five days," she said, panting.

"And you're gallivanting across the Curragh?"

"I've got to see Isaac. I can't wait any more!"

The sky was beginning to lighten, though it was still a cold colour, and I could see that she was small and dumpy, though I couldn't tell much more about her. What frightened me was the way she was standing, as if she could become suddenly uncoordinated and collapse. "Are you sure you're all right?"

"We've got to get across before it's too light," she said in a scratchy voice.

"Drink some of the water."

She leaned back her head and squeezed the water into her mouth without letting the bottle touch her lips. "Oh, that's triff. I love that plasticky taste. You won't believe it, my boobs are starting to prickle. I was parched. There now, Fergus, you'll have breakfast after all."

"Have more."

She managed another long squirt, then handed the bottle back to me. "You're a pal. Thanks. We'll go, so." There was a new bounce in her walk; she reminded me of Sinead.

A rail fence, broken in places and scarcely showing above the long grass, straggled beside us, and there was a huge square of darkness further on. "The stands," murmured Jennifer. "It's the race course."

I remembered my father sharp and shouldery in a tan suit, my mother in something the colour of raspberry ice cream – oh, God! – and a shiny straw hat. My mother hadn't wanted to go to the races, but Dad wheedled and pushed and got cross until she did. I minded Conor while the baby-sitter talked on the phone, and got into trouble for calling her a "stupid cow". My parents arrived back happy and relaxed, talking about a horse called Brandy Butter that ran like the wind.

"Penny for them," said Jennifer.

"I was just thinking … isn't it strange there's not a horse or sheep or anything on the Curragh?"

"Sure, there are only ghosts in this place, and we're almost out of it. We go that way," she added.

We had slowed to a shuffle. It was only a few hours ago that Dominic had left me, but it seemed days. My tired mind clung to him and to Conor, and I was trying so hard to concentrate on them that I didn't hear the hoofbeats until Jennifer grabbed my arm.

"Into the ditch! Hide!" She jerked at my jumper, then scurried into the grass, hunkered down and disappeared. I dived after her, but slipped and fell against her. Fergus woke with a squawk. "Oh, you eejit!" she hissed at me. She pulled frantically at her clothes, but not before Fergus gave full cry. The heavy hoofbeats slowed and stopped, and a deep voice said, "Hold on, now."

Jennifer kissed Fergus as if she never expected to see him again.

There was a thud, like someone jumping down on the road. "What did you hear?"

"Mark!"

He was no more than a yard from me, his knife in his hand. When he saw me, he threw up his eyes.

Bishop McGlinchy sat on his black hunter, a quizzical look on his face. "I thought I heard a child," he said.

"You did. It's Bishop McGlinchy, Jennifer." I pitied her, she looked so bewildered. The morning light showed her face to be small, freckled and terribly young, and Fergus only a scrap in her arms.

"Em, Bishop McGlinchy, this is Jennifer, em … "

She blinked at him, then shrank back when she saw

Mark with his knife.

"He's all right," I said.

Mark smiled, and she gaped at him.

"You wouldn't be young Isaac's girl," the Bishop said, leaning confidingly from the saddle.

Mark took his sharpening stone out of his pocket and honed his knife while they talked. He looked bored.

"Well?" I said.

"'Well,' what?"

"Well, where have you been? Have you seen Conor again, or Dominic?"

He made a play of examining the blade, as if to look for blood. "Since you ask me so politely, yes, I've seen both of them. Which one do you want to hear about first?"

I peered at him more closely, and was horrified. His eyes were sunk, and his cheekbones stood out as if chiselled. "Have you slept at all?"

"No, mother dear, I haven't. Conor's up past Rathangan, and at the rate we're going, we'll catch up with him in Boston."

"Ha bloody ha."

"But you may yet prove your worth."

"I haven't been moving in Margaret Kilcoyne's circles lately, Mark."

"Margaret's circles are also somewhat circumscribed by circumstance."

Bishop McGlinchy cut in. "I'm putting young Jennifer up on the horse with the baby here," he said. "I'll bring them to Rathbride, only a step now. You'd better come, too, hadn't she, Mark? You don't mind walking?" he added to me, with a gleam.

"Oh, no," I said.

Jennifer sat sideways on the hunter, clutching Fergus. "Come here to me." I sidled as near the horse as felt safe. "You're older than I thought."

"Twenty."

She giggled. "You never said."

"You might have only liked young people," I told her.

Mark gave the Bishop a stirrup, and he was up behind Jennifer in a single, lithe leap. He took the reins and they were off, the hunter walking gently, but with long strides.

"Mark?"

He stared down unhappily. "There's not much to tell. Conor's still all right. They've slowed down a little, that's good for all of us. It's just ... a lot of patrols are out, lads on the road holding things up. They'd support the slavers over us, most of them – it's their orders, they have to. It makes things trickier ... " He stopped and yawned. "What's this you'd a dream about An Fásach?"

"Dominic told you that?"

"He tells me everything," he said. It was his most arrogant look, which meant he was unsure.

"Then you don't need to hear it from me."

We sparred a little more, but it was only habit. "And you didn't see who it was," he said at last.

"No."

"Bloody useless."

"It is. Mark, will you walk slower? Surely they don't just bring people to that place on a whim? Kids?"

"Not often," he said almost gently. "It's Jack Rourke, Maura. He's out of control. Ach, he'll be toppled, but – . What's wrong with you?"

"Did you ever see my mother's pictures? In her room?"

"No."

"She'd a picture there she said was Jack Rourke. A black-haired man, with a scar." I showed him with my finger.

"That's him. Who'd have thought your mum would have a *grá* for Jack Rourke?"

I explained our experience in the cottage. Dominic had

told him about it, but Mark had never put it all together.

"He'd never recognise you again?"

"Ten years," I said doubtfully. "I was a child. No."

"Well," he said with a sigh, "we're bloody careful anyway near Athlone." He gave me a combination pat and shove on the back that almost sent me flying, and we tramped along towards the safe house.

I woke some hours later in a room with wallpaper that had a design of pink birds and trellises. Curtains with the same pattern were pulled across the window, and I lay there in sharp happiness, teased into a time warp where breakfast followed waking and you opened your hall door and met men and women and children; children in prams and push-chairs, children walking and cycling and running, instead of living hidden and swaddled like the sweet perishables they are. Fergus's cries woke me. They struggled through the air, mere shadows of the forthright squalls of the babies of long ago. Suddenly I couldn't wait to leave this room that mocked our lost plenty.

Mrs Riordan, the woman of the house, had put Jennifer to bed with Fergus alongside her. They both looked scrubbed and even smaller than they had in the dark. Their bedroom was larger than the one I had slept in, and it too had papered walls, multicoloured flowers in bouquets. There was a wistful blue carpet on the floor.

"It takes you back, doesn't it?" said Jennifer.

"How are you?"

"Not bad. But he's got a cold." She looked anxiously at Fergus, whose tiny face puckered in identical lines; he delivered an exquisite sneeze, followed by a wakeful glare.

"I think he's all right. Really."

"They've gone to find Isaac," she said. Her eyes shone. "I wish you could meet him."

"Me, too. Will you go back to the farm?"

"Oh, yes." Then, "Maura! That fellow we met with the Bishop – Mark – is he the one they all talk about?"

"Probably."

"I wouldn't have believed it if I hadn't seen him. Wait till I tell Isaac there's someone better looking than he is!"

I stood up to go. "Take care of yourself and Fergus."

"You'll find Conor safe, I know it. Maura!" She struggled up in the bed, her eyes bright. "Get Bishop McGlinchy to marry you and Dominic! He loves it, he marries everybody. Everything will be all right," she added, in answer to my look.

I nodded and backed awkwardly out of the room. Perhaps it was her combination of childlike frailty with womanly kindness, or just that I liked her and we'd been frightened together, but I already missed her.

I had been so tired when we arrived in late morning that I'd only a shadowy impression of Mrs Riordan. Now she moved forward, a strong-looking woman with greying hair and a frank smile, and brought me into her kitchen for a dish of succulent stew. "It'll put heart into you, and you need it, dear." She was a big woman, but very thin, with bony knees and ankles that showed through her knitted stockings.

"We're taking food you must need yourself."

"I've always been thin," she said comfortably. "Thyroid's a bit on the go; see my eyes. If it weren't for the War, I'd have done something about it; at any rate, when you see Seamus, you'll know there's food around here!"

When I was going, she offered gentle condolences on my mother, and for the second time that day I was touched beyond words. I wanted to cry on her warm, clean shoulder in her clean rooms like pearls in the grit of our universe.

As we left, Jennifer shouted from the bedroom. "Remember, Maura, he'll marry you if you ask!"

The Bishop – "Call me Teddy – " had trotted off ahead of Mark and me, "to reconnoitre."

"Why couldn't the same Teddy rescue Conor on his bloody horse?" I asked. "They'd never catch up with him."

"That horse is known over Ireland. So's Teddy. The religious work with the slaves, see; any time they're associated with a getaway, they're thrown out, and some girl or boy is punished."

"But we're all against the slavers, for God's sake, so how … ?"

"Ach, nobody wants them, and there they are. If you're bad enough, no-one can touch you," he said. "Unless it's someone as bad as yourself."

"Then nobody I know is bad enough."

"Are you sure?"

"You're all bluff, Mark."

"And if I wasn't?" He said this with his usual casual bravado and perfect smile.

"I never said you weren't tough, I used be scared rotten of you. You're not wicked."

"All I need is the love of a good woman."

"Sandra Touhey."

He roared laughing, but then he quirked his eyebrow at me and said, "You used not to like me, Maura."

"I used not."

He glanced at me from under his lashes. "Well, the next hour or so should be interesting."

"Yeah?"

"It promises interesting juxtapositions."

"Go on," I said, starting to feel uneasy.

Mark started to whistle.

"What bloody juxtapositions?"

"Yourself. Our Dominic. And a Bishop," he said.

My ears burned. He must have heard Jennifer.

"Will we take bets?"

"You're mean, Mark."

"This is your chance."

"Sure it is. That's why I came here, of course, to get married."

He laughed, but then, suddenly, he became serious. "I tell Dominic, 'why are you so cautious?' What's it the fellow wrote, 'Life is nasty, brutal and short?' Did you read that one?"

I shook my head.

"Well, it is, right? So it's take what you can. I don't want to get old in this kip, anyway. Now, Dominic – !"

"What do you mean, he's cautious?"

"Well, four guesses: Jackie, Sinead, and two girls down the country you don't know about. Both dead."

"What do you mean?"

"I mean that for a place where very few babies seem to get born, lots of people get pregnant, and the results aren't fantastic."

"Sure you just saw Fergus."

"Dominic didn't.

"So what happened to the girls down the country?"

"Croaked. One was dead when we were passing, and her man ran out the door and begged us to help him bury her. You're sure you want to hear this?"

"Yes."

"Wait, now. Look at that hedge. Did Dominic ever tell you about that stuff? See? The dark green leaves?"

"Mark – "

"Post-War nettles. The others are still all right to eat, and the bit of dock does the job, but those – don't try to eat them, don't let them touch you. They're bitches. See? They're darker. Smaller leaves."

"All right. Now, go on."

"You have to treat them immediately. The best is to find the dock – bind on some then and there, then soap and water, then compresses night and day. You should see the abscesses – "

"The woman was dead."

"Yeah. He hadn't even washed her, and she was there for two days. The baby was dying, we didn't know how it had lived so long. He'd done nothing for it; the bastard hadn't a clue. We dug a grave a few yards from the house, picked her up like she was and lowered her in. Didn't he come out with the child and make to drop it in with her?"

"Still alive?"

"'What can I do for it, I'm not well myself, it's more merciful,' he says. Our Dominic wrapped up the child and we brought him with us in case we'd find a wet-nurse, but the little fellow was gone before we were a mile down the road, so we took him back and put him with the mother. The father wouldn't even come out of his house. The other one, well, we were there. Staying in the house, and the daughter went into labour. Her parents had a couple of aul' wans in to help with the birth, and they were useless. The child was turned around, they said."

"So that's it."

"You've your work cut out for you if you want that fellow to do more than shake hands with you. But if you've a child, you see to it. Let your aunt and them take care of you. I don't want to be looking after Dominic if you go like those others."

"So you wouldn't mind."

"I've me own fish to fry." He smiled, flushing, then recollected himself and walked more quickly than ever.

I thought of Lizzie's story of how she found Mark. The Council had organised a search through all the flooded or damaged buildings to try to locate the people who had gone missing. Mark was shivering in the corner of a garage. He had made himself a barricade of garden chairs, an old lawn mower and a table, and he'd a garden fork beside him. Lizzie looked into a pair of cold, frightened and very angry grey eyes. He was fourteen; he had started the growth spurt that was to leave him six foot three, but when Lizzie found him he was all knees and elbows and ragged clothes. He was also covered with bruises.

He would never say what had happened to him or how he came to be there, and Lizzie, after leaving many openings, accepted he wouldn't. He told her only one thing about himself when she persuaded him to shelter in the convent, and that was that he was gay. 'Queer' was the way he put it.

Mark's arm shot out and stopped me in mid-step. There were voices around the next curve in the road, then laughter, and the loud snort of a horse. He sneered. "That fellow's made great progress!" he said.

We rounded the curve and before us, partially concealed by the jutting hedge, were the Bishop, a strikingly tall, skinny boy, and Dominic.

CHAPTER TWENTY-TWO

HE'D GROWN THINNER IN A DAY, AND THERE WAS A NEW RENT AT the knee of his trousers. If I hadn't known him, he'd have looked dangerous. He moved over to me and gave me a little shake as if to say, "It's all right," though his eyes said the opposite.

"We're going to Athlone, is that it?"

"Bright lights," he said. "This is Isaac," he added. The tall boy gave me a nod and a cautious look.

"I was hoping to meet you. You don't look like I thought. Jennifer never said you were tall."

He smiled at this and suddenly looked angelic.

"Fergus is a little dote," I said.

Dominic shifted restlessly beside me. I realised they were all three staring at him.

"Well?" said the Bishop. He took an ancient watch out of his pocket and looked at it.

"Do it," said Mark.

"Fuck off," said Dominic quietly.

The Bishop sighed, put back his watch.

Mark said, "She's got all her teeth, right, and the requisite number of arms and legs, and let me tell you, she's like an ox."

"Yeah," said Dominic. He simply turned to me, lifted

181

me in the air like a sack of sugar, and put me down again. "An ox, right."

I held my tongue.

"She'll have someone, and I hear James McEvoy wouldn't mind."

"That's true," I said. "He wouldn't."

"You love me," Dominic said scornfully. "Look, Maura, this isn't the time or the place."

I pulled him close to me and whispered, "What if this is the only time and the only bloody place?"

The others blinked placidly, waiting. He glared around at them.

"All right."

"You'll want to wash him when you get him home," Mark said pleasantly.

"Don't push your luck, Meehan!"

The Bishop raised his eyebrows.

"I see I'm doomed," Dominic said. Then he gave me a kiss, to take the sting out of it.

"Hold the horse, Isaac, please," and the Bishop dropped off the big gelding in a sliding scuffle. The horse flicked his ears. The Bishop rummaged in the pouch behind the saddle and produced a worn black book that was held together with old elastic bands, along with a bottle of holy water. These he handed to Isaac, who looked amused.

The grey sky, the wild green tangle of the hedge, the black horse, and the Bishop taking the faded purple stole out of the pouch, seemed to have happened before. The tasselled silk hung in the air unfurling, the Bishop's hand became languorous, and Dominic's profile was etched forever against the green hedge.

"Don't lose your nerve," he said, still not looking at me, as I started to tremble. I wanted Conor, I wanted my mother.

"I take it you've not been walking around Ireland with a ring in your pocket," the Bishop was saying. Dominic shook his head. Mark pulled the gold signet off his little finger and handed it to him.

"Just for the ceremony," he said.

Dominic squeezed my hand, but his face still brimmed with conflict. Then I remembered my mother's words about taking the decision for both of us, and suddenly felt at peace.

"Are you right?" said Bishop McGlinchy.

"We are," I said.

He raised his hand, then dropped it again. "This is real, y'know. As far as the Church is concerned, this is it."

"Go on," said Dominic.

"In the name of the Father and the Son and the Holy Spirit ... Maura and Dominic, you are here today to seal your love in this sacrament ... " The first day I ever saw him, outside the cottage, turning away towards some other fate ... "in the presence of God and of all these people, em, your friends, are you willing to accept each other as husband and wife? Say, 'we are'."

"We are."

"Will you love and honour each other in marriage all the days of your life?"

"We will."

"Are you willing to accept with love the children God may send you, and bring them up in accordance with the law of Christ, and his Church?"

"We are," I said.

"We are," Dominic muttered. Isaac looked away, his expression bleak. Mark moved towards him and whispered something.

"I invite you then to declare before God and his Church your consent to become husband and wife."

"I, Dominic, take you, Maura ... " His eyes were clear.

" ... for better for worse, for richer, for poorer, in sickness and in health, all the days of our life."

"What God joins together man must not separate. May the Lord confirm the consent that you have given and enrich you with his blessings." He nodded at Dominic, who slipped Mark's warm ring on my finger.

It was over while I was still trying to make sure I'd remember it all. "May God bless you, then, Father, Son, Holy Spirit," Bishop McGlinchy was saying. "Congratulations. Kiss for the bride – " a whiskery scrape on my forehead – "groom – " he shook Dominic's hand.

Mark, eyes gleaming, gave me a decorous peck on the cheek; then he and Dominic hugged each other. Something wet splashed over us all, the Bishop's holy water. "I'll do a blessing for you when you're back home if you want, so the others can see it," he said. "But you're married now. Well done. Are you right, Isaac?"

The boy nodded. I wondered if being at a trial run of a wedding had done his nerves any good, but when our eyes met, his were disconcertingly mature. "Congratulations," he said.

"You, too. I hope we'll meet again."

He smiled then, and his young-old face was radiant. "I'd say we will," he said.

The Bishop remounted his horse, Mark gave Isaac a stirrup behind, and they were off at a rocking canter, the boy's long legs hanging loosely on either side.

Dominic kissed me. "He forgot that," he said, "but I didn't."

Mark held out his hand.

I pulled off the ring, kissed it and handed it to him.

"Right, wife. Now let's see what I married you for." Dominic wiggled his fingers. "Your map," he said, smiling.

They knelt on the road to look at it, Dominic's hands moving knowledgeably over its veined surface. "We go to ó hAnnluain's. Pick up the suss."

"Bring a long spoon."

"Ach, she's all right as long as she doesn't see you. Mark isn't Mrs ó hAnnluain's favourite person," Dominic said to me.

"Thee doethen't like my thort."

"It's not the best place for women, though, sure it's not."

Mark shrugged. "If you say she's your wife ... ?"

"That mightn't make a difference. Do you think she'll pass as a boy?"

"Hello," I said.

"Mind you," he went on to Mark, "the only time I was asked about her was Pakky, and he'd his dirty aul' hands on her."

"You may be right. Just better put off the honeymoon, or Mrs ó hAnnluain will think you're of my persuasion after all. He's her golden boy," he added to me.

"Who's Mrs ó hAnnluain?"

"The business magnate in these parts. She runs a hotel and a laundry," Mark said. Dominic was silent, studying the map.

Finally he stood up. "We meet you there?"

"Right. See you tomorrow morning." Mark left. We watched him disappear around the bend and wished him back.

"Are you sorry?"

Dominic looked at me intently, started to speak and then stopped. "I don't know what the fuck to do about you," he said. There was amusement, love and panic in his eyes. He put his arms around me almost experimentally. Then we kissed. In a moment, his lips parted and then his tongue touched my lips and went into my mouth. My knees started melting; I held him harder to keep from falling, or perhaps if I did, to make him fall on top of me.

He groaned, straightened up, and wrenching himself away, kicked three different stones in the road. "Let's find Conor," he snarled.

CHAPTER TWENTY-THREE

WE FOLLOWED A NUMBER OF INCREASINGLY CRABBED AND featureless roads until at twilight we finally arrived at a dead-end. I could hear and smell water. We edged through a strong wooden gate towards a big farmhouse, a sturdy dwelling the shape of a shoe-box with a pitched roof. The patch of grass in front of it was nondescript, but not wild, and although the front of the house was dark, it was full of the energy a place has when a number of people are in it.

Dominic whispered, "Wait here," and showed me where I could stop under a tree, hidden from both the house and the laneway.

In a while I heard voices, Dominic's and another's, and a general low buzz of talk from deeper within the house. The conversation had a musical rise and fall, and suddenly I realised it was Irish.

I'd never known Dominic had Irish, not so fluent as this, only the bits and pieces we'd left from the school – though I'd heard him talking to Brigid once, and then he'd sounded less halting than the rest of us. There was much I didn't know about him. Now he was approaching with something light over his arm. He tossed it to me, and I saw he'd another one himself. It was a towel.

"We're all right. We've a room in the house. We'll wash and then eat."

There was a wide, swept yard at the back of the house with outbuildings, an iron pump with a number of chipped enamel basins beside it, and an open building with a concrete floor and a corrugated roof held up by rough timbers, the sort that might have been used as a cow parlour when cows were plentiful. There were rough, low frames with wires across them arranged in a line like beds in a dormitory. Dominic saw me looking at this and whispered, "The 'outside hotel'. It can get fairly rough in there." He filled one of the basins, and we washed our face and hands. "Mrs ó hAnnluain's very particular," he said, grinning.

I had a crawling feeling at my back. "Dominic. That man there. He's looking."

Dominic said something very loud in Irish. Two men came out of the house and there was a heated argument. One of them pulled our intruder away. The other spoke quietly to Dominic.

"They'll remove our informing friend." He laughed. "It's an ill wind .... Now ... Get out whatever you've got to be washed. Socks and knickers? God, you've nothing. Don't know how we'll dress you up for Athlone."

There was a long extension at the back of the house with a smoking chimney at the end. A smell of hot, clean cloth billowed from the half-door and a woman with a flushed face moved around inside, adjusting the pulleys that held sheets and clothing. Steam rose at the end of the room where flames roared in a huge fireplace, and there were special runnels in the floor where the water could drain away. Two large tubs of wash water at the back of the room added their own steam to the atmosphere.

"Coming to add to my rheumatism!" the woman roared gaily. "Come here, Thomas!" to a young boy who was trying to slip behind the sheets. He looked around Conor's age, but he was black-haired and seemed slightly simple. "You'll not be looking for these before tomorrow, surely to God?"

"Tomorrow, but very early."

"I have you. They'll be ready for dawn. Thomas! Come here to me."

When the lad came, smirking, she gave him our few clothes, a washboard and a long, wooden spoon and waited until he was busy at the hottest tub of water. "Tomorrow morning, so."

"Why would that man want to spy on us?" I asked Dominic, when we moved away.

He shrugged. "Any reason and none. So he'd have something to offer in any conversation with the Army ... just little pennies of information he collects. Well, it's backfired on him now because Mrs ó hAnnluain hates that, it's bad for business. It's good for us because it puts her a little in our debt, which is a good place to have her."

"Go on."

"Ach, she's never liked Mark. It was just that because of his looks, any lad who was that way inclined, you know, and Mark was always with me, so she was never ... You wouldn't always know what way she'd jump."

"I see."

"We have to go in now, she's got food for us."

"Food? Just like that?"

"Maura, this is her business! Let's just say I've done her a few favours. She's probably one of the best-off women in Ireland. This is a going concern."

"I didn't know there were any left."

"There's still a bit to gain and to lose in the Midlands. Just stick with me now, and say nothing. It's no harm for people to think you're a bit simple. If you want to use the privy, tell me. In fact, take it you go nowhere without me.

Nobody lets a young brother or sister around the place unguarded any more. Ah, sure ... " he said, and wiped my eyes with his sleeve.

I woke in the middle of the night in the small, bare room we'd been given, regretting Mrs ó hAnnluain's stew. Dominic was gone; cold air occupied his place. I turned over and curled up on my side. Despair was a luxury when you needed sleep.

Later I heard him breathing in the bed beside me, and felt the discreet warmth he radiated. I put my hand out to touch him, to be sure, and he gently returned it to my side. We lay there, sleepless and miserable, until it was light.

CHAPTER TWENTY-FOUR

I STRAINED TO LOOK PAST HIM, TO SEE LANDMARKS, ANYTHING THAT would show where he was. Nothing, only impenetrable hedges and the morning sky and a man with a torn leather jacket, who walked between me and Conor and jerked him up from the ditch where he'd been resting. Rough yellow hair and a scar on the back of his left hand. The jacket was black with dirt, but the inner creases showed brown. Conor had a cut lip; it was swollen.

I half-fell out of the bed and got sick in the pot. When it was over, Dominic was beside me.

"I'm all right." The thought of last night's coarse stew, so different from Mrs Riordan's, made my stomach heave again.

He helped me back into bed and sat beside me.

"Were you sick yesterday?"

"It's Conor. They've hit him. His lip is split. And I still couldn't see where he was."

"Next time, try – "

"Do you think I didn't?"

"Try harder," he said abruptly.

"I'm useless here, aren't I?"

He shook his head.

"What way am I useful? I hang out of you and see useless pictures in my mind."

"You will be useful," he said carefully. "We wanted to get Conor before Athlone, but we're too late for that."

"You were dragging me around like a lovesick stone."

"No, it was really my ankle. It's the times, also. Anyway, Maura, you'll be useful in Athlone. That was probably the best plan from the start."

"I turn up at Margaret Kilcoyne's Debs dance, assassinate Mad Jack Rourke … "

"What's the matter with you, is it the stew? We go to Athlone, and you talk to Margaret Kilcoyne."

"Those days are long gone."

"How many people from your school do you think survived? That Margaret might have met since?"

"I doubt she even remembers me, Dominic."

"Unhappy people think about the past."

"Is Margaret unhappy? How do you know?"

"She must be. Mad Jack has his eye on her."

"Him? He must be in his fifties!"

"He's about forty."

"But she's – "

"He'd be a hundred, Maura," he said impatiently, "and he could have her if he wanted."

"Her father – "

"Kilcoyne's not the man he was. He's not able for Jack Rourke."

"Poor Margaret," I said, horrified.

He stirred restlessly. "Could Margaret link you to the cottage in Offaly?"

"She was never there. We invited her once, but the country was so unsettled – her parents wouldn't let her anywhere without two bodyguards. It was the time he was Minister for Agriculture, and there were all the threats … "

"All right," he said thoughtfully.

"I still can't believe that man who came to our cottage is Jack Rourke. It's like knowing somebody before they were famous."

"You'll know him again if you see him, Maura."

"I don't want to see him – ever."

"You may have to, love. What was Margaret like? Was she – ?"

"She was sweet. Not spoiled, like you'd think … she was timorous, Dominic, anybody bullied her. If her own father can't stand up to Jack Rourke – I mean, I don't see how she can really help us."

"They say he's mad about her."

I thought of the man I'd heard all those years ago on the road, and remembered my mother's words to Lizzie – "Then he looked at her, and I just knew." He had hurt Conor, a baby, hurt him quite casually to tease my mother.

"He's mad full stop. God help her. Dominic, I don't see how – "

"You don't! What are you, embarrassed? Are you shy? Are you just too nice to go ask 'Poor Margaret' for something? The Kilcoynes are living on our backs. They're colluding in what's going on! Use Margaret, for fuck's sake, that lot are happy enough to use kids like Conor!"

"I'm afraid of Jack Rourke! So would you be if you remembered anything about him!"

"Fuck Jack Rourke! Can you remember Conor?"

I swung wildly at the contempt in his voice, catching him under his right eye with my fist. The colour leached out of his face; for a moment he looked blind. He had slapped the side of my head with his open hand before I even saw him move. Then he was halfway to the door. "You'll meet Mark outside," he said. "Everything's paid." Then he was gone, the door slamming behind him.

Mark was lounging outside the gate. Mrs ó hAnnluain

hurried after me with my few clean clothes – that was her penance for our being annoyed by the man at the pump – but she almost kept them when she saw Mark. She hesitated, then pushed them at me with a knowing glare. "Woman's knickers! You got what you deserved, didn't you? Should have kept your hands to yourself!"

"Oh, Mrs ó hAnnluain – no way to speak to a bride," Mark called. "Come on, my little fairy, your Uncle Mark's looking after you now." He beamed at Mrs ó hAnnluain, bowed like a courtier, offered me his arm, patted my hand. Mrs ó hAnnluain made an outraged noise between a squawk and a wheeze. The gate slammed behind us.

"So much for Dominic currying favours with her," I said.

"Do I see the first prezzies, the matched set of blackening eyes?"

"Are they both black? The pig!"

"One of yours, one of his. His right, your left. I'd forgotten you were a *ciotóg*."

"Mark – "

"It'll blow over. Really. Oh, you're not – ! Don't cry, Maura, it gets on my nerves. Give it a rest. Marriage is marriage. This is only the beginning. You'll look wonderful for Athlone."

"Stop that act. Where's he gone?"

"Oh, just ahead. He'll see a few people. I take it that's an excuse for the maintenance of his celibacy."

"You can't be 'celibate' when you're married. You can only be cold, and cruel!"

We walked for a while without talking.

Finally Mark said, "Are you just going to cry all morning?"

"What's got you so bloody chipper?"

"You can take it my love life's going better than yours."

"Good! Where are we going next?"

"To collect Eoin – my friend. He's coming with us to

Athlone." For the first time I could remember, Mark smiled straight into my eyes.

"Congratulations," I said, meaning it.

"Don't worry about our Dominic," he said after a while. "He's crumbling. I can tell." He nudged my arm. "It's unnatural, the life he's leading."

As much as he tried to modify his stride, Mark continued to pull ahead of me. Finally I stopped him.

"I'm too slow again, Mark. I was sick this morning."

I got him to show me on the map where to meet him; it was just off the main road near Eoin's farm.

"We'll meet Dominic farther on," he said. "He'll have cooled down by then. Oh – the Militia's out. You're a boy and a bit simple, right? And you know nothing of me or your husband. If you see them before they see you, scarper, it's easier." Then he swung away from me. I couldn't have kept up with his joy.

He left me alone in a landscape which once had a gentle loveliness, but which now seemed vacant and bleak. Even before the wars there had been decay here, so many had left the land; now the hedges frowned across rough fields gone to seed, where drainage had failed and tractors, finally abandoned, rusted to cobwebs in sour meadows. I repeated Mark's directions to myself again and again, then set my own pace, hoping to find a rhythm that would take me to Eoin's farm at the right time.

I saw two small groups of men in uniform during the afternoon. I wasn't fast enough for the second lot; they shouted at me and motioned me to come to them. I slouched over, letting them see my reluctance. There were three of them, in their late teens or early twenties. The uniforms didn't fit well and emphasised how thin they were.

"Who are you?" said the oldest-looking one. He had a

worn-looking baton hooked to his belt.

"Maurice … Maurice Byrne."

"Where are you from, Maurice?"

"County Wicklow."

He frowned at the other two. He took a couple of steps to the side and looked at me over his shoulder. I felt I'd seen the gesture before somewhere and that he had, too.

"Wicklow."

I ducked my head, nodded.

He unhooked his baton, and I stumbled back.

"And what brings you so far from home, Maurice?"

The eyes of the other two were bright, waiting.

"Me ma died!" The tears took me by surprise. I sobbed with grief and fear.

The older youth reattached his baton to his belt. "And where'd you get your black eye?"

"Me da," I sobbed.

"Jesus, Wicklow," said one of the other two youths.

"Why'd you come here?" pressed the leader.

"They say there's work in Athlone." I wiped my eyes and nose on my sleeve.

They looked at one another. "Not for you, lad."

"Why?"

He turned to the other two, casting up his eyes. A consensus of boredom and pity was forming among them. "You haven't a craft or some big skill, no?"

I shook my head, shuffled. Then I said, "I'm good with hens."

"You mean you can find them?" The other lads laughed. "Look, Maurice, you're better off back in Wicklow."

"Me da'll kill me."

"Call into farms along the way, Maurice. Somebody may have the odd hen. Don't go to Athlone."

They moved on down the road. I saw they were wearing their own shoes; one of them was limping.

After that, I concentrated on avoiding people rather than making the best time. Yesterday we had passed two or three people on the road and seen a few farmers out in the fields. Today I didn't see any locals except one man driving his cow to be milked. He jumped when he saw me.

"Open the gate, Mister?"

"Thanks very much," he said. I held it while the cow swayed slowly past.

"Sup of milk?" he asked gruffly.

"Thanks, Mister, I must be going," though I was ravenous. "One thing – "

"What?"

"Mister, I was stopped by soldiers. What's the matter here?"

"Seen many of them out today?"

"Two lots."

"Wait one minute, lad. I'm getting a cup." He hurried into a gap in the hedge, the cow pushing after him, and returned with an enamel cup full of foaming milk.

"Thanks. You're very good."

He looked at me more closely for a moment, then said, "Where were the soldiers, lad?"

"I met them an hour ago. Near a crossroads – I came on them suddenly around the curve. There was a broken-down farmhouse on my right, reddish-coloured."

"Big pillars into the yard? No gates?"

"That's right. An old tractor inside."

"I have you."

"There were three of them, lads. They warned me not to go to Athlone."

"God help them. Recruits. You were lucky."

"I was. Why are they out, Mister, do you know?"

"Do you not know yourself?"

I shook my head.

"There's a chance of fighting." He glanced at the cup,

which I had emptied, but I held on to it. "And it's said they're looking for criminals as well."

"Criminals?"

"Depends how you look at it."

I handed him back the cup.

"You needn't be frightened," the man said. "The so-called criminals wouldn't hurt you."

"You know them?"

"Jaysus, no, word gets around. Anyway, those young lads were right. Stay away from Athlone, boy. There'll be trouble there." He nodded at me and turned towards his house. I could hear a woman's voice behind the hedge.

"Thanks for the milk."

He put up his hand. "You won't mention the cow?"

"No." I waved and hurried on, fortified by the milk, my heart pounding.

By late afternoon, I'd seen two more groups of men, and I was wondering if I was lost. The second lot delayed me terribly; I took cover behind a hedge, and they decided to stop for their break directly in front of me. It was only luck that most of them chose to relieve themselves on the other side of the road, and I decided to hide farther back in future.

There were six of them, older and more experienced than the recruits. They were mid-twenties to mid-thirties, and well fed. Their uniforms were very worn, and some of them were incomplete, a uniform shirt with ordinary trousers, or the other way round. All but one of them had boots; the last was wearing what looked like a very old pair of ordinary men's shoes. They'd have made two and a half or three complete soldiers among the lot of them. I'd have seen very little of this, only they moved around before they got settled.

" ... the middle of nowhere on a wild goose chase."

"Intelligence!"

There was harsh laughter.

"There's no good going to come of this," said a quiet, nervous voice.

"So you've said, Patrick."

"The people are getting annoyed."

"I'm fucking annoyed!" This man had a red face, and in the old days he'd have been fat.

"What'll you do, then, Elvis, start a petition?"

"I'll start a fucking petition."

"Put Elvis here in a dress and see if we can land the big one that way," said another.

"It's not me dress he'd be interested in."

"T'wouldn't be the rest of you, either, if he's the fastidious devil he's told to be."

"Fast wha'? I suppose you think you're the pretty one here?"

"He could be in the area. They say he comes here."

"Take it easy, Patrick. There's six of us. We won't let him have his way with you."

"The whole thing's a farce. Do you know why we're put looking for this fellow?"

"Elvis needs a friend."

"Go on, why?"

"Because he's the only person in the entire population that we might be able to recognise."

"I recognise me wife. Sometimes."

"I recognise Elvis!"

"You don't even have to see Elvis to recognise him!"

"You'll be cleaning the jacks, Andy me boy."

The man named Patrick said, "This fellow's nobody, only he's big and tough and maybe a faggot. What's he done? He's only a bloody ratcatcher or something."

"Maybe we need him, so," said a quiet voice.

"Yeah."

"We should be home in our beds."

"Arragh!" This was Elvis, disgusted. "Fucking cowards, the lot of you! Anyway, the Specials take care of all the hard-cores."

There was a rustling of packs opening. The three quieter men sat down, their backs to the ditch.

"It's daft," said one of them.

"And who'll they take it out on? Us."

"There's very bad feeling. My own brother-in-law won't talk to me."

"He never did."

"That's the other one."

"Count your blessings. My one lives in my ear. 'Where's the good market next weekend?' I tell him how the fuck should I know."

"You know what I mean."

"Who is this fella anyway, Patrick?"

"Big man. Over six foot. You wouldn't want to cross him, I hear, but he's said not to look for trouble. "

"His side-kick's the one to go for if you ask me, but when half of Ireland has brown hair and a beard ... "

They were quiet. From across the road came a series of loud farts.

"D'you think Elvis is a candidate for spontaneous combustion?"

"I hope so," said the quiet man.

"Come on, ladies, work to do!" Elvis was back.

"Yes, sir!"

They turned in unison and relieved themselves into the hedge. Mercifully, they had moved down a bit and a little only went on my shoe.

CHAPTER TWENTY-FIVE

THE OVERCAST HAD CLEARED, BUT THE TWILIGHT THAT TOOK ITS place was no comfort; as the light thinned, the landscape became transparent, a dim membrane over shadows of darker lives, darker landscapes. Twilight sounds started in the fields like a whispered medley of forgotten languages, the hedges drew closer and the road under my feet was almost invisible. Suddenly the land seemed limitless and unfriendly, and the blackening hedges the steep sides of a maze.

A cow lowed suddenly in the field beside me, and Mark glided forward, motioning to me to be quiet. "We might not be alone."

"Who? Soldiers?" It came out as a gasp. His wraithlike appearance in the halflight had frightened me half to death.

"I'm not sure." He turned away and gave a low whistle. Another figure stepped through the gap in the hedge. It was a lad of about eighteen, stocky, of medium height. Even in the twilight I could see that he had crisp black hair and a high colour; he shifted nervously on his feet.

"This is Eoin," Mark said briefly.

"I'm Maura."

"Hello," he said, ducking his head. He seemed

smothered in shyness.

"All right, so go back!" Mark burst out. "All you'll do is upset her – "

"She'll be more upset if she doesn't know," the boy said doggedly.

Mark smouldered. "I'm wondering why you're here at all, Eoin – "

"I was late. I was putting in the cows."

"Jesus! Ten minutes! I mean it, love, the place is crawling – "

"I'm gone," said the boy. He smiled at me, a sudden, puckish grin, touched Mark's cheek, and ran silently down the road.

"Eoin's coming," Mark said nervously. "He just has to say goodbye to his fucking mother. I wouldn't mind, she's such a bitch." He picked up a small stone and shot it into the hedge.

"Some soldiers were talking about you today. They've got your description, some of them; they're looking – "

He made a large, dismissive gesture. A few moments passed, and then he began prowling up and down. I could scarcely see him.

"Should we go get him?"

"No. It would only make things worse."

A dog barked far away, the sounds like light blows on the air. Then there was another noise, percussive but lifeless. The shot reverberated through the night, quelling all other sounds. Mark was already running.

My lungs were bursting when he stopped to listen; I could hear nothing but the pulse in my ears, but after a few moments the small night noises resumed in the grass. A breeze lifted, died. Then, where? A field, two fields away? It was indistinguishable as a voice, but a human cry it must be, just too brief to quite penetrate the breeze. We ran.

The night air was opening the dying smells of leaves, of cooling fields, the edged, secret scents of autumn. Among these came the intruder, threading its acrid way.

I slowed as my foot skidded on moss. The sky above the hedges went opaque, then pink, then red. The brightness was full on Mark's face metres ahead of me as he turned into the farm gate. I reached it just as there was a muffled thump, and sounds of glass shattering.

The house, flaming, shimmered with heat. There was a movement in the darkness at the other side; I prayed it was Mark, prayed he hadn't run inside for Eoin. I ran around to the back, hugging the cooler verge beyond the dreadful red light. There was a rough, neat yard, lit by the flames from the house, but less intensely than the front. Here the fire in the house had settled to a lonely crackling, like a giant hearth left untended. Smoke stung my eyes. There was no sign of Mark.

I turned towards the outbuildings in hopes he had survived, even to crawl away. I could see into their open doors: tools stacked neatly in one; an orderly agglomeration of bits, pieces, all sorts of reusable parts, in another. A good farm. A smell of hay. I ventured out the other side of the yard, tripped and sprawled, and for a moment could see nothing, only feel soft, filled fabric warm under my shin. "Mark," I whispered, weeping. "Oh, Mark."

A filthy hand clamped over my mouth, and there was a prickle of steel below my jaw. I grunted, and the fingers spread to cover my nostrils as well. Then the hand loosened as suddenly as it had grabbed, and the man's weight made me stagger. "Hold him up!" said Mark's voice, sharp. He manoeuvred the man into a slumping crouch, and tied his hands behind his back. I stood back, shuddering. Another man, the one I had fallen over, lay on the ground.

"Mark – Eoin?"

He nodded towards the fire. I couldn't see his face.

"Mark?"

"Leave it!" With quick, fierce movements he attached a noose around the man's neck and threaded it through the bindings at his wrists. His legs twitched. Then he shook his head, dazed.

"Get up. Get up, you bastard. Mark Meehan has you now."

The man sucked in his breath.

"How many others? How many?"

The man stumbled against me. The roof of the house caved in behind us, and the triumphant leap of the flames lit his face. He was terrified.

"Do you want to go out again?" Mark's fingers were at his neck. "Will you know yourself when you wake up?"

The man groaned, moved his eyes piteously. "I didn't do it."

"I can smell it on you! How many?"

"They made me – " He cried out, an astonished, frightened howl.

"How many?"

"Four of us!" cried the man, cowering.

"Four like fuck!"

"All right – five! Six!"

"One under your feet. Yourself. Where are the others?"

"How would I – they're scattered. We're to meet at – at – will you for Jesus sake stop it, stop it!"

"Where?"

"Near Farnagh. They won't now … "

"Who's in charge?"

"Mick was, the man you … We had to, you know how it is!"

"Why Floods?"

"They – they harboured criminals!" the man cried.

Mark yanked his ropes.

"Mark – "

"Shut up." His eyes were blank. He was out of control. I could feel our hostage's fear all over my body, as penetrating as acid.

Mark dragged and pushed him towards the front of the house. He paused at the gate. Long flames still shot through the roof, but the light was less intense and parts of the house were beginning to smoulder. There was a worse smell on the air now.

"Four of them," Mark said. "The parents ... the daughter ... the son. What did they do?"

The man made a choking noise.

Mark manhandled his prisoner down the road. His rage gave him eyes for the dark. I stumbled after him, thinking I heard the man's heart racing as fear stripped him to childishness. Finally Mark pushed into a field which rose steeply, then dropped, making a hidden place from the road. There was rough ground on the other side, a circular rise and a fall – a rath. "Well, well," he said in a purring voice. "A fairy fort!"

The man froze. "Oh, sweet holy God!"

"I believe he knows something about me."

The man trembled. "You make me sick," he quavered.

"I like a slender man, a daring man, a man who will take risks, who will – incinerate an entire family alive like a litter of hedgehogs."

"I didn't – I didn't plan it, I didn't mean to do it," said the man. His voice shook. Mark gave him a vicious jerk, spilling him into the centre of the rath. There were grunts, a scuffle. "I can't – breathe!"

"Tell me more about my one-time friends, the Floods."

"Stop it!" the man whispered.

"Get off the top of the rath," Mark said to me coldly. "You'd be seen."

"They'll be looking for me," the man said. "Oh, I wouldn't like to be you, boy, when they – "

" – find you?" Mark, in his scary, silky voice. "It's you they'll find. You know?"

The man was silent again. Then he burst, "They'll find you – and your black-haired friend."

"You make me so angry when you threaten my friends, fry them – " Mark said in his mad, pretend-petulant voice, "when I only want to talk about your friends."

"Let me go, I've told you – !"

"Mark, don't play with him, please, Mark."

He pushed the man's face into the soft grass, and I yanked at his coat.

"Stop it! You'll kill him! We have to go," I whispered. "Leave him tied up if you've got to. Come on, Mark. Remember Conor. Please."

The man groaned, but he had taken hope; a stagey quality crept into his voice. I tasted the smoke on my lips.

"You tell him everything you know, everything, or I'll beg him to kill you!" I snapped.

With this his resistance seemed to break, and oddly, he regained some of his dignity. "Six of us ... They were always asking questions, Floods were, and the young lad never stopped nosing around. You can't have that now." He cleared his throat. "I'm – I'm sorry."

I heard Mark rubbing his hands back and forth on the grass as if to clean them.

"Mark," I said. "We should go."

He got up as if the man no longer existed, and I followed him back to the road. The man had the sense to stay quiet in his bonds and not call attention to himself, but I knew Mark wouldn't have hurt him any more. I wondered what I'd have done if it had been Dominic – or Conor.

I don't know how many miles we walked. The only sounds were our boots on the road and Mark's ragged breathing. His grief radiated such raw, negative energy that it took me over. I breathed in his rhythms, and my heart was ready to burst. When we reached impenetrable darkness under a canopy of trees, I had to stop, hearing the scuff of his boot as he turned. "Please, Mark, speak or cry – something."

There was silence. Then a soft sound in front of me, and he seized my shoulders and shook me like a dog shakes a rat. "Mark, please!" He hurled me away from him; I sprawled on the road. "You'll break!"

He caught his breath and moved towards me. It was I who would get broken, I reckoned, and I tried to roll towards the ditch without making a noise. Then he howled. It was an inhuman sound – there was no intelligence in it, only pain. The hair stood up on my neck.

Far away in the dark, someone was running towards us, a man by the sound of it. Near me, a sob. I put out my hand, felt Mark's hair. He was crouched on the road, crying. He moved away from my touch. I edged around him to get between him and the person who was coming.

The steps slowed. I knew the gait with its slight limp. "Dominic?"

"Maura?"

I moved towards him, hands outstretched, finding his sleeve, then his own warm hands. Mark still sobbed, oblivious. "Eoin's dead."

"Oh, Jesus." He was next to Mark now, and I heard the rustle as he dropped to one knee. "Jesus, Mark, I'm sorry. Jesus."

Mark seemed to be rubbing his face on his sleeve. "Fuck." His voice was thick with tears.

"You all right?"

"Yeah, yeah, I'm great."

"Jesus, what happened?"

"Ach, Eoin, you know, he – Eoin talked. Jesus, he

bragged! So ignorant. I told him and told him – stubborn little prick!"

"They burned the house with them all inside," I said.

Dominic made a sound. He held Mark.

After a long while, Mark said, "What are we doing in this bloody place? It's like a pit here even in the daytime."

"We'll move on, so," said Dominic.

"Right," said Mark.

A long while later, I heard Mark saying, "Hey. Hey look, Dominic, she's asleep!"

I rubbed my eyes; the hedges on either side had small chinks of light in them. Dominic put his arm around me. "Back this way, love," he said. They had turned in at a gate, and I had kept walking.

I reached up and touched his hair, ran my hand down his face. His right eyelid was purple, fading to yellow at the corner. He looked down lovingly, resignedly almost, and kissed me gently. For that moment I stopped existing except where I touched him, lip to roughened lip, hands to hair, the sensation of my own clothes on my breast, his warmth the other side of them.

My hands fell away, though, and when I woke up in a dim, small room, it was getting dark again. The bed I was lying on had a lumpy mattress that smelled of clean straw. A faint light came from the next room, and the sound of Mark and Dominic talking. They sounded rested, though Mark's voice had a sad frailty in it I had never heard before. Dominic's was gentle, matter of fact. Tears stung my eyes; it wasn't fair. It wasn't fair.

A chair scraped. The room brightened. Mark poked his head in the door, and I sat up. "See you tomorrow," he said, in his new fragile insolence.

I held out my arms to him.

"You're taking too many liberties," he said, but he gave

me an awkward pat. "There's a stream a few yards away."

"Are you telling me something?"

"Yes. And your husband could stop a train. 'Bye." He was gone.

When I paused between the bedroom and the main room of the cottage, I saw Dominic still with his hand on the latch. He was staring into space.

"Will Mark be all right?"

"I think so."

"He says we're filthy," I said.

He shook his head, but he was smiling. "The stream outside's as cold as a witch's teat."

"Worse than the one in the Wicklow Gap?"

He looked at me strangely, almost shyly. "No use putting it off," he said. He held the door open and let me pass in front of him. "Wait," he said. He returned with two rugs, worn threadbare. "To dry ourselves."

We could just see our footing in the twilight. The dry weather had hardened the ground and dried the stream's verge, which had widened as the water dwindled. There was a small pool below a place where the water tumbled over stones. "It only comes up to your waist about," Dominic said. "You nearly have to sit down in it."

He hesitated a moment, then folded the rugs and laid them together on the grass. "You have the top one," he said, smiling.

"Thanks."

He pulled off his jumper, dropped it on the grass. He seemed uncertain. I looked at him, raised my hands. He pulled my jumper off over my head. He did it gently, stood a moment with it in his hands, then dropped it on top of his own. He'd his old blue shirt with the sleeves rolled up. I remembered Lizzie finding it for him. I unbuttoned it, his heart beating under my fingers. I laid my palm against his chest, feeling his warmth and the steady beat of his heart.

He slipped off the shirt, dropped it, pulled mine over my head. He caught his breath, sighed. Gently he touched me, pulled me close and kissed me. I held him, trembling. We broke apart to step out of our clothes.

Then when we kissed, we were so urgent we almost hurt each other, yet I felt only a fierce joy when he entered me – it was the seal on my love for him, that he'd changed me forever.

When he lay quietly beside me, I trailed my hand down his back, over his shoulders, down his ribs. Over the hard sinews, his skin was as soft as a girl's and I was terrified at how frail a covering it was. His vulnerability filled me with fear, yet at the same time I rejoiced in every sensation I had from him, the warmth of his body, the stinging soreness between my legs, the ache of the small, smooth stone under my shoulder. If he left me again, I would still have all that.

He stirred, kissed me. "You're bleeding," he murmured. Carefully, he pulled away from me.

"It's nothing."

The cold of the stream made us gasp. We washed and splashed one another relentlessly, whooping, but only for a minute or two; it was unbearable. We helped each other out, wrapped ourselves in the rugs and staggered back to the cottage, clutching our clothes in numbed fingers.

Dominic barred the door. We curled together in the bed then, limb on limb, whisper on whisper, growing deliciously warm. Before long, warmth turned to desire, and we loved one another slowly, for every parting and every sad uncertainty. Now there was a fluttering throughout all my body, as if something trapped had been awakened and released into flight, and soon, quivering, I felt the warm pulse of his coming.

He was still inside me when we slept, but our limbs

were like water, and it was only later that I woke up hot and cramped from a dream in which Conor gazed at me out of huge eyes in a haggard face.

CHAPTER TWENTY-SIX

I WAS LAST IN ATHLONE WHEN WE WERE AT THE COTTAGE; IT rained all one weekend, and my father bundled us into the car and brought us to the museum in the castle there. Suddenly I could smell the leather of the seats, my mother's perfume, and the baby shampoo in Conor's hair. The windscreen wipers had eased back and forth with that perfect rhythm of mechanical things while the landscape hunched, notional, under the rain.

Now there was sunlight, the scuff of feet and creak of the odd cart; two were passing when we walked out on the highway, one pulled stoically by a farmer with a makeshift harness across his chest and shoulders, the other by a donkey attended by an old man. The highway itself was almost dazzling after the narrow, hedge-bound roads we'd been travelling. The land rolled away on either side of us, and I felt hopeful and exposed.

There were more people on this road than I had seen together since we left Wicklow, and I gazed, fascinated, until Dominic squeezed my arm. Then I realised that everyone else seemed to be observing the old decorum of cities; they watched their footing, or looked ahead with calculated vagueness. Even those travelling together seemed to speak out of the sides of their mouths to one another, in tones that nobody else could hear. I wasn't long discerning the reason for this. There were some whose oblique alertness separated them from the rest and these, I reckoned, were informers of some sort.

One large group of people tried feverishly to connect. The beggars were everywhere, threading fitfully through the travellers, hands held out. One girl paced beside me, peering up into my face with feral blue eyes, mumbling steadily, holding out scrawny palms.

"And who are you?" Dominic said to her. She shrank away from us.

"You took notice of her, Dominic; why did she do that?"

"I'm a man, so she's afraid of me." He shrugged. "You've only to look at her."

I watched her frantic, random progress along the straggle of travellers, always approaching the women. Most ignored her. She drew too close to one, who was stumping along with a heavy hessian bag over her shoulder, and the woman simply swayed the bag at her and knocked her flying. She struggled up again, a jumble of rags and pale, brittle-looking limbs, and scuttled to the side of the road, pulling at her clothes to cover herself, eyes darting, terrified.

I tugged at my pack. "No," Dominic said.

"One mushroom." We had found some on our way.

"You'll have my work cut out for me," he said, looking over his shoulder, but he slowed while I darted over to the girl and gave it to her. I had the soft, grey wheel into her hands while her eyes were still widening with the fright of my approach.

In a moment there were three young boys at our elbows, one actually trying to fumble at my pack, and Dominic rounded on them, sending them scurrying back. "Didn't I tell you," he said, but he was more sad than annoyed.

Then there was a sudden flurry, and half the people on
the road melted into the fields on either side, while
Dominic and I drifted with the others to the verge. A
clattering got louder behind us, then became deafening as
two great dray horses came into view, pulling a long truck
piled high with turf.

They were magnificent creatures, massive, glossy,
bursting with health. I wondered why the people watching
looked so glum, savouring as I was the might and energy
of these animals, the rich tang of their bodies and their
leather trappings. Then the truck was past us, and I saw.
Half-strapped, half-clinging to the back of the load were
five, no six, children, their faces and arms and clothing
dusted and browned to the colour of the turf. There was
something half-formed about them, the way they lay
listless, heaped together with exhaustion, as inanimate as
the turf itself. They looked around Conor's age or a little
older.

A woman on the other side of the road ran into the
middle of it, wailing and screaming. One of the children
struggled to sit up, pulling his neighbours with him. The
turf behind them shifted a bit, and they scrabbled feebly to
keep their balance. They sank back again, and he turned
his face away.

The woman couldn't keep up. She faltered, then
stopped in the middle of the road, crying loudly.

"Walk on a bit, Maura, I'll catch up with you."

"All right." I was too stunned to query him, too shocked
by the sight of the chains, the chains threaded through
leather-covered rings on their wrists and legs.

There was an ugly atmosphere on the road now, and
thank God for it. The only sound was the woman crying
behind us, but the air was alive with rage, silent but no less
communicative for that. I had begun to wonder if the other
travellers were starved and depressed beyond all reach of

empathy or desire.

Dominic caught up with me.

"What did you do?"

"Ach, just told her to get in touch with Liam Murphy or Rachel O'Farrell; they try to help people like her in the town. There are a couple of women with her now, neither of them smell like informers, so ... "

"Is Conor in chains?"

"I doubt it. Really."

I said no more about it; I didn't believe that Conor was not miserable. I knew he was.

After about an hour, the beggar children dropped back and then disappeared altogether. The reason for this became clear around the next curve in the road. A large, makeshift shed had been built of rough timber. There were shutters at the sides of the windows, which when closed would make the building like a squat wooden fortress beside the highway. There was a similar shed on the other side of the road a bit farther on, and between these a number of staggered partitions, made of upright lopped logs, stretched across it.

The travellers were filing through them without comment, watched by soldiers in the same disparate uniforms I'd noticed before. There were a few youths among them, but most of the men were middle-aged or older; some looked consumptive, and one had lost an arm. What physical weaknesses they had were belied by their eyes, however: these were sharp to a fault.

The woman with the hessian bag was a few yards in front of us. One of the older soldiers motioned her aside with a slight movement of his head. She hadn't seemed to be looking at him, but she walked over to him immediately. He and another man turned out the contents of her bag on the verge. There were a few poor vegetables, what looked like six or eight small carrots and about a half-stone of new potatoes. There were two pairs of knitted socks, rough and bunched-looking, and – I craned to look, and Dominic took my elbow, rough – a doll, a lovely doll with washed clothes that they'd dumped into the dust. The woman went still.

The younger man, who had upended her bag, pushed at the doll with his dirty boot, and the woman said something. His face hardened. He picked up the carrots and a pair of the socks and stuffed them into his blouse. The woman looked away. Then the older man, who had watched sardonically, pushed her against the wall of the building, pushed her until she was spreadeagled, arms up, legs wide, leaning. He ran his hands down her arms, her sides, her legs and between her legs. Then he pushed her around and plunged his hands into the front of her clothes, rummaged. "Maura," Dominic said between his teeth. His fingers were hurting my arm above the elbow, hurting so much that I gasped. "You'll make things worse for her if you stare."

I looked up at him, beseeching. He gazed straight ahead, his face relaxed, almost dreamy, as if he'd been commenting on something quite neutral. "You're hurting me."

"When you react – it's like holding up a sign, it's like holding up meat in the middle of a dog-pack, Maura. In situations like this, you go invisible, do you hear me? She wouldn't have been searched if she hadn't commented … I'm hoping none of these boyos recognise me now … "

"They'd know you?"

"Sh-h-h," he said, and his hand still on my arm, he led me into the partitions.

My neck began to prickle with fear; I could see now that they were hinged, that they could be shut behind and ahead of us if someone raised an alarm. We were like rats in a box. Dominic shuffled placidly along beside me, his expression still abstracted and dreamy, but his hand on my arm was tight. My mouth dried. The wooden palings were so high, so dark, the people, slowed, were becoming a crush, the air was thickening. Dominic gave my arm a slight shake; I felt the rough silk of his beard at my cheek. I leaned against him, concentrating on the living hardness of hip and ribs, his heart beating strongly behind the shabby jacket.

At last we were at the other side of the partitions, or "inspection area", as I heard one man calling it, and we could see the the highway ahead of us unravelling into the outskirts of Athlone. In the end it was like going from one trap into another when we entered the odd warren of streets that form the centre of the town. I clung to Dominic's hand. I felt if he were jarred away from me by the crowds, I would never see him again. Our new closeness made us vulnerable; it was like a beacon to attract disaster in this luckless place.

We followed the streams of people towards the river, Dominic telling me it was best to merge with the crowds for a while at the fair. Also, he hoped to meet Mark there, Mark's idea; Dominic's was to spirit him out of sight immediately he found him.

The Shannon announced itself with brightness, the sense of great space around the corner, and I caught my breath when we jostled into view of it; I'd forgotten how wide it was, how massive the main bridge over it, how heavy the huge bulk of the castle frowning across at us. Now the bridge was obstructed in much the same way as the highway outside Athlone, with a series of gates and blockages, but this time they'd an odd, glinting texture; they were bristling with nails. The people weren't going to the bridge, however, but to the fair on a vast, cleared area on our side opposite the barracks.

This was all changed from what I remembered. There had been aging and derelict buildings here when I had gone to Athlone with my family. My mother had been interested in their lines – "melancholy" – and had sketched them with a few flicks, a line of old warehouses and offices that seemed only feebly haunted by their one-time dignity. These had been razed, along with the whole area around the castle and barracks opposite; this was scraped clean of so much as a bush that a dog could hide behind, and the high brick walls surrounding the barracks were festooned with barbed wire.

Before the War, this had been a dignified place, with an atmosphere of stolid but warm reassurance. We had walked along the road between the river and the barracks, and my parents had let me push Conor's pram. With hindsight, I'd have said the whole place felt benign and above all, Irish.

Now it had sickened, as if we'd joined Europe un-vaccinated when we gave up our neutrality all those years ago. Lizzie had told my mother, "It wouldn't have made a blind bit of difference; we were never really neutral, sure we weren't. We'd have been hit."

"Something was changed … " my mother said. "The atmosphere changed."

I leaned closer to Dominic. All around us looked like another place, another time, when my parents watched the news on television, the picture dipping crazily on scenes of stony buildings, squares full of people, nightmare expressions of rage. Older, more intractable hatreds grafted themselves on to us; we took on new shapes, new capabilities. I thought of the children, chained, on the truck. I thought of myself, a child sticking a knife into a grown man, scalding another with a kettle.

Dominic scanned the crowd and the stalls thickly scattered around us. If I saw him now for the first time, would I dream he was gentle? Would I meet his eyes? I would see his wolflike leanness, his watchful expression, the scars across the back of his left hand. I would see his beauty, all right, because he was a lovely man, but I might give him a wide berth. And myself, looking: what was I?

As we moved among the stalls, I whispered that some people seemed to be watching us. He shrugged. "That's what they're there for. Take no notice; we're bog-trotters in their eyes, too stunned by the bright lights to notice them … They lose interest after a while."

"Don't compliment yourself that you look like a yokel; you look like a terrorist."

"You're nervous, love. Don't worry."

"And don't smile like that, either."

He laughed.

I poked him in the ribs, and he put his arm around me, just as if we were two lovers with nothing more on our minds than the fair. He leaned down as if to kiss me, saying "Keep an eye out for Mark – just let me know if you see him, but maybe you shouldn't recognise him."

I grabbed his collar. "Since you're here, you might as well."

He kissed me in a glancing sort of way and when I laughed, muttered, "You don't want to get me going in the middle of Athlone." We moved farther into the untidy rows of stalls, our clasped hands warm together, and I saw that the man and woman who had been watching us had drifted away.

The stalls – I call them that, for want of a better word – were a motley assortment of planks, wheelbarrows, ancient prams, folding tables – whatever you could think of to display meagre and bedraggled bits and pieces. There were far more vegetables in this big fair than I'd ever seen together in Wicklow, but they were at least as poor in quality as the ones we produced. Mind you, not everything was bad. On one table were four pairs of knitted socks in greased natural wool. I wished with all my heart I could get a pair for Dominic – the work in them was beautiful. But I had nothing to barter except Lizzie's jacket. That was far too valuable. A woman sat behind the table, knitting steadily. She seemed to be daydreaming, looking straight ahead as if it didn't matter whether she attracted customers or not.

"I'll leave you a mo' while you watch the entertainment," Dominic said, meaning the knitting, and he slipped away before I could follow him.

The woman dropped a stitch, picked it up with one practised turn of the wrist. I opened my mouth to ask her was it the wool of her own sheep she was using, but a voice cut across mine:

"You wouldn't be looking for such big socks for yourself."

The woman's mouth curved in a small, scornful smile. The darting needles never slowed.

It was a young man who had spoken to me.

I turned my back to him, picked up a pair of the socks, turned them over, looking.

He had a round, pink face and small eyes, and he reminded me of a tall, shrewd pig. Not that he was fat: he was lean, but he'd all the signs of being well-fed, even prosperous. He wore a saffron-coloured shirt of soft wool, and tweed trousers. Both were new and without a patch. His shoes were post-war, but they were leather and made by a craftsman. All this I saw at a glance, along with the soldier's scarf pinned at his neck. He stood out in the crowd, startlingly colourful and sleek, but the thing that separated him most was his confidence. I had never felt before that my own shabbiness made me naked.

"Cat got your tongue?" He smiled, showing a full set of good white teeth.

I gave him my haughtiest look, borrowed straight from

my mother, and continued to watch the woman knitting. "I was wondering do you use wool from your own sheep," I said to her.

"I do," she said, knitting briskly. "A middling herd. Good wool, good enough."

"Your work is lovely," I said.

"What would you want for them?" said the young man.

"I'll come back when you're not so busy," I told the woman.

She gave me an odd look, pitying I thought, with a hint of warning.

"I can show you the best thing at this market," said the soft voice at my shoulder.

I moved on, pretending not to hear him.

"You've not been here before. I'd have seen you." He touched my hair, as if testing it for quality. I realised the people were parting in front of us, keeping away.

"If you weren't new here, you'd be – polite. To me."

I turned and faced him. The chat stilled in the stalls nearest us. "Yes, I'm very new here. Too new to know that pigs can talk!"

There was an appreciative murmur from the crowd, but I knew I was out of my depth; his expression hadn't changed at all. "You'll be very used to that, and soon," he said.

I gave him my best curled lip as I turned, but my legs felt numb from knee to ground. I marched away from the area where I'd left Dominic, praying he wouldn't get involved.

There was a crash and a rush of breath behind me, and titters here and there.

"Oh-h-h-h," said a surprised voice. "The pretty shirt all spoiled!"

I slipped behind the people watching until I found a vantage-point from the other side of the crowd. Porko, as I called him in my mind, had his back to me. Mark, wide-eyed, was helping him up, standing much too close to him. He gave him a broad, simple grin. "Much better now! Still lovely!" His eyelids drooped. "Let's get off some of this mud. A shame about the shirt. And the trousers." He dusted at him with huge, shapely hands. "Tck … !"

Porko's face was white with fury. He pulled away so violently that he almost fell again. Soft laughter like will o' the wisps swelled, dissolved as soldiers approached. He looked plainer than ever beside Mark, and he was vain enough to notice that the girls among the crowd were staring at his tormenter, transfixed.

"Get off me, you bloody great butterfly!" Porko's face reddened, and the little white teeth snarled.

Mark stood over him and blinked down into his face, bewildered and rather menacing. "Butterfly?"

Porko turned on his heel, motioned curtly to the three or four soldiers who had arrived on the scene, and walked quickly away. He made some angry comment, but there were only a couple of whistles from the crowd.

I was caught out by the direction he took so suddenly and only hid myself in time. The people in front of me closed ranks without a word, and I'd a sudden stab of hope. The very air of Athlone was thick with resentment and collusion. Surely someone, someone would help us when we found Conor?

In a few moments Mark swaggered around the side of a stall.

"You'll be in horrendous trouble now, Mark."

"Not at all," he said. "Now, my reward." He picked me off the ground and gave me a long, hard kiss on the mouth in full view of all who cared to look. "I'm in disguise," he whispered.

"Have you never heard of French kissing?"

"There are limits."

"You'll have to put your arm around me now."

"Enough is enough." He looked over my head, started to speak, stopped. Dominic was walking towards us, his face tight with rage.

CHAPTER TWENTY-SEVEN

DOMINIC GRABBED MARK BY THE FRONT OF HIS JACKET. "WHAT the fuck!"

"You saw what was going on." Mark was unperturbed.

"So did everyone – Jesus, man, would you remember where you are!"

"My moment of chivalry, and look."

"I didn't know what to do, Dominic," I said. "Whoever he is, they're all afraid of him."

Dominic was still scowling at Mark. "All you had to do was trip him, boyo, and instead you had to give him – an autograph and a poster of yourself. He thinks nobody notices him," he said to me. He turned to Mark again. "You're leaving town, and now isn't soon enough."

"Make me," said Mark, beaming.

"Dominic, he's coming back. He's got soldiers with him."

"Leg it, you bastard!"

"Liam Murphy's, tomorrow at dawn," Mark said, widening his eyes dramatically. He began threading his way through the crowd. His head bobbed above almost everyone else's, and people turned to look at him as they always did; so much for anonymity.

"We meet again," said Porko.

"Well, now I've my husband with me."

"I thought the other lout was your husband," said Porko, showing his little teeth. "Though I was thinking he preferred me."

"You were annoying my wife," said Dominic. His demeanour had changed. He seemed taller, older, and sternly disapproving.

"He was," I said. "He had me badgered until he put me in the way of that other one." I shuddered. "God knows how Margaret survives in this place! I thought it would be civilised."

"Well? Can a married woman walk through the fair before going to meet a friend? I'd have thought you were the lout," said Dominic in a mild voice.

"You have to excuse me," Porko said. "Your wife … doesn't look like the married women here. In fact … " he shrugged.

Dominic gave my hand a warning squeeze.

"In fact … ?" I prompted.

Porko gave a sly smile. "Have you met your friend yet?"

"That can hardly be of interest to you."

"Well, it is. We're very hospitable here. My men will help you find your way," he said, and giving me a last, insolent look, he walked off.

The two lads that Porko detached from the four he had with him looked almost as sleek as himself, and only a little less unpleasant. If he was a pig, these would do as spoilt rats. They seemed to be sharing a quiet joke. "I'm not ready to go yet," I told them coldly. "I want to look at the stalls."

A middle-aged woman with articles in a pram had been beckoning me with her eyes, and I wanted to talk to her.

"Dominic?" I said. He had been looking calmly at the other two, whose demeanour got less relaxed, but he came with me. I picked up a chipped plate and looked at it.

"Very nice, isn't it?" cried the woman. "A little chip, is all. You won't find them better now."

Dominic shifted and looked bored. The two soldiers talked behind their hands. "I believe I once saw your young man with Liam Murphy?" she went on, in a hushed voice. She pushed a cup into my hands. "The handle's cracked, but tis solid."

Dominic looked at her with interest. "I recognise you. We're in a bit of a bind here."

"Oh, that fellow. You must look out for him, no little tit-bit of cruelty would be too small for him. He has the girls tormented."

"Enjoying our chat?" said a voice at my elbow. One of the rats.

"I was," I said.

I turned to the woman. "Would you know my friend Margaret Kilcoyne?"

The soldier's eyes widened.

"Miss Kilcoyne is well known in Athlone," said the woman, delighted. "I know where she lives, of course."

"I'll bring you to Miss Kilcoyne," said the soldier uneasily.

"You'll come to my house first," said the woman, who now had a glint in her eye. "You'll want to wash."

"Thanks. I think we'll go straight," said Dominic.

The woman's eyes flicked over our clothes and she looked doubtful, but she said, "You're right." Without further ado, she folded the makeshift cover on the pram. "I'll come along with you," she said, "just in case these young ones don't know the way."

"We know the way," said the brasher of the two lads, giving her a hard stare.

"Then it's very queer," she said, drawing out the word, "how often you bring people to the wrong place."

The soldiers tagged behind. I could see one shrugging to the other. Both of them looked nervous.

I was surprised at the state of the town. The centre of power of the Midlands seemed almost as shabby and derelict as our own small village. The narrow streets were darkened by the shutters that boarded up many of the shop windows and doors, and many of those buildings seemed to have become dwellings again. Everywhere I felt constricted and watched, and gradually I began to realise that there was a tension in the air that came from something other than the spies and soldiers. The two lads stayed close behind us, however, and we could say nothing.

"Be sure now to tell Margaret Kilcoyne how thoroughly you were escorted here, and by whom," the woman told me.

The soldiers looked extremely uncomfortable now. Dominic turned to the woman and said casually, "There seems to be a bit more than fair day in the air here."

"Oh, indeed there is," she said with a fierce smile. "All rumours, of course. Sure we'll be well protected, won't we, lads?"

The two behind us gave her twin looks of loathing.

"Oh, all of southern Ireland's on its way here, isn't it, lads, to take us over and put us to work. Only rumours, aren't we lucky."

"What's your name!" said the brash lad, enraged.

"What's yours? Mind you tell it to Margaret Kilcoyne," she said to me, grinning back at him.

The rats smouldered.

"Almost there," she said. We were passing fine old houses now, houses which were well kept.

"I'm surprised Margaret lives in the town," I murmured to her.

"There are no amenities out of it," she said in low voice.

"And no safety, either, for Brian Kilcoyne. He'll never leave Athlone. Margaret's popular enough, she's not blamed for what goes on, but ... "

We stopped at a large, double-fronted house with scrubbed steps and fresh-looking paintwork. There was a brass knocker on the front door. The woman seized it and gave it two resounding thumps.

"Are you all right?" Dominic whispered to me.

I shook my head, numb. The memories were crowding back. I couldn't see Margaret without seeing Sister Imelda, Mrs Mulcahy, our whole class at school, home, everything. The front door opened.

A middle-aged man stood staring at us. He wore very clean clothes, a jumper with a shirt underneath, trousers and a long white apron that looked as if it had been boiled. He had light, but good shoes on his feet.

"Is Miss Kilcoyne at home, please?"

"Have you an appointment?" he said.

"I'm a friend of Miss Kilcoyne's from her old school in Killiney," I said. "Would you please tell her Maura O'Keeffe is here?"

He shut the door. One of the soldiers tittered.

Dominic put his arm around me for a moment, just that, but there was everything in it. I began trembling, and when the door was finally flung open and Margaret, white-faced, stared into my eyes and threw her arms around me, crying, I burst into tears myself. For those few moments, we clutched at one another in the full bitterness of our first loss.

CHAPTER TWENTY-EIGHT

SHE LOOKED STRANGE IN A WAY THAT WAS DISTURBINGLY FAMILIAR; it was the way the light in the hall spilled over her hair, draining it of its subtleties and leaching the colour from her cheeks. Dominic, too, had this hard pallor, and so had my hands that scrubbed my eyes and came back wet and glimmering.

Margaret watched me anxiously. "Maura?" She put out her long, white hand that I remembered so well.

"It's the light," I said stupidly. "It's electric. It's been so long."

"Have you no electricity?" she said wonderingly.

"Not for houses or lights ... Have you – have you your own generator?"

"Oh, no," she said. "There's quite a large one, it covers these few streets. It's run on turf somehow. My God, we're talking about electricity, when – Maura, come into the sitting-room, and – " she gestured, smiling.

"Oh, I'm sorry, this is my husband – Dominic Moore."

"You're married! Oh ... ! Please ... " She opened the door to a large, high-ceilinged room which was flooded with natural light from the long windows at the back. "Declan!" she called to the man with the apron, who was still hovering outside the door. "Declan, please bring us coffee. Open a tin if you need to. Sit down," she said to us, her blue eyes shining. "Maura O'Keeffe, I can't believe it!"

"Do you know, you haven't really changed," I said slowly. It was true – her hair was still soft, long and white-blonde, she was still slim and ethereal-looking, but it wasn't so much a matter of physical appearance as of manner. There was still something vulnerable about her, and it was emphasised rather than lessened by the luxuries around us.

"You haven't, either. That last day at school you helped me put the books in my bag, remember? You were the last person in our class I ever spoke to. My God," she said, swallowing. "Dominic," she went on, "I hear Dublin in your voice. Are you one of us?"

"I'm from Dublin, yes," he said quietly. There was a tiny pause.

Margaret blushed. "Where do you live, then, Maura? What brings you here?"

There was a knock on the door, and Declan came in with a tray of cups and saucers, coffee in a very large glass container with a rod of metal down the middle of it, a small jug of thick cream and a bowl of honey. The cups and saucers matched, and there were matching silver spoons as well with fragile stems. It was the smell of the coffee, however, that struck me like a blow; it suffused the air like a rich tide. My mother took coffee from a flask in her studio, steam billowing in the cool air, the brown-black scent of it unfurling past that autumn's picture, one she had started up near the turf allotments. Not the Dutchman's picture, but a smaller one, an abstract design of footed turf on the hillside. The undersides of the sods, patterned on the left of the canvas, were the same colour as the coffee. I'd never tasted it – she said it wasn't good for me – and had never thought to see or smell it again.

Dominic's face was inscrutable as he accepted the cup and saucer from Margaret. He shook his head a little, smiling, when she offered him cream and honey. I too refused these things, wanting to know the true taste, black like my mother learned to take it one time in America, and I was shocked by its bitterness.

"From petits fours to coffee," I said with a gasp.

"You find it very strong," Margaret said, anxious.

"It's just a bit strange," I said, "coffee and electric lights in five minutes of each other. Margaret – "

But she was asking me about my parents, her eyes widening in sympathy when I told her about my mother. "But that's only what – three or four days ago? In Wicklow?"

"Yes. You see – Margaret, I left Wicklow before my mother was even buried. Dominic and I met on the road and came here as fast as we could with a friend." When I told her what had happened to Conor, her expression changed. For a moment she looked horrified, then distant and almost bored.

"To be honest, I never thought to leave Wicklow," I finished, chilled. "I never expected to come so far ... "

"And you believe Conor is here?" she asked, looking into her cup.

"He was seen up as far as Moate. The men seemed to want to get him here very quickly." I had finished my coffee without realising it. The cup chattered in the saucer when I put it back on the low table in front of us, and my heart pounded.

Margaret looked at Dominic out of the corner of her eye as if she expected him to say something. He looked politely back at her and sipped his coffee. I realised, quite suddenly, that she was nervous; the boredom and the distance were only camouflages she'd acquired.

"Is it embarrassing for you, my coming to you like this?"

I demanded.

She turned pink. Then she laughed. "Yes! Well, not embarrassing, exactly – shattering!"

Still, things weren't right. She was uneasy. "Maura, I know it's terrible these things – it's terrible about Conor. I think I can – Here." She poured more coffee into our cups, slopping it a little in her haste. "I'll – I'll be back in a few moments." She hurried out of the room, closing the door behind her.

For a few seconds, Dominic and I sat speechless, as if we had lost permission to talk. Then he said, "I don't think you should drink more of the coffee."

I put the cup down so quickly it spilled. "Do you think it's – "

"No, I don't think it's poisoned," he said, grinning. "It's the caffeine in it. I saw your hands starting to shake."

"Dominic, is it all right? Should we have come? Margaret seemed so – "

"This is what Mark would call a 'social situation', love. I'm sorry he's missing it. Think of it – Margaret's only remaining friend from the old days appears in Athlone to ask Margaret to help her rescue her brother from Margaret's Daddy. I'd say Margaret manages to go days on end without reminding herself that nearly everyone she knows is implicated in the slave trade."

"But is he? Is Kilcoyne?"

"You had to come to Athlone to see an electric light burning in a house, never mind in broad daylight."

"It was dark in the hall," I said foolishly.

"All the blinds are drawn in the front of the house," said Dominic softly. "They're drawn all along the street. It's a kind of tact, maybe, so the hoi polloi can't see them drinking coffee inside, or won't know when to throw a rock, or so the people inside can't look out and see the hoi polloi outside."

"Well, I think Margaret wants to help."

"She's friends in high places," Dominic said.

"She's not bad, Dominic."

"She's not needed to be bad – there's enough without her."

I was quiet. I thought he was too hard on her. The dregs of the coffee had chilled, and the aroma was no longer seductive, but bitter and thin. I looked around the room. A huge rug covered all but the polished margins of the floor; it was a thick Chinese rug with a turquoise background and pastel flowers clustered in bands around the sides and in the centre. The upholstered chairs we were sitting on were covered in a silky, pale green brocade, as was a sofa on the far side of the room. The fireplace was as imposing as an altar, lined with pale marble and surrounded by a graceful carved mahogany mantelpiece. An enormous gilt-framed mirror hung over this, and the room reflected in it looked somehow inviolable, except that we were in the centre of it, two dark-haired invaders from another life, a hard-looking young man and a wild girl. Deep in the house, a clock chimed softly, and there were quiet, neat footsteps on the landing upstairs.

"We'd better plan," Dominic said. "I doubt they've risen to electronic listening." He got up and paced restlessly around the room, flexing his shoulders a little. My heart pounded irritably. I stuck out my tongue at the big mirror and crossed my eyes. Dominic laughed and arrived beside me. He made a hideous face by pushing up the end of his nose with his palm, and glaring down at it. "Wedding photo!" he said.

"You wouldn't want the wind to change," said a silken voice. We jumped like rabbits.

A man had come into the room with Margaret. My first thought was how striking they were together; he was fair-skinned, but his hair was black and his pale blue eyes, very bright. Margaret had put her flaxen hair up to go out, and she now looked like a young queen instead of a fairy-tale princess. She was still slightly breathless. "Jack, this is my friend Maura and her husband Dominic."

"Dominic Moore," said Dominic, taking the hand that was briefly held out to him. He was taken aback, and I thought it was because we'd been caught out at the mirror. Then the man turned to me, and I saw the scar. It was no more than a gleam, a small irregularity across his face that made him more handsome. The caricature on my mother's wall had refined itself to this. One thing, however, was still right, and that was the smile in his eyes. When he saw me notice his scar, his eyes smiled into mine as if we shared a joke, a joke that was too intimate to put into words.

There was a short conversation, but I remember nothing about it. Nobody seemed to find my behaviour odd, so I must have played my part. It was only when Jack Rourke had left that Margaret turned to me and exclaimed, "Maura! – oh crumbs, I've been so thoughtless, you're as white as a sheet; you must be exhausted."

"We haven't eaten much on the way," said Dominic drily.

"Of course! I'll get, I'll get – would you like to eat first, or rest? Or wash? There's hot water. I'm sorry Jack's so tied up, but he is looking for Conor, he'll have people looking for him, I mean ... But he doesn't expect to have news before late tonight, and he wants us to come to him. I mean, he's having a party for Charley Mullan, he's just been made Captain. It's to cheer up the Militia lads, Jack's very good about that."

"I thought the Militia lads I saw today looked cheerful enough," said Dominic. "A very sprightly one had us escorted here."

"Oh, they're very lively, poor boys, but it's all tension. I mean, you've heard what's going on."

"Are you expecting fighting, or what?"

"I don't know. No, not really." She looked distressed. "Jack doesn't say much because of Dad, Dad gets too upset."

Brian Kilcoyne was ill. That explained a lot to me; I couldn't imagine him entertaining Margaret's engagement to Jack Rourke in any normal circumstances. "Anyway," Margaret was saying, "I hardly think the sky will fall on us tonight!"

She brought us upstairs to a room at the front of the house that had a bathroom beside it. She took my clothes and brought me a soft red dress to wear, and a soft black jumper. Dominic wanted to keep his clothes, so she brought him a clean shirt and socks.

"Something tells me we're meant to take a bath," he said. "Before we present ourselves in the holy of holies."

"Do you suppose we share the water?"

"It's quite small," he said, smiling. My heart turned over, but I thought, 'There will be other times.' "You go first," he said gently. "I'm no stranger to cold water."

There was a cake of scented soap in a dish beside the bath, and a bottle of water laced with vinegar to help rinse our hair. The water was hypnotically warm.

Conor had loved bubble baths when he was a baby, that was our game together. I taught him to cup the bubbles in his palm and blow them into the air. He laughed so hard, I had to put my hand behind him so he wouldn't topple over. Then I had to be very careful lifting him out of the bath, he was so slippery and so excited. Perhaps we could come back here before we went home; perhaps Conor could have one marvellous bath in his life.

"If you don't get out now, you'll have no time to rest before tea," Dominic said. He kissed my mouth and my tearful eyes. "It's no wonder you're in a state. Don't worry.

I think the bastard may well see it through. We'll get Conor and show our heels to this place."

"What about Mark?"

"I'm to meet him at dawn," he said, imitating Mark's delivery, "at Liam Murphy's."

"What if he's not there?"

"You're a disgrace, woman. Look at the colour of that water."

"No, really – what if?"

"He'll be there."

"When he left the fair, they were all looking at him."

"He moves fast, love."

"Don't get into that! Run fresh!"

"I doubt even the princess's boiler runs to two baths," he said.

"Bets."

He sighed, turned on the taps. The water was as warm as before. I rubbed my hair dry with the thick blue towel and crawled naked between the clean sheets. I woke again to a dazzle of light and Dominic, dressed and clean-shaven, was standing beside me. "You'd best get up, Cinderella, if you want any food before the ball."

CHAPTER TWENTY-NINE

THE WINDOW OF THE BASEMENT KITCHEN WAS BLACK, MADE AS flat and opaque as a sheet of paper by the glare of the electric light. Margaret sat with us at the table, which reminded me of the one in the convent kitchen back in Wicklow. This too was massive, its deal surface smoothed and whitened from a hundred years of scrubbing. There was a blue linen cloth thrown over our end of it with matching napkins at each place and, again, matching cutlery and plates. There were huge potatoes in a dish, their skins black and brittle, and in another dish, steaming disks of carrot. Then Margaret brought a third plate to the table; piled high with pink, flaked chunks of fish, it exuded a haunting and delicate scent. "Salmon," she explained, seeing me frown. "They've been coming up the Shannon these past few years; a great sign of hope, aren't they? They were tested early on. They're all right."

I almost cried to see and smell such food, but in the end Dominic had to eat most of my portion along with his own. "I'm sorry," I said. "I don't think I'll be eating until we find Conor."

"You want to keep up your strength," Dominic said, but there was nothing I could do.

Margaret's eyes were huge with sympathy and disappointment.

"I'll regret this all my life," I said to her. "It's only beautiful."

Margaret's shyness had lessened and given way to confusion and distress. She kept smoothing the side of her hair with the back of her long, white hand, a gesture I remembered from school. Dominic didn't help. He was both wary and abstracted, and his small talk had dried completely. I had a mad feeling that the next time I looked at the window it would be light, that the black night was draining swiftly into days upon days in which we would not find Conor or help him. We would wander around Athlone for months, tasting coffee and making conversation while Conor's wrists wore away under his chains and his spirit died. And wouldn't it be like the Jack Rourke I had known to play with us?

A shy young recruit from the country accompanied us to Jack Rourke's house. He was very different from Porko's crowd; he could scarcely bring himself to speak to us. He walked ahead of us with an oil lantern whose pale light showed the footpaths like black-shadowed relief maps, and glided over stale-painted hall doors as if checking that they were shut tight. Most of the windows, like Margaret's, were heavily curtained; where there was a gap, there was sometimes the airless glow of electric lighting.

I had never been more aware of Conor. I could almost feel his presence, and my chest ached with claustrophobia and impatience. Dominic showed his own tension in the tightness of his shoulders and his silence.

"Jack said there would be a surprise at the party," Margaret was explaining. "I know you can't even think about such things under the circumstances, Maura, but ... maybe after, when this is over, you'll remember ... "

In that moment, she sounded so lonely that I wanted to hug her.

"I'll remember. Oh, Margaret, I wish we'd met under better circumstances."

A large group was approaching from a side street. At first we couldn't see them; we could only hear the slap and thud of their marching feet. Then they were passing us like a great dark human machine, and I could feel Margaret shrinking a little like I was. "Where are they going?"

"They're heading towards the Birr Road I think," said our escort. He seemed transfixed looking after them.

"Something starting?" asked Dominic.

"Ach, I wouldn't know. We're told nothing." He set off with the lantern again, disconsolate.

There were about twenty soldiers milling around outside Jack Rourke's house. The steps to the hall door were lit with oil lanterns, which flickered in the gathering breeze, making the eyes of the soldiers disappear into their sockets while their limbs and clothes, fretted by shadows, seemed to have a bizarre life of their own. At least two of them were drunk, and there was a savage edge to their laughter.

Our lad approached them apprehensively, but before he could say anything, the others saw Margaret. They quietened and straightened themselves, and the two drunks faded to the far edges of the group. As we approached the steps, however, there was another commotion in the street.

This group was travelling north. They also were soldiers, but they were far less orderly than the marchers, and they attracted a spate of catcalls from the crowd near the steps. Margaret caught her breath, murmured something, aghast. I glimpsed the tall, fair-haired figure who stumbled in their midst before the little rabble, half-walking, half-trotting, disappeared in turn.

"We'd best go inside, had we?" Dominic sounded

very far away.

We were at the door, we were inside the door. The house blazed with light. "Isn't it wonderful?" Margaret cried pleadingly. "Doesn't it remind you of Before?"

"The light does," I said.

The tall rooms were filled with people, mostly young, mostly healthy-looking and sleek. There were more men than women, and Margaret and I seemed to be among the youngest women there. People looked a little too long at me and Dominic; we were the angular ones, the outsiders. I think Margaret was struck by this for the first time. We weren't disdained – a few girls hovered near so that Dominic would notice them, and the men tended to give him very direct stares when their eyes met his. I had an admirer, too – Porko, in the corner, getting drunk.

Dominic continued to get looks because of his long hair and ordinary clothes, but more, I thought, because of his quiet independence. In this group of underlings – for this was plainly what they were – he had authority. While my head ached and my flesh screamed to be on the roads again and well away from this terrible place, it helped me to look at him. For a few wild moments I doubted he had seen Mark among the gaggle of soldiers, he seemed so calm. Then our eyes met. The banked rage in his reassured me.

Margaret's face lit up. "Here comes Jack now," she said.

He moved towards us, his hangers-on parting in front of him. It was utterly effortless, because people watched him with their eyes, their backs, their shoulders, their very feet. The room was one big smile, and they were all so afraid of him they were rotten.

He took poor Margaret, blushing, by the hand and turned to the rest of the room. The talk stilled. "Mr and Mrs Moore!" he said, gesturing to us. "Make them at home!" There was a smatter of applause, which stopped when he turned to Margaret again and lowered his voice. "What kept you? Was your father bad?"

"A bit. It was – it was all right, because Maura really needed to sleep and have supper. I thought you wanted us late, though, Jack? Have we upset things?"

"Oh, no," he said. I was looking for some spark in him, some gentleness towards Margaret, but I didn't like the way he said it; there were nuances in his dirty-silk voice that I was certain Margaret didn't catch. *I wouldn't allow you to upset anything; you wouldn't do it twice.*

"I should have some news for you in about an hour," he said to me. "Margaret," he said drolly, "are you quite sure I haven't met Maura before?"

"N-n-o … ?" Margaret said doubtfully.

"Were you ever in Wicklow?" I asked.

"No. That wasn't where I saw you."

Dominic's hand arrived, very casually, on my shoulder.

"Any long-lost twins?"

"No," I said. I tried to smile. Jack Rourke's bright, pale eyes held mine.

"Jack never forgets a face," Margaret was saying.

"Must be very useful," Dominic said.

"Oh, it is," said Jack Rourke. "When I've news, you'll have the letter of release." His expression was pleasant, but I sensed that Margaret had used up some of her currency with him in helping Conor, and that it was all the more dangerous for her being unaware of it. What in the name of God could we do about Mark? I was sweating by the time Jack Rourke moved away to talk to other people.

"There, now!" said Margaret, gazing after him. "Come and I'll introduce you to Mrs Allen. She's the civilisation here." She dragged us across the room to a pleasant-faced woman in the corner. Margaret blurted out my predicament with her usual simplicity, and Mrs Allen pounced at once.

"Isn't she very good?" she said to me and Dominic. "Now, you'll take the advice of an old married woman," she told Margaret. "You'll not ask that man for another thing for at least a month. Don't ask a man for a favour unless you have to, isn't that right?" she prodded me. "Take it from two married women, eh? Though the young men do not be counting like the old ones. The old ones count. I should know."

"Jack's not old," Margaret said, blushing.

"He's old enough to be counting, dear, isn't he – Maura? Oh, it won't be long, Maura. Now, Margaret, you're a good girl and let him ask you for favours in future."

People were beginning to drift out of the room and across the hall. Margaret's eyes shone. "It's Jack's surprise! Do you know what it is, Mrs Allen?"

"I'll bet – " she pursed her lips – "he'll have his telly going, with some tape in it. Would you take her arm there, Dominic, and we old wives will follow you." Dominic gave me a warning glance, took Margaret's arm and moved slowly into the throng. I was glad to see that he was making an effort to talk to her.

"Would you be planning to ask Margaret for any more favours?" Mrs Allen asked me sharply.

"I can see the way it is. Has she got to marry him?"

Her eyes softened a little. "Sure, she loves him. What she thinks is him. A 'crazy salad,' eh? Yeats," she added. "The poet. *Fine women take a crazy salad with their meat.* We'd best join this lot going in. He's something on; the rest of the houses were told not to use their electricity tonight. He hadn't even the decency to ask those people to his party – he hasn't got to be decent, of course, and I'm sure I needn't ask you not to repeat any of this."

"Wait a moment – please. Margaret's interceded for my brother. Another friend is in trouble as well, but … I don't want Margaret involved again. What should I do?"

"Have you got anything to give them? They'll do anything for a Swiss knife, say, or an implement. Sure, you know. Clothes?"

"No," I whispered.

"Well, Margaret's none to give you."

My face went hot. "I wouldn't ask!"

"There now," she said. "I shouldn't have said it like that, I didn't mean it like that. I'm worried about Margaret, you understand, don't you? She's no mother, and she needs one." She gave me a bright, hard look. "It depends what the trouble is, how bad. All the camps are along the Ballymahon Road. Come now, we must be moving, I don't want to talk to you alone too long; it's not done here. Hello, Enda, when's the wedding?"

A brown-haired man, very flushed, got even redder and called back, "Next Friday!" His friends cheered.

"Everybody asks for their friends at the camps, you can do that. They keep the immigrants – fancy that, dear, we don't have slaves any more, only immigrants – immigrants to Athlone, eh? – in the camps nearest the town. They're looked after a bit. Useful. The farther on you go, camp by camp, the more useless the body or the more serious the crime. The last is the nearest to An Fásach, and I pray your friend won't be there, because you won't get him out. Please don't judge us all by that, dear. We were here before this lot. Seán Óg is giving you an almighty stare. Do you know him?"

I had felt the stare. "He tried to pick me up at the fair."

"You stay with me then until we get beside your husband. You needn't be exposed to that fellow's dirt … Just wheedle them, dear, that's all you can do. And any little thing you could give them, if it isn't too small … "

"I suppose Margaret wouldn't leave. With us."

"She wouldn't. She looks after her Dad. And she wouldn't be able. And she'd not be allowed. She's his; he wouldn't let her away, oh, not for a million years. Like a big spider. He hasn't touched her yet. He just has her all wrapped up in his web, ready. Are you ill? Are you all right?"

"Headache. They go away after a bit."

"Your wife's not very well, Dominic," she said after we had threaded our way to him. Margaret leaned over, concerned.

"It's all right, really," I said. I moved around to stand beside her without knowing quite why, then feeling I might never see her again. Weak tears gathered in my eyes.

"Are you sure you don't want to go upstairs and lie down?" she whispered.

I shook my head. "We mightn't have much more time. Oh, Margaret! I wish you weren't marrying Jack Rourke."

She drew away from me, looking more hurt and offended than anyone I'd ever seen. Then she looked ahead, rigid.

Although folding doors had been pushed back and this room ran the length of the house, it was still too warm. Jack Rourke was lounging beside a very large oblong screen at the far end, watching an older man fiddle with knobs and wires. In a moment someone turned off the lights, and we were left in cave-like darkness.

The screen flared into action with a burst of loud music. A printed message, too low for me to see, appeared and faded in the lower left corner. Then there was a wail of instruments – guitars – and harsh, yet strangely harmonic, singing.

Two pale-faced young men sang; they were strangely beautiful, with their knotted hair and leather clothes. Their faces were as white as the leukaemia children's, but not so bluish – this harbinger of our lives was only a pretence.

The men in the room were laughing, why? "The cartridges," Dominic whispered, and I recognised the metal bits stuck into the singers' belts like ornaments. The music continued, but there was a confusion of beautiful faces on the screen, appearing and fading as if trying to escape.

Soon skulls begin to gleam under the flesh, eyes to darken and hollow; the chords continued, indifferent, as the eyes hollowed and holed, and maggots slid in and out of them. The two young men brayed on, smiling defiantly as if nothing was happening. Little bright-coloured cartoon creatures like triumphant mutates spilled jeering across the screen, but I was transfixed by the other images, trapped in that time and its queer, cold pain.

The sounds had diminished to throbs and came from somewhere below us. Dominic sat beside me on a bed, stroking my arms, his forehead creased with anxiety. High on the wall behind him was a small light; the rest of the room was in shadow. I struggled to get up, but he stopped me. He was wearing his jacket again, and our packs were beside me on the bed. He took a large envelope out of an inside pocket. "Conor's release," he said. "They've found him. We're to collect him. They're not even insisting on one of their escorts, thank God. There's something happening, Maura. The party's still going, but the younger men have left. Rourke's left, too, and he sent Margaret home. She says goodbye."

"I won't see her again."

"Maybe. Someday." He paused a moment, still stroking. "Was it the video, or was it something else?"

"It was in daylight, and we've just seen him … "

"It'll be daylight very soon," he said grimly.

"We're still in Rourke's house, aren't we?"

"Yes. Upstairs."

"I can feel him everywhere. I want to wash … "

"He never so much as touched you, Maura. I wouldn't let him, don't you know that?"

"He wouldn't need to. He's in the air."

"What did you dream about him?"

"It wasn't about him," I said, sick. "It was about Mark."

CHAPTER THIRTY

I DIDN'T SEE THE PICTURE UNTIL I STOOD UP. THE SMALL LIGHT ON the wall was for it.

"The picture!"

Dominic turned to look at it, impatient, started to speak, stopped. Then, "It's lovely," he said. "Come on."

"Dominic – it's my mother's, it's the one!"

It was more beautiful than I'd remembered. It was stronger and more cajoling than ever. The warm contours of the Sally Gap coaxed me all the way back to the centre, where the lines of the hills converged, then released me into flight on the luminous horizon. It looked finished.

"Do you want it?"

"What do you mean?" I said, gazing at it, touching it.

"I mean we've no time, Maura. It'll be getting light soon, and there's about to be anarchy."

"Take it down," I said.

He did, and I tapped it out of the heavy frame. My mother had fixed it to the stretchers with staples, and Dominic simply ran his knife along them, peeling the canvas away. I rolled it up, then looked for something to cover it. The canvas was joyously alive under my fingers, its textures teasing at every nerve. Dominic took a sheet off

the bed and tore it in half, and tore off more rough strips
to bind it. We worked so furiously that this took only a few
moments. We lashed the picture to the back of my pack
and left the room with its now sinister light on nothing. We
got only a few desultory glances when we were going, and
finally we were in the street, a wind off the river pushing
between the houses.

"We'd want to get Conor before our friend finds his
picture gone," said Dominic.

I was so convinced that the picture would bring us luck
that I didn't even comment, but said, "What about Mark?"

"Mark will find his own way out."

I stared at him. "He won't!"

"He always does, Maura." Behind us, the town
darkened. Dominic turned to look. "The electricity's gone."

I didn't answer him.

"Whatever you saw, he'll get out."

"I saw him in An Fásach."

We could hear the river now, and feel its chill. There
was a circle of oil lanterns in front of the first gate onto the
bridge; a number of soldiers stood just outside their dazzle.
Two stepped forward to challenge us, their faces hard,
until Dominic showed them Jack Rourke's letter. They
waved us on almost hastily after that, showing us to a
walkway on the side of the bridge that was separated from
the series of heavy wooden gates down the middle of it.
We walked in silence, hearing the Shannon purring and
slithering powerfully below.

On the other side, we walked through quiet, dark
streets that seemed all the more still because of the din
from the barracks by the river behind us.

"Mrs Allen said you can go and ask about people."

"I know all that. I talked to her after Margaret left." He
was walking faster and faster; finally I realised that he was
angry – I had never seen him in such a rage.

"What did she say?"

"That pig-faced fellow has done for Mark! He's on their permanent 'Interrogation' list, and someone's found out he was at Flood's. They had him within minutes."

"But I thought … "

"He grinned at me all evening, the shite – he knew. I was sure he'd come after us, Maura. I thought we'd never get out of there, only – Jesus, these 'spells' of yours, I say to myself maybe they're protected – maybe you can't be harmed on account of them."

That was more than I thought.

We were now on the outskirts, where the houses had shrunk to cottages. The wind brought the smell of leaves and faint sounds of people talking, and I was reminded of the time Mark and I had paused, listening, down the road from Eoin's house. I reached out to Dominic and stopped him. "It's the way things are, I know," I said. I pulled him to me and touched his face and hair, and in one fluid motion, he lifted me against him, and we clutched at each other, flesh to flesh, bone to bone.

"I love you!"

"And I love you."

"We're like strangers in all this."

"We're not," he said. Then we kissed, quick and hard, and were on our way. A cock crowed somewhere to the right of us in the dark, and we hurried faster.

"We'll have to get Mark," I said.

"First things first. Conor's in the second camp along here."

There were night sounds behind the hedges – children crying, both waking and sleeping, dull chink of metal, a sudden, feral growl from a big dog. Two men shuffled out to accost us, but they weren't really pushed. One stretched and scratched at himself while the other looked nervously down the road and asked what was going on in the town.

"Something's up," Dominic told them. "You'd do as well to let this lot go if you hear troops coming down this road."

"What have they got in there at all?" I asked, when we were out of earshot. "Did you hear them all crying?"

"With any luck those fellows will release them."

"But they sounded so young – where would they go?"

He tugged at my arm to hurry me. We could see the next set of lanterns down the road. Behind us, the sky was lightening. There was a dirty pink tinge on the horizon, which seemed to have moved a little closer.

Conor wasn't there. We didn't believe the warder at first when he told us, not even when the other three backed him up. They produced a clipboard with dog-eared sheets of paper on it and showed me Conor's name, misspelled, with a pencilled note beside it, "Camp 6".

"Where is that?" Dominic asked him.

I snatched a lantern from one of them and ran along the straggle of tents and huddled blankets, screaming his name. "That boy Conor, he's gone," one sleepy, sad young voice finally called.

"Yeah, he is," came faintly from the other side of the field.

I stumbled back to Dominic at the gate. The warder was talking. "Sure, we don't like to let any of them go under those circumstances, but what can we do? We'd do a runner ourselves only for Liam Murphy, but he says who will they get after us, it's better to have someone who cares. Show us the letter."

Dominic gave it to him warily.

"Hold up the lantern there, Emmet."

"He's not there, Dominic," I said. My teeth were chattering.

"Sh-h," he said, nodding at the man.

"It's got everything, his stamp and signature and all," said the man, "and it's not specific, is it? My God, you could turn out the whole lot of them with this. Look here, Emmet, who's in charge at Camp 6 on a Monday?"

A crackly voice behind them said, "Myles McDermot."

"Right. You ask for Myles by name and tell him I advise him to release the lot and clear out. Half the lads he's got there are from Tipperary, and if that crowd are really set to invade us, he won't want to be found herding them out to An Fásach. My name's John Baker. John Baker, right? And you ask for Myles McDermot. And I wouldn't, like, tarry along the way. I'm a Dublin man myself," he added, nodding and giving the letter, carefully folded again, back to Dominic. "As a matter of interest, who was it you annoyed?"

"Could have been Seán Óg O'Mahony," said Dominic.

John Baker lifted the lantern and peered at me. "Sure to be him, all right. Off with you now, and good luck."

I'd no trouble keeping up with Dominic's long strides. I could have run. The whole area had a rank, marshy smell. As the darkness thinned, we were able to see more of the deserted sites of camps that had been abandoned, desolate squares of trampled grass strewn with petty debris – bones and bits of rags like soggy scabs on the ground. There was a stench from these places that rose and fell with the breeze, and I reckoned the prisoners were moved on when this became unbearable.

Houses had been scattered among the campsites nearest the town, but they were very scarce now, and the quickening light showed them to be uninhabited. We reached a fork in the road. Dominic swore.

"Wait!" I said. Half-hidden in the hedge was a plank with a white scrawl on it: "An Fásach."

"Do we believe it, that's the question," said Dominic.

"They haven't been taken there, have they?"

"No, but they'll be close to it." The wind stirred the

hedge. He grasped the sign with his hands and pulled at it. It was firmly anchored to a stake set in concrete hidden beneath the weeds. "Well, that's it," he said. "They want to make sure there's no messing about that place."

"They've already taken them," I said. "They're gone." I started to cry.

"You saw it?"

I couldn't answer him.

"Did you see it?" he yelled, shaking me. "Like a bloody vision?"

"No," I said, "but it's too quiet!"

"Maura, you bitch, don't do that again! Come on, now!" and we plunged headlong down the road.

The hedges on either side of us were the wildest I'd seen, stretching long, awkward branches into the road and thrusting up others against the sky, which seemed itself to be disorganised, streaked as it was with queer swirling shadows. There were voices on the wind. Someone was shouting and cursing, but all we got of it was a broken staccato.

"You stop here," Dominic said. "You'll go no farther."

"Don't you be ridiculous!"

"I shouldn't have let you this far – go back to the crossroads, Maura, and wait."

"I'm coming! We haven't reached the camp!"

"We've passed it, Maura! You didn't see. They're gone. They've got them almost to An Fásach."

There was the unmistakable sound of a rifle shot. Dominic ran. "Go back, Maura!"

The road curved and straightened to reveal a straggle of figures ahead. Dominic pounded towards them. A man turned. He had a long rod in his hand, the rifle. "Myles McDermot!" Dominic screamed. He held up the letter and waved it. "Myles McDermot! John Baker has a message for you!" One man left the group and trotted towards him. The others moved forward again.

I caught up, gasping, as the bundled figure arrived. He looked like a creature from another world; he wore a thick one-piece suit that covered all of him, dirty leather gloves with great gauntlets on them, and something like a balaclava over his head, except that it was canvas instead of wool. "What does Johnno want?" he said crossly.

I left them and ran towards the pitiful cavalcade ahead. The man with the rifle, as cocooned in clothing as Myles McDermot, turned and took aim. "It's all right!" I cried. "We have clearance. Look, Myles McDermot has seen it and he's coming."

The man motioned me to come closer. I stared wildly at the small group in their chains. Conor and Mark were behind the others. Mark was sprawled on the road, and Conor was kneeling beside him, shirt tail extended, mopping at a cut over his eye. "Conor!" I cried, and I couldn't understand when he wouldn't look at me, but hung his head in shame.

The keys were produced by a third man, as heavily clad as the others, and their desperate prisoners, free at last, fled back down the road. The warders weren't long after them. They set off at a run, pausing only to fling off their gloves, then their headgear, then their all-over suits, the signs of their trade. "I never thought we'd see Irish executioners," Dominic snarled after them.

Conor still slumped beside Mark. "I'm sorry we were so long," I whispered. I put my arms around him very carefully. Slowly, almost cautiously, still averting his eyes, he let his head drop on my shoulder and started to cry.

CHAPTER THIRTY-ONE

TEASED BY AN INVISIBLE HAND, THE DUST FROM AN FÁSACH ROSE and fell, eddied and whirled with sinuous grace. Wistful fingers formed, fingers that splayed and faded as they dissipated into the sky, always moving towards us.

"What happened him?" Dominic was asking Conor.

"They hit him with the rifle, for nothing. Oh, he said something, but they didn't even hear. They didn't even hear what it was! And he was already bad."

Dominic leaned close to Mark's ear. "You and your big mouth!" he said loudly. Mark's eyelids flickered. Dominic felt all around his head. One side of it was matted with dried blood, and Dominic's fingers were sticky when he finished. "His skull doesn't seem to be cracked."

"I think he's just tired," Conor offered.

"Tired?"

"They made him run up and down all night to see how strong he was. They took bets on him, they wouldn't let him stop. He wouldn't talk to me; he said I'd be in more trouble if we talked, and I could do nothing."

"He was right, and you couldn't. Don't worry, Conor, we'll all be fetching and carrying for him when he's healing." He leaned over Mark again, his face pale. "Hello in there!"

Mark did not respond.

For a moment it was as if I were looking at the four of us from far away, a huddle of figures on a desolate road, squatting around a fallen god, while the sky rose above us like some vast abstract canvas, full of swirls and magic, shadows of snakes.

Dominic was opening Mark's shirt. "He could be bleeding inside," he muttered, wiping his forehead on his sleeve. "Jesus, Mark, wake up! An Fásach's coming after us here!"

The broad chest was a mottle of bruises, but only one looked really dangerous, and it was along the ribs. Dominic probed there, but he could find nothing broken. "Conor, did you notice anything when he was walking around? Was his back okay?"

Mark's right arm twitched. His eyelids fluttered, but his eyes did not open. He tried to scratch his chest. "He does that when he's sleeping! The bastard's asleep!"

We were elated, then somehow furious at him. I tore open Dominic's pack, found the Our Lady bottle and squirted fierce jets of water onto Mark's face. His tongue went out: he tried to lick it.

"Get up!" Dominic roared at him.

Mark's eyes opened. "Who are you?"

Conor started to giggle.

"This is your friend who's getting cancer while you snore. This is my wife who's probably pregnant. This is my brother-in-law who's twelve and getting a right dose for himself, so would you for Christ's sake get off your arse so we can leave."

Mark struggled to his feet. "I was waiting till you'd undress me entirely," he said, swaying a little.

"Ha, ha," said Dominic.

I handed Mark the Our Lady bottle and he squirted the

remainder of the water into his mouth, his bottom lip starting to bleed again. When he handed the bottle to Dominic, I refastened the buttons on his shirt. He hadn't been able to hold the bottle in his fingers, but only between the heels of his palms. "If you hadn't done that for me at the fair, they'd have let you alone."

"Ach. Well. I doubt it."

"Anyway, thanks and all that," said Dominic, his eyes red. "Now let's go."

Retracing steps usually shortens them, but not this time. Our legs were like lead as we struggled to outdistance the claws of dust above us. The wildness of the hedges near Camp 6 now showed itself for what it was – a bevy of mutations that made some shoots long and straggly and others stunted and clenched tight together like fists. Mark sweated as he passed them. Conor seemed too relieved to notice. I didn't know how I would tell him about Mum; how could he bear any more?

"Why in the name of God did they send you to Camp 6?" I asked him.

"I don't know. They wanted me for the turf before. Then these soldiers came along and said Seán somebody said I was for Camp 6. Mr Baker said 'who was to know if I stayed with him', but the other two were scared this guy would find out. Sure, I was delighted when I got there, because there was Mark, only – " His face crumpled.

"You thought you'd lose him like Morrie?"

He stared at me. "You know about Morrie?"

I told him how I had found Morrie and made his cairn and how Dominic said that each person passing would add a stone. "You'll see when we're going back," I said. "We'll say a prayer."

Again, he had that shamed, stricken look. "Mum's dead, too, isn't she, Maura?"

"She is, Conor. I'm sorry, love."

"I knew you wouldn't have left her otherwise." Tears poured down his cheeks.

"I would, actually. She'd have made me! She died before you were gone, Conor. While we were all sitting in the church. She was happy."

Conor said nothing then, but he let me put my arm around him. He smelled different to me; he had a sad, sour defeated smell. "The sooner we get to running water, the better," I said. "You're due for a wash, my love."

"Some things don't change."

As we neared the town, the wind shifted. Black smoke billowed from something burning beside the river. The wind blew it towards us, and at the same time, the strange configurations from An Fásach receded. "Thank God it didn't rain that time," said Dominic.

Conor looked so scared that Mark said, "There goes my last chance to be Tinkerbell."

"Who's Tinkerbell?"

"A fairy that glowed in the dark, Conor. Very small."

"Good luck on the 'small'."

That was the way we talked until we arrived at the outskirts of the town. We were too uneasy to be serious.

"What if we meet that Seán fellow?" Conor said.

"I doubt we will."

"What if we do? He'll see Mark."

"I think our Seán will be under wraps," said Dominic.

"I'd like to meet him again, but not just now," said Mark.

"If you so much as think you see him, turn your back. Pretend to be a horse or a barn. Go near him, and I'll kill you myself!" Dominic said.

"Don't fight him, Mark."

"I'm only annoying Dominic, Conor; it's my poor substitute for mincing our Seán into something Ógger."

The wind must have veered again, because although we

were still north of the town and moving through its western outskirts, we got a sudden strong stink of smoke. Here the streets had lost their reticence. People, mostly women, were out standing and talking, and four or five children frisked excitedly in the road. There was celebration in the air. Conor began to brighten a little.

A woman who had been laughing and talking with two others turned and called out to us. I walked over to her, while the others waited. The women looked shocked by Mark's bruises and cuts, but seeing him chatting to Conor and Dominic seemed to reassure them.

"Can you tell us what's happening? We saw the smoke," I began.

"That was Mad Jack's farewell!" All three started to laugh, and the one who had called me over, a strong-looking red-head, gave a whoop.

"He was burnt up?"

"Ah, you poor dote! No, dear, you've missed the Revolution. It started without you!"

"It started without us, too!" shrieked one of her friends, and they roared laughing.

"Are you saying there's no more?"

"No more Mad Jack, true enough!"

"Where are you coming from?" one of the other two said suddenly.

"Is it over?" I persisted, nervous. "Can we cross the river?"

A little knot of youths shot around the corner, pulling and tugging at a lad in a Militia uniform. He was laughing harder than any of them. They all scrabbled with their hands, himself included, and the shirt was in the air, then the shoes and the trousers. He hadn't a stitch on underneath, and the whole lot of them jumped and capered around the road, whooping, the ex-soldier in the middle of them like a white stick-figure.

"That's what was bossing us all the years!"

"That's only poor Gerry Doyle," another woman said. There was a little ripple of silence.

"It's a pity she didn't live to see him out again."

"It's a Federation now," the first woman said to me, without taking her eyes off the lads in the road. "The lads from Tipp are running us now."

"The main bridge is a gaol! They have them all there, Jack Rourke and Peadar O'Mahony and the whole lot of them. And they let go all the children, except they say now they'll have to find them again or nothing here will get done. But I hope they're well on their way, don't you Sarah?"

"It wasn't right," said her friend. She turned and hurried into the house beside us. She had been staring at Conor's chafed ankles. She returned immediately with food in her hands, two wrinkled apples and a piece of cold meat. She gave the piece of meat and one of the apples to Conor, who thanked her and offered the meat to the rest of us before starting to tear into it. The women looked at him approvingly.

Directions were given and repeated, and we were on our way.

"No, you eat it," Dominic said when I held out my apple. "I don't want to be carrying you home."

It had a sad, delicate flavour, as sweet as the past. I chewed the frail core until it tasted like old hemp and broke. Then I couldn't seem to throw it away, so I put it in my pocket.

We passed terraces of older houses with small groups of people hovered outside, quieter and more anxious-looking than the women we'd met. They watched us intently as we passed.

"They won't let you go down there!" a voice called.

"Who won't?"

"The soldiers, are you cracked? The Cute-hoor-arians!"

It was a long, swarthy man who spoke. He was sitting against the gable wall of a house, his legs stretched in front of him. This man had managed to get drunk.

"Well, we'll see."

"You'll see all right!" he cried, and then began muttering to himself.

"He's legless," I said.

The man waved a dirty bottle for emphasis. "I'm telling you!" Then he shrugged, took a last draw, and flung the bottle to one side.

Conor's eyes were enormous. He chewed his lip and looked at me nervously. I nudged him and pointed at Dominic and Mark, who were smiling like conspirators.

"Will we meet some Tipp-hoor-arians?" Mark said.

"Will Mark be all right?"

"He will, Conor," Dominic said. He pulled me close to him. "The Tipps are a bit mellower than this lot here. We may even know some of the lads, isn't that right, Mark?"

"It's our civic duty to have a look, so it is."

Conor seemed reassured again, but only just. He walked ahead with Mark. We followed them, Dominic's hand still on my shoulder. I put my own over it. "Do you think it's almost over?"

"We still have to be careful ... but yeah, the worst is, almost ... " He rummaged under his jumper, found his shirt tail and dabbed at my eyes with it. "Jesus, I wish I could cry," he said unsteadily.

We hurried a little to catch up. Neither of us wanted to let the other two out of our sight. "This must be what having children is like," Dominic said.

"There are hardly any birds over the Shannon."

"It's true. Not like the Liffey."

"Not like home, either."

"No. I like the aul' gulls."

"Dominic, I'm still scared. It's like – nothing's happened."

He laughed so hard that Mark and Conor turned and stared, half-smiling themselves.

"Nothing's been resolved," I argued. "We meet Jack Rourke again after all these years, and somehow we never – I never ... Do you know, I thought his own skin would cry out to him who I was. I was so afraid to be in the room with him that I thought he must – must smell it, like an animal."

"He'd hardly pick out your fear from all the others."

"And the only person who really hurt us was Seán Óg."

"That's all it is, Maura – we're small enough to be hurt by someone even smaller. We're almost invisible now to a man like Jack Rourke. Mind, the bastard fancied you."

We had come a different way back, and I was surprised to see the castle glowering over our heads. Some local people had gathered near the gates of the bridge and had trapped two harassed-looking men. Some soldiers in blue uniforms were restraining a woman who was trying to skewer the men on her pitchfork. Six children around Conor's age, chained together, cheered her on.

"I understand, Missus, but we need them to tell us how to release the children there – "

"If you'd heard what I've heard," cried the woman, lunging again.

"Sure we have, it's a scandal countrywide – there now," and the new soldier took the fork from her with an ease that bespoke layer on layer of health and strength.

More soldiers were approaching from the barracks. The crowd quietened and drew back as if the marching men were something solid that could run over us.

These drew up beside us with rigid faces and a stamping of feet. They wore their own clothes, but they all had blue scarves to identify them. A small man, their officer, turned smartly and saluted the man with the fork, who saluted in return and told him to stand at ease. There was a light snigger from the people beside the road, and a rash of cheering from the children. "Up Tipp!" screamed one of them, and another quavered into a song in Irish; two other frail voices took it up, and there was a murmur like a growl among the men on the road. When one of them joined the song, his voice loud and tearful, the children howled with joy, shrieking out the words of the song, which was some anthem of their own. The tears stood in our eyes, happiness for them and loneliness that we didn't know their song.

The small officer delegated one of his men to escort us back over the bridge, and Dominic, Mark and Conor feasted on news with him. I put my hand to my pack to make sure the picture was still there and walked out to the side of them to make sure I could see what was coming.

CHAPTER THIRTY-TWO

THERE WERE HORSES ON THE BRIDGE. WE COULDN'T SEE THEM YET because the main gates, shut fast, blocked our view, but the side gate was open and the hoofbeats rang sharply. The first thing we saw, however, were some men walking. Mark laughed beside me, and I looked to see what had amused him.

He too had been noticed. "Mark," I said, "better kiss me again."

He pointed to his sore lip, which was oozing – it did every time he smiled – and put his arm around me instead. The sorry figure in chains kept gesticulating to the man in the blue scarf, his warder, and finally this man approached us, laughing.

"Is it Mark Meehan?" He grinned up at him.

"It is," said Mark carelessly. Dominic murmured something disapproving.

"Our friend there thinks he's seen a ghost. Says we should be arresting you, too."

"Sure, he only wants company."

"And who's your accomplice?"

"Me sister-in-law, kind of."

"Well, you can let go of her now because none of us

are after you!" said the man, laughing, "And next time you come to Tipp, you can bring her with you."

"No chance," said Dominic. "And don't be so free with yourself in future, Mark, unless you want to go back to Camp 6."

The man returned to his charges, gave the furious and filthy Seán Óg a dig in the back, and moved on in the direction of the Ballymahon road.

Someone was looking at me.

My head turned towards the river, and I saw him. His hands were bound, attached to a rope held by a man on a tall horse. There were others behind him, but he was the one I saw. His face had reddened in the cold, and the scar, livid, now divided it from brow to cheek.

The crowd behind us surged forward, and he actually smiled, as if my being pushed towards him was the last exercise of his power.

"I was right. When I saw you'd taken the picture ... You're her daughter, aren't you?"

I nodded.

His eyes lingered on Conor for a moment. "And this is your brother."

Conor stared back at him.

Then his pale eyes sparkled into mine. "I looked for you for a while," he said. He traced his scar with his forefinger, ending with it on his lips; he kissed it and pointed it at me. One of the blue-scarved men jerked his tether. They moved on, their horses' hooves stinging the silence.

"Who was that man?" Conor whispered.

"The nasty old thing who pinched you when you were a ba'."

Conor wanted the whole story, but I told him I'd like to be sure it was over before I began it again, so he had to be content with that.

It was different going back. Anyone coming from the direction of Athlone was waylaid and asked the news, brought in and warmed and – when possible – fed. We stopped at the Riordan's – we owed them that – and even managed to find Jennifer and Isaac, who were back on the farm with Jennifer's brother, James. They were all three so happy, and so daft, that we spent the night laughing in their kitchen. Fergus the baby, looking even more intent, was there for all of it. Mark sat quietly during these visits; the reason we gave was that he was recuperating from his beatings, but the real reason was that he was grieving. "That's how he got caught, of course," Dominic said. "He didn't give a toss."

It was hard going back to the empty house, cold because they didn't know when to expect us, and motherless. Yet we're healed by these walls. We gave Mark my mother's room because he loves it; it's too much for the rest of us. The other day I noticed something different about my mother's drawing of him, then realised he had written "Eoin" over the heart of it, very carefully and beautifully.

Conor will always miss Morrie, but Mrs Kenny has been very good to him. She tells him that, terrible as Morrie's ordeal was, it would have been worse to watch him dying over an entire winter. "I know you took care of him," she says. She's very subdued now, which makes me sad, but Sinead doesn't think it will last for long. She is beginning to take an interest in her grandchild, "now that she knows he has the right number of heads, hands and feet," Sinead says. "And nothing I do is right! And you won't believe this, Maura – she and Mrs McEvoy have teamed up. The cord wasn't cut before those two got their claws out of each others' hair and into me and Ciaran."

Lizzie assures me that there isn't a quota on healthy

babies. I told her what I had dreamed about my daughter, how she was more like a flower than a person, with little buds for her arms and legs, and Lizzie told me she was supposed to be like that early on.

Lizzie was the only one to know until Mark, innocently observant, blew the gaffe. Dominic was agonising over birth control, and Mark said, "Surely the horse has bolted?"

We'd a horrific row. I finally realised that Dominic thought I'd told Mark before him. When that was sorted out, it was all right. "I'll worry when you start into labour," Dominic says. He's good that way.

I think my visionary dreams are going. The last I had was of our daughter, and I've a feeling there won't be any more. I'm not sorry. There was just one on our way home, and that was of Jack Rourke. He was in An Fásach, looking straight into my eyes like he always did. The dust slunk around him as if tasting him. He still smiled as if we shared a secret, but I looked back at him and said, "We'll never be like you." Sometimes I pity him. Almost.

I do dream about my parents, our house, my old school by the sea, about all the people. Every night they come, more vivid, almost, than they were in life. Perhaps it's because we're threatened with another move, inland this time; but in my heart of hearts, I believe the dreams come from my daughter – that as she grows, she re-creates the world.

THE END